THE KILLER INSIDE

Lindsay Ashford was born in Wolverhampton and now lives on the coast of west Wales. She worked as a BBC journalist after becoming the first woman to graduate from Queens' College, Cambridge, where she studied Criminology.

She has written three other novels in the Megan Rhys series: *Death Studies*, *Frozen* and *Strange Blood*, which was short-listed for the Theakston's Old Peculier Crime Novel of the Year Award 2006. All three titles are published by Honno Welsh Women's Press and are available from all good bookshops or online at **www.honno.co.uk**.

<u>Praise for Lindsay Ashford</u>:

"Gritty, streetwise and raw, Frozen *takes us into a labyrinth of deviant murderers, crooked cops and hapless young female victims with an authenticity and detail borne of Ashford's own journalistic experience"*
Denise Hamilton, author of the Eve Diamond crime novels

"Patricia Cornwell has patented the persona of the doughty heroine who bucks the system, but Ashford is closer to her personal demons" **The Guardian**

"Ashford's excellent understanding of society gives this exciting book an added depth" **Big Issue Magazine**

"Chilling... Will appeal to those who enjoy the forensic procedurals of Kathy Reichs" **Library Journal**

THE KILLER INSIDE

by

Lindsay Ashford

HONNO MODERN FICTION

Published by Honno
'Ailsa Craig', Heol y Cawl, Dinas Powys
South Glamorgan, Wales, CF6 4AH

The author would like to stress that
this is a work of fiction and no resemblance
to any actual individual or institution
is intended or implied.

A catalogue record for this book is available from The British Library.

ISBN 13: 978 1870206 921
ISBN 10:1870206924

The publisher gratefully acknowledges the financial support of the
Welsh Books Council

Author photograph copyright Nicola Schumacher

Cover image: Getty Images
Cover design: G Preston
Printed in Wales by Gomer

For Mum and Dad

ACKNOWLEDGEMENTS

I would like to thank C. K. for allowing me to talk to him about the experience of spending a year in jail. I know that he found it difficult to discuss the trauma of being imprisoned but I hope that sharing it with someone has helped him to come to terms with it.

I gained further valuable insights into prison life from *A Life Inside* by Erwin James (Guardian Books) and *Bang Up For Men* by Adrian Rudesind (Starborne).

Thanks go to my editor, Caroline Oakley, for her sound advice and to Helena Earnshaw and Janet Thomas for their suggestions and unwavering support. Also to my children, Ciaran, Ruth, Isabella and Deri for putting up with a mother who writes about murder rather than magic.

Finally, thank you to Steve Lawrence, who has contributed to this book in so many ways and whose love and encouragement make writing a far from lonely experience.

Prologue

Sometimes I wish I'd never found him. But somebody had to. He shouldn't have been left like that. Unburied.

The sight of his face, wizened and unreal, sent spiders scuttling from some dark corner of my mind: images of a place I don't remember. And now, every time I close my eyes, I go back there.

I'm climbing out of bed but it's not my bed. It's a cot with white-painted bars. My legs are just long enough to straddle them and slither over the side. I can hear my own footsteps, bare feet padding along a hard surface. Wooden floorboards or lino, maybe. It's light outside, but not very. The hallway has an eerie grey pre-dawn look about it. I pause in the doorway of a kitchen. I'm about to step in something but I stop just in time.

It looks like ketchup. A big sticky pool of red. Curious, I move closer. Dip my fingers in it. I don't lick them, though. It smells funny. Then I see him lying behind the door. His eyes are closed. 'Daddy,' I whisper, tugging at his vest. 'Daddy!' He doesn't move.

I back away from him and turn round. The door to another room is open. I take a step towards it. I see her lying on a settee in a black nightie with little red hearts for buttons. Her eyes are closed, too, but they look strange. They twitch like a dog chasing cats in its sleep.

I touch her arm, then tug it. Her head moves a bit but she doesn't wake up. I go to the other end of the settee to tickle her toes because that always works when she doesn't want to get up. But there's something on her legs. Red stuff . Then I see something lying by her feet. It looks like a doll. But its face is a different colour from other dolls. Sort of bluey-white. Its body is wrapped up. Not like a present. Like fish and chips. I want to unwrap it. Give it a kiss. But there's something scary about its eyes.

Now I'm back in bed. My own bed. Blinking back tears as I stare out of the window. The sky blurs pink and orange. Tiny clouds swim out of the sun. On the horizon, like a black paper cut-out of a castle, is Balsall Gate jail. 'If only you were here, Dad,' I whisper. 'You'd know what to do.'

Chapter 1

HMP Balsall Gate was a squat, grey, Victorian monstrosity of a prison. Monstrous not only in appearance but for what went on inside its walls. To reach it Megan Rhys had to walk through the equally depressing graveyard that bordered its west side. The derelict church overlooking the graveyard was almost as forbidding as the prison, its stained glass windows smashed to jagged shards.

She could have driven to the prison and parked her car in the inner courtyard but it was only fifteen minutes' walk from her office at Heartland University. Hardly worth it. And she needed the exercise. She felt bloated and her trousers were uncomfortably tight. She could no longer fit into half the clothes in her wardrobe.

The very thought of the way her waistline was expanding made her dive into her bag for her latest prop: dried prunes. She was snacking on them instead of the *Maltesers* she'd become addicted to after giving up smoking. The problem was the packets were so hard to undo you could starve to death trying to get at the damned things. So she'd taken to carrying a pair of nail scissors round with her, which she fished out along with the prunes. Cheeks bulging like a hamster, she picked her way past gravestones choked with weeds. Lucky there was no one about. She must make sure there were no telltale bits stuck to her teeth by the time she reached her destination.

The weather had been very hot for April. The closer she got to the prison walls the more oppressive the air seemed to become. She glanced up at the sky. Today was the kind of day the forecasters described as quiet: notable more for what wasn't going on than what was. There was no rain, no wind, no sunshine. It was as if the elements were holding their breath, waiting for something to happen.

'Good morning, Dr Rhys!' The security man in the office at the prison gate beamed at her as she handed over her bag. She'd only been coming here for a few weeks but he greeted her like an old friend. Probably because the majority of people he met in the course of his working day were sullen, miserable and aggressive. And who could blame them, she thought, glancing back as the huge wooden gate thudded shut. It was the entrance to hell.

Megan knew prisons like some people knew football grounds. She had visited all the high and medium security jails in the UK, as well as several in the States. In her head she had a league table and Balsall Gate was at the bottom. She was here to investigate the unusually high rate of suicide among the inmates. During the previous six months no fewer than ten men had taken their own lives. It had been too much for the resident prison psychologist to handle: he was on long-term sick leave after a year on anti-depressants.

She was in the inner courtyard now, a cobbled area the size of a tennis court enclosed by towering stone walls coated in the grime of inner-city Birmingham. She could hear the shouts of men through tiny, barred windows. Barked conversations between inmates desperate for a way to pass the time. The shouts were peppered with obscenities. Then a chorus of wolf whistles as someone spotted her walking across the cobbles. She closed her ears to the lewd catcalls that followed. She'd heard them all before and she knew that any female under retirement age was likely to get the same treatment.

It wasn't difficult to understand how despairing a person

could become in a place like this. But the frequency of the deaths was alarming. There were hundreds of other Category B prisoners housed in cramped, outdated conditions – so why had this one driven so many to take their lives?

At the inner gate she was met by Fergus, the prison officer who had escorted her the previous day. Fergus was possibly the tallest man she had ever met. At six foot seven he had to bend his head to get through the doors to the cells. Not fat, but solid, he had the look of Jaws – the James Bond villain – minus the metal dental work. Not the sort of man any inmate would want to get on the wrong side of.

On her first day at the prison Fergus had taken her to the governor's office. She had known in advance that Malcolm Meredith was a member of the old school of prison management, not impressed by the efforts of prison psychologists to rehabilitate inmates. As far as he was concerned, prison was all about retribution, not rehabilitation. He had a world-weariness that she had seen in many men at the top of their profession who were nearing the end of their careers. Malcolm Meredith had less than a year to go before hanging up his governor's hat for good. It was pretty clear that all he was thinking about was escaping the daily grind and getting out onto the golf course. His leadership was lax and his staff appeared to be taking full advantage. All prisons had a pecking order amongst the inmates, but Megan knew that in Balsall Gate there was also an unofficial pecking order amongst the screws. Someone was wielding far more power than they ought to and that, she believed, was the key to the misery in this place.

'This way, Dr Rhys.' Fergus unlocked the door to a long corridor, holding it open as she passed through. His size and build would have made him a natural candidate for top dog among his fellow jailers but Megan had decided within seconds of meeting him that Fergus was not the type. He

was the archetypal gentle giant. She guessed that from an
early age his sheer physical presence had been enough to
get him by without resorting to bullying of any kind. In her
experience it was the smaller, less physically impressive
warders who were likely to cause the most grief to inmates;
the weedy kids who had been picked on in the playground
and who saw a guard's uniform as the perfect way to get
their own back. She followed Fergus down the corridor, its
walls newly painted in pink gloss. *Pink.* Not a colour you'd
expect in a prison. It had been done on the recommendation
of an interior design team who said the colour would lower
aggression among the inmates. Like everything else tried to
date, it had failed.

She glanced at her watch. 'You'll be unlocking soon,
won't you Fergus? For association, I mean.'

The guard shook his head. 'Not today, ma'am.' He cocked
his head to the left. 'Bit of trouble last night, so they're on
twenty-three hour lock-up.'

'What trouble?'

She heard the guard's tongue click against the roof of his
mouth. 'In the Segregation Unit. You know what it's like.'
He glanced at her over his shoulder as he unlocked a door.
'They sometimes go a bit crazy.'

'What happened?'

'Oh, the usual: some guy screaming his head off, waking
everyone else up. Course, they all start bawling then, don't
they?'

Megan frowned. She could just imagine what the noise
must have been like, the way the walls in this place echoed.
The stress levels must be at an all-time high after a night like
that.

'Here we are, ma'am.' Fergus showed her into a small
room with the kind of furniture not in evidence in the rest
of the prison. Two new-looking armchairs upholstered

in green dralon faced each other across a round, wooden coffee table that bore a tray with cups, saucers and a plate of digestive biscuits. As she stepped across the threshold a head appeared from behind the wing of one of the armchairs. Dominic Wilde was only three years older than her but his shoulder-length wavy hair had gone completely white. His face had the inevitable prison pallor. She thought, not for the first time, what an odd pair they must look; with her black hair and olive skin, he was almost like her photographic negative. A lifer with thirteen years under his belt, Dominic was the most serene, well-balanced prisoner she had ever encountered.

'Morning, Megan.' His large eyes were the colour of rain-washed slate and the creases at their lower corners deepened as he smiled. She settled into the chair opposite. There was a tangible warmth from the man, melting the cold fear that seemed to leak from the very walls of this place.

'Morning Dom.' They had been on first name terms for the past few weeks. She had first met him two years ago when she'd visited the prison to interview another inmate for a book she was writing about sex offenders. Dom Wilde was what people in the prison service called a Listener. An inmate trained by the Samaritans to counsel fellow prisoners. He was now so well-respected by the other inmates that he had been made Listener Co-ordinator, which meant he was on call twenty-four hours a day, seven days a week, dealing with anything from marriage break-ups to threatened suicides.

Dom was Megan's cover; her excuse for getting into the jail regularly over a period of weeks. It was a plan she had suggested to the Ministry of Justice. She wanted to find out what was causing the alarming suicide rate in Balsall Gate and so did they. The Ministry knew that if they sent an inspector in they would be presented with a sanitised version of what was really going on. So Megan had suggested investigating the prison herself on the pretext of carrying out a research project to monitor the effectiveness of the Listener service.

She had marked Dom Wilde out as someone who could give her the answers she was looking for and all her subsequent meetings with him had reinforced her initial instincts about him. He was the only person in Balsall Gate who knew the real motive for her research. If he hadn't agreed to co-operate she wouldn't have gone ahead. There were only two conditions: the first was that she wouldn't ask him to repeat any conversations held with inmates he'd counselled. The second was that the results of her findings wouldn't be published until after his transfer to open prison, which was due in three months' time.

'I've been reading one of your books,' he said, eyeing her over the rim of his coffee mug.

'Oh?' Her hand went to her face, her index finger finding the diamond stud in her nose. Rubbing the stone was an idiosyncrasy, a gesture she performed unconsciously the way some people chewed their nails or flicked back their hair 'Which one?'

'*Profiling Serial Killers*', he replied. 'You're very modest, if you don't mind me saying so.'

Megan gave him a puzzled smile. 'Modest?'

'You never told me you'd been inside every maximum security prison in the UK.' He cocked his head to one side. 'Or that you were the youngest person ever to become head of a university department.'

She shook her head with a soft hiss. 'The prison thing isn't something I tend to brag about – it's a bit of a conversation-stopper at dinner parties.'

'I can imagine!' His wide grin revealed even, white teeth. 'Has to be a damn sight more interesting than saying you're an accountant or something, though?'

'I suppose.' She nodded. 'But I sometimes get the feeling it's the only reason I'm invited – know what I mean?'

He nodded back. 'I sometimes feel like that. When they bring people here – government officials, that sort of thing – they trot me out like a prize poodle.'

Megan could picture it. The model inmate, wheeled out to prove that prison *could* work. She was fairly certain that the person Dom Wilde had become was down to his own strength of character, not anything or anyone he had encountered during his years inside. Prison nowadays was more about warehousing than anything else. There were few attempts at making inmates feel good about themselves.

'I hear you had a bad night.' She settled back in her chair, waiting for his version of events.

'Yeah.' He shook his head slowly. 'Young guy called Terry. Someone found out he was in for trying to kill his mother.' He pursed his lips. 'Course, the lads in here, well, some of them have got the word "mum" tattooed on their fingers…'

Megan drew in her breath. They might as well have thrown him to the wolves.

'He came to see me,' Dom went on. 'Turns out he'd put a pillow over her head because she had Alzheimer's. They didn't want to hear that, though, did they? So he ends up on Seg and on the first night he just loses it, poor sod.'

'So now they're all on twenty-three hour bang-up?

'Yeah.' He shrugged. 'That's nothing new, though. Happens more often than not these days, for all kinds of reasons. Staff shortages, staff training, any excuse, you know?'

'Can't do much for the atmosphere…' She looked him in the eyes. There was a wry smile on her face but she was digging. She had learnt early on that Dom was the sort of person who took time to open up. Talking to him was like panning for gold. His mind held nuggets of highly valuable information, but bringing them to the surface took patience. Ask him outright about something controversial and he would clam up. Despite the deal they had struck over the publication of her findings she wasn't sure she had won his trust yet.

As if echoing her thoughts he gave her a long look before replying. 'Well,' he said, 'the vibes in here have been pretty dire ever since Charlie got done over.'

'Charlie?'

'One of the screws. He was attacked by an inmate in the laundry. Smashed his head against one of the washing machines.'

Megan held his gaze, her face betraying no emotion, waiting for him to go on. This was good. This was something he hadn't mentioned up to now.

'There were others there. They saw what happened but they did nothing. Left him for dead.'

'But he didn't die?'

'No. But he was brain-damaged. He'll never work again.'

'How long ago did this happen?'

'Nearly a year ago.'

'Do you think it's had an effect on the suicide rates?' She wasn't going to say it outright, wasn't going to ask him to grass anyone up. Not yet, anyway.

He nodded. 'Oh yes,' he said. 'And how.'

'Dom,' she ventured, 'did you ever…I mean, have you ever thought about…' She hesitated, searching for the right words.

'Topping myself?' he finished the sentence for her. 'There was a time, yes,' he said softly, stroking his chin. 'It was five years into my sentence and I'd just had a knockback. They told me I was looking at seventeen years minimum before any chance of parole.'

She nodded, waiting for him to continue. Wondering if he could talk about it.

'I did the usual, you know,' he grunted, his mouth twisting into a half smile as his eyes met hers. 'Tore my bed sheet into strips and plaited them. Tied one end to the top of the window and looped the other round my neck.' He sniffed, glancing at the scuffed grey lino on the floor. 'I sat there on the edge of my bunk. Ready to jump. Four, five times I must have got right to the edge, closed my eyes and thought *This is it!*'

Megan waited, but he was just staring at the floor, his eyes glazed over. 'What changed your mind?' Her voice was almost a whisper.

'Having the choice,' he said, his mouth turning up at the edges as his eyes snapped back into focus. 'It suddenly came to me that this was the one thing I *did* have a choice about. And somehow, once I'd realised that, it was much easier to bear. Does that make sense?'

'Yes,' she said. 'Was that when you decided you wanted to do the degree?'

He smiled. 'When I was first here I couldn't even string a sentence together. Never even tried reading, bar page three of the *Sun*. Now the library's my favourite place. Can't imagine life without books.'

'There's one thing I don't understand about your life in here, though.' Megan looked into the twinkling grey eyes. 'You've got all this responsibility, the respect of the staff and the governor, but you're still on the wings. Why aren't you on enhanced status?'

'Ah, that's a sore point,' he chuckled, sitting back in his chair and rolling up the sleeves of his blue denim shirt. 'Me and one of the other lads – Carl Kelly – are both up for transfer to the enhanced wing, but there's no beds. There's only forty available out of a total of six-hundred and fifty, so you can imagine, there's a bit of a waiting list.' He shrugged, still smiling.

Megan tutted under her breath. How frustrating it must be to know you were entitled to sleep in a decent pine bed with a normal mattress instead of the metal cots with their thin, stained pads. Entitled, but not able. Not able to walk freely to and from a cell with no locks; look out of a window with no bars...

'I wouldn't be surprised if I don't actually make it to enhanced,' he added. 'The transfer might come sooner than free beds in here.' He rolled his eyes to the ceiling. 'S'pose it doesn't matter that much. What's a few more months after thirteen years?'

Megan pursed her lips. What was there to say to that? She sometimes had nightmares about prison; dreamed that she was on the other side, banged up with the people she'd been interviewing for a book or an academic paper. She would wake from such dreams bathed in sweat, her heart pounding, her eyes searching the outlines of the furniture in her bedroom for reassurance and comfort. Her ex-husband, Tony, had teased her about talking prison talk in her sleep; regurgitating the slang she had heard during the day. Going into a jail was like visiting another country. The language, the way of life, the whole culture was something set apart from the world outside. And each prison had the same language: Wormwood Scrubs or Parkhurst, Strangeways or Dartmoor – the slang was identical. And to get to know the inmates, you had to learn the lingo. Sometimes they would test her out, as Dominic had at their first meeting. He had told her there was a 'jugging' or a 'chibbing' in Balsall Gate at least once a week. She had nodded in silent assent. A jugging was an attack by one prisoner on another, involving pouring a jug of boiling water over the victim. It was usual to mix sugar with the water so that it would stick to the skin, causing the maximum possible damage. A chibbing, on the other hand, involved an attack with a blade. These would be manufactured by inmates, usually by melting the end of a comb or some other plastic object and inserting a razor blade into it.

'Carl's really pissed off about the enhancement.' Dominic's voice cut across her thoughts. 'His cell's much smaller than mine. Don't know how he stands it.'

Megan had had a guided tour of the prison and she knew that cells differed according to which wing they were on. The Victorian architect who had designed the place must have had a particularly mean streak, giving Balsall Gate the distinction of having the most cramped accommodation in the country. But she had only seen the cells when they were empty. It would be useful to hear just how pissed off Dom's fellow inmate was. If she went to Carl's cell with Dom, she might be able to persuade Fergus the guard to give the three of them a few minutes on their own. She gave Dom a sympathetic smile. 'Can I take a look?'

'Yeah, course you can.' Dom rose from his seat. 'Don't s'pose Carl's going to mind.' His eyebrows flicked upwards. 'He's been on his own the past few days 'cos his cell mate was released last week. It'll be a bit of light relief for him, talking to you.'

Megan looked at him. Her years of assessing the worst offenders in the criminal justice system had made her an expert bullshit detector. She had a lot of respect for Dom Wilde. He'd talked to her about the murder he'd committed but he'd also told her things he needn't have, like the fact he had a grown-up daughter he hadn't seen since the day she was born. The opinion she had formed was that he was a man who said what he meant and didn't try to massage egos to get what he wanted. She hoped the motivation for his helpfulness right now wasn't about providing a bit of titillation for a mate on twenty-three hour lock-up.

The giant Fergus came to escort them from the relatively civilised section of the prison that housed the counselling room to the wing occupied by Carl Kelly. The smell hit her when they reached the end of a winding corridor and Fergus unlocked a connecting door. It was a rancid mix of stale sweat and cigarettes, so powerful it made Megan want to gag. The smoking ban had not extended to prisons. They, like hospices and care homes, were considered in law to be private residences, so prisoners were still allowed to smoke in their cells and in the exercise yard. The reaction from prison officers to this decision had, in the main, been one of relief. There had been dire warnings of riots breaking out amongst inmates if they'd been prevented from smoking during the long periods of lock-up.

As she stepped across the threshold the sound of banging and shouting echoed behind the row of locked doors. The men nearest the entrance had heard the rattle of Fergus' keys and their catcalls spread from cell to cell. It was like standing next to a huge, bubbling saucepan that threatened to boil over at any second. Dominic turned to her and grinned. 'Welcome to Delta Wing – aka Baghdad. Quite quiet this afternoon, actually, isn't it Fergus?' he said.

The warder cocked his head on one side and listened. 'Yeah. Not too bad.' He looked at Megan and winked. 'Reckon they saw you out the window, ma'am – they're on their best behaviour!'

Megan grimaced. Fergus had made it clear from the first time he'd escorted her around the prison that he found her attractive. The comments he made were so obvious and were said in such a guileless manner that she found it impossible to take offence. She glanced at Dom and saw that he was grimacing too. 'Which is Carl's cell?' she asked him. He jerked a thumb towards the far left of the corridor and she followed him, Fergus trailing in their wake.

'I'll just make sure he's decent,' Dom said, flipping up the rectangular panel that covered the perspex observation window in the door. He bent down to peer into the cell. 'Shit!' He jumped back as if the metal flap had burnt his fingers. 'Fergus!' he yelled. 'Get in there – quick!'

'What is it?' Megan saw that his eyes were wide with horror and his face was drained of what little colour it had had. Then the guard was between them, keys rattling as he fumbled for the right one and thrust it into the lock.

'Jesus Christ!' As the door swung open Fergus stopped dead, his huge frame blocking Megan's view of the cell. Then his hand shot to the radio pager hanging from his belt. Through the gap created when he lifted it to his mouth Megan saw what Dom Wilde had seen through the observation panel. Carl Kelly was slumped on a chair, naked apart from a pair of blue boxer shorts. There was a syringe lodged in his left thigh. His head was tipped back at an angle against the wall of the cell and his arms were locked together, the elbows sticking out at unnatural angles and the fingers clawing at the air. As the guard lumbered towards him she got a full view of the face. The mouth was contorted into a ghoulish grin.

Chapter 2

'Carl! Christ, mate!' Dom Wilde pressed the pale flesh at the neck, feeling for a pulse. Megan was still staring at the lifeless face. The eyebrows were raised and the open, grinning lips were blue round the edges.

Fergus was barking into his radio pager. Seconds later there was a thunder of footsteps in the corridor outside. Half a dozen guards crowded into the cell. A few minutes later the prison doctor arrived to confirm that the inmate was indeed dead.

He pulled down the boxer shorts and shoved a thermometer into BG 199718 Carl Kelly's anus. Death, he estimated, had occurred within the past two hours. This was confirmed by Dom, who said he had been chatting to Carl about an hour and a half ago, just before he went for the interview with Megan.

'Why is he...*smiling*?' Dom had turned away when the doctor was making his examination. His question was addressed to the cell wall. His voice, calm and matter-of-fact up to now, was bitter, almost accusing.

'It's what's known as *risus sardonicus*.' The doctor wiped the thermometer and slid it back into its case. 'Common symptom of tetanus – otherwise known as lockjaw.' He beckoned to the hospital orderlies who were waiting outside the door with a stretcher. 'Heroin addicts are a high-risk group for it. Dirty needles...' He trailed off as the orderlies prepared to lift the dead man.

'Could the tetanus have killed him?' Megan asked.

'Possible, but unlikely,' the doctor replied. 'Cause of death is much more likely to have been an overdose. Of course, we can't be certain. Have to wait for the post-mortem.'

Fergus and some of the other prison officers removed their caps as the corpse was carried out of the cell. Megan watched the two who didn't. One was short and stocky with a grey moustache. The other was taller with ferrety eyes. She saw them exchange glances as the body went through the door. Ferret-face mouthed something to his friend. Something like, 'Stupid bastard.'

Megan looked at Dom as they waited to be questioned by the police. He was so different from the man she'd got to know over the past few weeks. He had always seemed so calm, so in control of his emotions. She had seen him with other prisoners, men who were literally shaking with fear after being threatened by another inmate, or weeping like children after receiving a 'Dear John' letter from a wife or girlfriend. Dom had a knack of pouring oil on troubled waters. He was always able to find the right words and say them in the right way to put others at ease, no matter how worked up they were. But he hadn't spoken since they had left Carl Kelly's cell. He was sitting, bent over, with his head in his hands as if he was racking his brains for an answer to what had happened.

'Do you think it was an accident?' Megan wasn't sure if he had heard. His shirt collar was up over his ears. 'Dom…' she began again, but in a quick movement he sat up.

'What do you mean?' His eyes locked on hers for a second before turning back to the floor. She couldn't read his expression. There was genuine grief in those eyes. But there was something else as well. Despair? Anger? Clearly Dom and Carl had been close friends. Just how close she wasn't sure. Did Dom blame himself for Carl's death? Did he feel he'd failed him some way?

'What I mean,' she said, 'is that the overdose could have been deliberate.' She paused, waiting for him to give her more.

'He told me he was off the gear.' The pale skin below his hairline puckered into frown lines. 'Carl was doing a lot of brown when I first got to know him. He'd done just over a year of his bird when I arrived.' Megan nodded. She knew Dom Wilde had been in three other prisons before being transferred to Balsall Gate. 'He had regular suppliers,' he went on. 'Screws, mainly.' He glanced at her again. Probably to see if she was surprised by this revelation. She wasn't. 'Anyway, he really wanted to get clean,' Dom went on. 'He knew he'd never get parole if he didn't. And fair play to him, he did it. Took about six months, but he really kicked it. Started going to the gym, reading books – even got himself a girlfriend.'

'A girlfriend?'

'Yeah.' He blinked, then rolled his eyes. 'This woman had been writing to him. Started visiting him a couple of months ago. She was...' He hesitated, shrugging again. 'She was what the lads in here would describe as "very fit".'

Had Dom been jealous, she wondered? He didn't sound it. Perhaps he and Carl hadn't been lovers, then.

'Are you sure she hadn't finished with him? I mean, that could've been a reason...' She tailed off. His pain was tangible. She felt uncomfortable about saying the word 'suicide' now.

'No,' Dom cut in, 'she hadn't. He showed me a letter she sent him this morning – she said she couldn't wait for him to get out.' His eyes clouded and he turned them to the floor again.

'Dom, what was Carl in for?'

'Dealing.'

'Heroin?'

'Yeah, and the rest,' he said. 'Carl was in and out of prison from when he was a teenager. He was on a five-year stretch this time.' His eyes narrowed and he opened his mouth as if to add something, then shut it again.

'What?' Megan asked.

Dom pursed his lips, shaking his head.

'Please, tell me.'

'It's not important. Not now.'

'Dom, if this was deliberate…if Carl overdosed on purpose…'

'I know what you're saying: you want to know if someone drove him to it. Well they didn't. Not anyone on this earth, anyway.'

'What do you mean?'

'Something he told me. I promised I'd never tell anyone. But now he's…Christ!' He broke off, cupping his face in his hands.

'What was it? Please, Dom, it might be important.'

There was a muffled sigh. When he answered her he uncovered his mouth but not his eyes. 'He said he killed a man and got away with it.'

'Oh?'

'Stabbed him in a row over money he was owed for drugs.' Dom rubbed his eyes and jerked his head at the tiny, barred window. 'He said the bloke was buried over there.'

Megan gave him a blank look. Then she twigged. 'In St Mary's? In that graveyard near the prison gate?'

'Yeah, it used to freak him out. See, if you stand on a chair you can see the graveyard through the cell window. Carl said he used to lie awake at night thinking the bloke was coming back to haunt him.'

Chapter 3

The police didn't seem interested in attending Carl Kelly's post-mortem. It was obvious from the questions Detective Sergeant Les Willis asked that he regarded the investigation as a waste of his time. As far as he was concerned a convicted drug dealer had died by his own hand – and good riddance. Whether it was suicide or an accident really didn't matter. Nor did the fact that the drug Kelly had injected had been smuggled into the prison. Megan got the message loud and clear: to DS Willis, that was the governor's problem, not theirs.

So she was the only person, other than the pathologist, to be in on the examination carried out in the hospital wing of the prison. Alistair Hodge was an old acquaintance of hers. She had watched him dissect the bodies of several murder victims, all female, but she had never seen him perform a post-mortem on a man.

'I'm surprised to find you here.' He glanced at her across the shrouded body, his broad Scots voice echoing round the bare walls.

Megan gave him the official line about her research. There was no reason to suspect that Hodge would go telling tales to Malcolm Meredith but there was no point taking any risks: for all she knew they could be golfing pals. 'I certainly never expected to find myself at a scene of death while I was here,' she added. That was enough to justify her presence, if that was what he was after.

'Well,' he chuckled, pulling on a pair of thin latex gloves,

'I've done so many post-mortems here in the past six months I'm thinking of renting myself a cell. Hell of a place, isn't it? Not surprising the poor bastards keep topping themselves.' His silver-rimmed spectacles caught the light as he pulled back the sheet covering the body. 'This one looks like a happy chappy, though, doesn't he?'

Once again, Megan found herself staring at the evil, open-mouthed grin on Carl Kelly's face. She looked away. The only way to take a dispassionate look at the dead man was to hold her hand up in front of her, allowing a view from just the nose up. His eyes were large and blue and the cheeks were plump. The hair was dark brown and short-cropped, slightly spiky. He bore more than a passing resemblance to Robbie Williams. She dropped her hand and immediately her eyes were drawn back to the mouth. It seemed to exert a horrible fascination. It was impossible *not* to look.

'Tetanic spasm,' the pathologist said as he moved around the head, inspecting it from various angles. 'Not uncommon in heroin addicts.' There was a pause as he ran his eyes over the rest of the body. There were tattoos on each arm, one in blue of an oriental dragon and another in green of a bare-breasted mermaid. 'This is interesting.' Hodge was staring at a small purple bruise on the dead man's left thigh. It was the mark left by the syringe that had still been in the vein when Megan, Dom and Fergus had found the body.

'What?' Megan moved closer, bending her head to inspect the bruise. The smell of tobacco smoke and rancid sweat seemed to have followed Carl Kelly from the cell.

'There are no other bruises. No other evidence of injecting.' Alistair Hodge's eyes met hers for a second before scanning the body again.

'So he wasn't a regular user?'

The pathologist shook his head. 'Doesn't look like it. Bit of bad luck, that, overdosing on your first time.'

'And unlikely,' Megan said, 'because one of the other inmates told me he'd been a regular user in the past. He must have known what he was doing.'

'Also unlikely that he'd have developed tetanus.' He raised his head and pushed his spectacles back up his nose. 'It takes time to kick in. Even if the needle he used was dirty, if this was the first time he'd injected in a long while…' He tailed off, the corners of his mouth turning down as he glanced at Megan.

'Could he have got the tetanus some other way?' she asked. 'From a cut or something? I mean, the conditions in this place are not exactly hygienic, are they?'

Alistair shook his head. 'I'm sure you could catch a lot worse than tetanus. We'll know more when we've done the tests.'

'What's your gut reaction to this, though?' Megan held his gaze. 'Do you think it could have been suicide?'

'I don't know.' He shrugged. 'We may never know. What I can say is that if it *is* suicide, it's the first one I've seen in this place that's involved drugs.'

'Could the heroin have been cut with something?' Megan asked. 'Something that could have killed him where the heroin alone wouldn't have?'

'Quite possible.' He nodded. 'Dealers are cutting drugs with all kinds of rubbish these days. The toxicology report's going to show that up, anyway.' He rubbed the skin between his lower lip and his chin, staring vacantly at the body as if he was weighing something up. 'You say you've spoken to one of the other inmates about him?'

'Yes – why?'

'Did you get the impression that Mr Kelly here had any enemies?'

'No one specific, but in a prison it's next to impossible not to rub someone up the wrong way.' She frowned. 'Why?

You don't think someone…' She allowed herself to look at the head again, at that awful, grinning face.

'Someone could have given him dodgy heroin on purpose, yes,' he said. 'How the hell you'd prove it, though, I've no idea.'

Megan stayed away from the prison the next day. Her teaching workload at the university had been lightened this term to allow time for the research she was doing but she felt unable to carry on with it until she was clear about exactly how Carl Kelly had died. If someone had deliberately set out to kill him and that someone was one of the prison officers, she needed to know. It would throw a whole new light on what was going on inside Balsall Gate, hinting at a level of organised crime and intimidation that went way beyond anything she had anticipated.

She wondered how much Dom Wilde knew that he wasn't telling her. He had hinted at things but she had the impression he was holding something back. His reaction to Carl's death had been a revelation. Was he more afraid than he appeared to be?

She spent the next day and a half organising the notes she had already taken. Despite the fact that she wasn't officially meant to be in her office, there were constant interruptions from various members of staff who had obviously been waiting to grab her the moment she reappeared. When she heard a fifth person knock her door in the space of an hour she groaned under her breath. This time it wasn't one of the departmental lecturers. It was an undergraduate called Nathan MacNamara.

'Dr Rhys?' He stood on the threshold, six foot two of skin and bone, his blond-streaked brown hair sticking out from his head like a tarnished halo.

'Nathan.' She tried to inject some warmth into her voice but her heart had sunk at the sight of him. She wondered what excuse he'd cooked up this time.

'I brought you something.' He ambled into the room, covering the space between the door and her desk in three long strides. Reaching into the pocket of his baggy, ripped parka he pulled out a brown paper bag with something bulky inside. Whatever it was had exuded grease while inside his coat, leaving translucent blobs on the paper.

'Er…thank you Nathan. What is it?' She took the bag between the nails of her thumb and forefinger, trying to avoid contact with her skin.

'It's a piece of birthday cake. As you couldn't come to the party I thought I'd bring you some.' He gave her a sheepish smile. 'It's fudge cake. With chocolate orange segments on top.'

She peered inside the bag, searching for something to say. He was leaning across her desk, so close now she could smell him: it was the kind of smell given off by so many male students, a mixture of beer slops and rancid trainers. It was so difficult. He was one of the brightest students in his year but he was becoming a complete pain. What did he see when he looked at her, she wondered? She was twice his age and probably about two stone heavier. But those moonstruck eyes made it quite obvious that he fancied her. Perhaps what he was really looking for was a substitute mother. But if he was, she absolutely was not going to be it.

'That's very kind of you – I think I'll save it for this evening.' She fixed her eyes on his. 'You probably won't be seeing much of me for the rest of this term and next – I'm off on sabbatical to the University of Ulan Bator.' She gave him the very faintest of smiles, hoping that a little levity might get the message across without letting him down too hard.

'Wow! That's like, really cool.'

Bugger, she thought. *Why are some bright kids so thick?* 'I was joking, Nathan,' she said. 'But I meant what I said about not being around much in the next couple of months, so if you need any help you will go and talk to Doctor Walker, won't you?'

He nodded and backed towards the door. The expression on his face said it all. Doctor Walker was his tutor. He was also a martial arts expert who didn't suffer fools gladly. 'I'll see you, then.' There was a definite tremor in his lower lip. She heard his huge feet shuffling off down the corridor. Guiltily, she deposited the brown paper bag in the bin.

When the phone rang she was staring out of the window at the distant walls of Balsall Gate, thinking about Carl Kelly. By now his body must have been transported to the city morgue. Free at last, she thought.

'Megan?' There was something in the tone of the pathologist's voice that warned her something unexpected was on its way.

'What is it?'

He gave a short cough before answering, as if he found the news faintly embarrassing. 'There wasn't enough heroin in the system to kill him. He died of strychnine poisoning, would you believe?'

'Strychnine?' She blinked at the distant, grey outline of the prison, wondering if she'd heard right.

'I know – bizarre, isn't it?'

'Sounds like something out of an Agatha Christie novel.'

'Well, it certainly explains the evil grin.' She heard a sort of grunty chuckle at the other end of the phone. 'I have to admit I've never come across a strychnine death before, which is why I went for the tetanus line. I thought it was a straightforward case of lockjaw, but it wasn't. You can also get *risus sardonicus* from the muscle spasms caused by strychnine entering the bloodstream.' The pathologist cleared his throat again. This time he sounded as if he was about to deliver a lecture: 'A fatal dose may be as little as 30-60mg. It's one of the cruellest poisons in existence because it causes excruciating agony whilst not affecting consciousness. The convulsions are sometimes so severe that muscles are torn away from ligaments and tendons...' He tailed off, leaving her with a vivid picture of Carl Kelly, locked up alone in his cell, writhing as if being tortured as the poison took hold.

'They used to use it on rats,' he went on. 'But now the only mammal you can use it on in this country is moles. It's strictly controlled, though, and quite hard to get hold of.'

'So where did it come from?'

'Well, the only people who are supposed to have access to it are licensed pest controllers. But there's a black market for it like any other restricted drug.'

'But why would any drug dealer *want* to cut heroin with a substance that kills?' Megan persisted. 'I mean, it's not exactly good for business, is it? Bumping your clients off.'

'God knows,' Hodge replied. 'It could've been a mistake. I've seen plenty of those in my time. All the dealers care about is diluting the drug to make a bigger profit. Washing powder, talc, you name it. If it looks like a mixer they'll use it.'

'Hmm.' Megan frowned at her reflection in the window pane. 'If it was a dodgy batch of heroin you'd expect a whole spate of deaths like this, wouldn't you?'

'You would,' he said, 'and your next question is going to be have I seen any more corpses with gruesome grins on their faces? Well, as I said before, this is the first strychnine case I've ever come across. Doesn't mean to say I won't be seeing more in the near future, though. It's going to be a waiting game, isn't it?'

* * *

Five minutes later Megan was on the phone to Detective Sergeant Les Willis of West Midlands police.

As she waited to be connected she reached for the stash of prunes in her desk drawer. *Investigate*, that's a joke, she thought, popping a couple into her mouth. She swallowed them without chewing them. Would the toxicology report have any impact on Sergeant Willis' indifferent attitude, she wondered? It didn't.

'As far as I'm aware,' Willis said in his slow, rather ponderous voice, 'there have been no recent cases of that nature in the West Midlands force area. Of course, it's not the kind of information we have to hand – it'd take time to check the statistics of drug-related deaths…'

Megan listened as he explained exactly what this would entail. By the time he had finished she had covered the whole of a page of her notebook with doodles.

'Yes, well, if you could let me know if you do come across anything,' she said. 'Because if you don't, we could be looking at a murder.'

'Oh, I think that's a bit of a leap of the imagination, don't you, Dr Rhys?'

'Why?' She didn't feel like being polite. In the past two years she'd spent more time helping the police solve major crimes than she had on academic research. She had been asked by officers far higher up the pecking order than Willis to profile serial killers and rapists. The majority of the detectives she had worked with had valued her opinions. She didn't appreciate being dismissed like some busybody with an overactive imagination.

'Well,' he persisted, 'deaths like this – we see them all the time.'

'I thought you just said that you hadn't?'

'Not exactly like this, but, you know…'

'What?' She felt heat rising from her neck to her face. 'What do I know, Sergeant?'

He hesitated a moment before replying. She knew she was being bolshy but she didn't care.

'Er…well, the dealers, you know.' She detected the effort in his voice. He was trying not to lose his rag with her. 'They're always cutting the drugs with new stuff and...'

'I just want you to keep an open mind,' she interrupted. 'Carl Kelly may have been a low-life smackhead, but I'm not going to stand by and watch this case being brushed under the carpet just because he was in prison when he died. He's entitled to the same justice as anyone else.'

There was silence at the other end then the line went dead. She stared at the receiver. 'Bastard's hung up on me!' she said aloud. She could phone back, of course. But no doubt DS Willis would say they'd been accidentally cut off. With a grunt, she replaced the receiver in its cradle. What was the point? If there was any detective work to be done here, she was going to have to do it herself.

Chapter 4

By late afternoon Megan was back inside Balsall Gate prison. Her nose wrinkled as she walked along the narrow corridors. The usual body odour and smoke was tinged with a greasy, burnt smell, like overcooked sausages.

'He's in the library – you'll have to wait in here while I get someone to fetch him.' The man escorting her today was Ferret-face, one of the prison officers who had not doffed his cap when the body of Carl Kelly was removed from its cell. He had not introduced himself to her, but she had heard the man on the gate call him Al. He sat down in a chair on the other side of the waiting room, his thin lips set in what looked like a permanent sneer. He turned his face away as he hissed into his radio pager. When he had given out his instructions he continued to stare at the wall, seemingly unable to make eye contact.

The atmosphere in the small, bare room was as thick as the smell in the corridor outside. His hand was in his pocket and he was fiddling with some coins. The jangle of metal on metal was the only sound she could hear above the distant shouts of prisoners calling to each other through the windows of their cells. He seemed on edge. Was it because of her, she wondered? Was he unnerved by her presence in the prison? Did he have something to hide? And if so, what?

It was clear from the conversation she'd overheard at the gate that the prison officers hadn't yet got wind of the fact that Carl Kelly died of strychnine poisoning. She could use this to her advantage. Find out just how much the guards *did* know about the narcotics trade in this place.

Ferret-face shifted in his chair, making its rubber legs squeak on the lino. She had to think of a way of getting him to talk. But loosening the tongue of a hard-faced prison officer of twenty-odd years' service wasn't going to be easy. She needed an angle. The jingling in his pocket intensified as she searched for the right words. She opened her mouth, then shut it again. No point in pussyfooting around, she thought. Go for the jugular.

'You know,' she said, shaking her head slowly for extra effect, 'I can't believe a waster like Carl Kelly managed to get hold of enough gear to top himself.'

No response. Not even a twitch of those tight lips. Too obvious, perhaps. She tried another tack. An audible sigh, then she said: 'They really piss me off, his type.'

The chink-chink of the coins stopped. His eyes were still on the wall but she sensed that she now had his full attention. After a slight pause, she went on: 'They're in here for a couple of years, Premier league football on the telly, regular food – all paid for by the likes of you and me – then they're back out to their BMWs and their Rolex watches...' She tailed off, watching him intently, and saw one eyebrow lift half an inch. 'I know I shouldn't say it,' she said, shaking her head again, 'but as far as I can see it's bloody good riddance when someone like Carl Kelly gets his comeuppance.'

She saw the lips part. Heard him draw in his breath.

'I thought you lot were all bleeding heart liberal *Guardian* readers.' He said it to the wall but she could see the faint trace of a smirk on his face.

'Yeah, right,' she said, clicking her tongue against the roof of her mouth. 'How long do you think airy-fairy shit like that lasts when you've spent half your working life listening to the lies these bastards tell you?'

With a grunt he cleared his throat. 'Tell that to the governor and these do-gooding prison visitors, will you? Always on our bloody case, they are. "Respect the inmates and treat them well," they say. "Be a role model for when they get out." Bollocks to that, if you'll pardon my French!'

She smiled to herself. It was beginning to work. Now she needed to move it up a gear. It was a risky strategy and she knew she was only going to get one chance. 'What I can't figure out,' she said, 'is how Kelly managed to get hold of enough heroin to overdose.' She paused. He didn't respond. 'I know you can get small amounts easily enough, but how would he have got his hands on that kind of volume?'

She heard a noise that was a mixture of a cough and a snort. When he spoke his voice was low and gruff. 'They don't need much and they all have their crafty little ways'.

She dug her nails into the palms of her hands, willing him to go on. But he fell silent.

'And what would those be?' She held her breath.

'Put it this way,' he said, with a slow nod of his head, 'Dealers aren't the only ones who want to drive round in BMWs.'

'What do you mean by that?' She went hot in the face as the words came out. It sounded clumsy. She'd overplayed her hand.

He looked at her for the first and only time since they had entered the room. 'Nothing,' he said. 'Nothing at all.' The lips clamped shut.

In the few awkward seconds that followed she stared at the pock-marked lino at her feet, inwardly cursing herself for getting so close and blowing it. What was all that innuendo about? Did he know about the strychnine? Was that what he and his mate had been muttering about when Carl Kelly's body was carried out of the cell? Had they been party to his death or turned a blind eye to someone else's involvement in it?

The crackle of a radio pager made her look up. A disembodied voice announced that Dom Wilde was out of the library and waiting to see her. With his customary grunt, Ferret-face got to his feet and pointed to the door.

The lids of Dom Wilde's soulful grey eyes were tinged red. She wondered if he'd been crying. Clearly she hadn't quite worked him out. Up until the day Carl Kelly had died, she'd had him down as a man who was totally unflappable. When she had asked how he could be so calm in such a stressful environment, he had told her about his discovery of Buddhism. Apparently he spent the hours of confinement in meditation, having developed a technique for switching off his mind to the noises around him.

'Are you okay, Dom?' she asked, as she settled into the armchair opposite him.

'A bit tired,' he replied. His lips turned up slightly at the edges. It was a ghost of his usual grin. 'It all kicked off again last night – didn't get much sleep.'

'What was the problem? Was it because of Carl?'

He nodded. 'It always happens when there's a death in here. Doesn't make any difference if it's a suicide or an overdose. It freaks people out, you know?'

'I can imagine.' She leaned forward in her chair, her eyes searching his. 'Dom, I know this must be really hard for you, because Carl was a mate. It must be doubly hard because you were the one who helped him get off drugs in the first place.' She hesitated, wondering if he was up to being questioned. 'There's something I need to ask you, though.' His eyes met hers. The weariness in them was tempered with the warmth he'd always shown her in the past.

'What is it?' he asked. 'It's okay.' He coughed and swallowed. 'I'm okay. Really.'

'Are you sure?'

He nodded.

'Well,' she began, 'what you said before, about there being nobody on this earth who might have driven Carl to suicide – what if it wasn't that?'

He blinked. 'What are you saying?'

'Did Carl have any enemies in here? Anyone who might have wanted him dead?' She watched his face change. The brow furrowed and the eyes narrowed. It was a look of incomprehension.

'You think he was murdered?'

'It's possible, yes,' she nodded. 'I'm going to tell you what the post-mortem revealed, but no one else in the prison knows yet, so you didn't hear it from me, all right?'

'Yes, okay…' Her words seemed to have knocked him off balance. 'What happened?'

When she told him about the strychnine his eyes widened. His look of disbelief changed to revulsion when she explained that agonising muscle spasms would have caused the fixed grin on Carl Kelly's face.

'Christ, if only I'd been there!' He shook his head. 'What a bloody awful way to die.'

'There was nothing you could have done,' she said gently. 'It only takes a tiny amount of the stuff to kill someone. And the effect is irreversible.'

He sat for a moment, his head bowed, staring at his hands. She had never seen him looking so lost, so vulnerable. She felt an almost irresistible urge to put her hand on his shoulder. But she fought it. To touch a prisoner, to step over the professional boundary, was an absolute no-no. Never before had she felt like doing this. But she had never met a prisoner quite like him before.

Here was a man who had been locked up for thirteen years in the most appalling conditions and yet there was some untainted, almost innocent quality about him. Two years ago, when she had first set eyes on him, her initial impression was of a powerful, muscular man who was not to be messed with. It had come as a surprise to learn that he was a counsellor – and a good one at that. But there had been a moment, just a week into her research here, when she had glimpsed what lay beneath the tough exterior. Fergus had been escorting her to the counselling room when a message had been relayed that Dom Wilde was with an inmate on the wing they were passing through. Fergus had taken her to the cell and lifted the viewing panel, allowing her to see what was going on inside.

A distraught man was slumped on a bunk with tears streaming down his face. As she watched, Dom reached out and took his hand. It was obvious from the manner in which he did it that this was the gesture of a man who was not afraid to be seen showing compassion.

Now here she was again, looking at him. His head was bent and his eyes closed. This time *he* was the one who needed compassion. She leaned closer, until there was only an inch or two between their heads.

Suddenly his eyes snapped open. 'Why do you think it was murder? I mean, it could've just been a dodgy batch of brown…'

Her face flushed as she straightened up in her chair. 'Yes… I…er…' She felt as if he'd caught her doing something underhand. She blinked and took a breath. 'I know that's the obvious conclusion, but if it was a batch of the stuff you'd expect more deaths, wouldn't you? If not in the prison itself, then in the wider community.'

He considered this. 'Yes, I suppose you would. You've checked, then?'

'I've talked to the police about it, yes. Not that they were very forthcoming.'

'Tell me about it,' he shook his head. 'I've seen it time and time again. They don't give a stuff about deaths in prison.'

'Well, they certainly didn't buy my theory about Carl,' she said. 'But the more I think about it, the less far-fetched it seems to be. The question is, who would want to kill him?'

'No one I can think of. He hadn't had any recent run-ins with anyone. Like I said, he was keeping his nose clean. Didn't want to screw up his chances of getting a transfer to an open prison.'

'What about that incident you were telling me about earlier? The attack on a prison officer in the laundry – was Carl involved in that?'

'He was there, yeah,' Dom nodded, 'but he didn't actually do anything.'

'But he didn't help the guy who was attacked? He walked out with the others?'

'Well, yeah, but there were ten of them in there. Why pick on him for revenge? And anyway, it was ages ago – why wait till now?'

Megan shrugged. 'Well, no. It doesn't add up, does it? It's just that if the screws are bringing drugs in for the prisoners and a screw wanted revenge on someone...' Her eyebrows framed the question.

He shrugged back, but said nothing.

'I was talking to one of them before I came to you,' she said. 'His name's Al. He as good as told me he was bent.'

'Megan...' Dom tailed off with a sigh. 'Please don't ask me to name names. I can't risk it, you know? I know I said I'd help you but that was before...' He shook his head and lowered his eyes, as if he was ashamed of what he was about to say. 'I might not always show it, but I'm desperate to get out of this dump. I've wasted so many years of my life and I don't want to throw any more down the pan. I want to be able to walk in the fresh air, get a job and somewhere decent to live. And I want to find my daughter.' He pressed his lips tight, as if just saying the word caused him physical pain. 'Do you know what I'm trying to say? It's different now. Carl's death has upped the ante. If I start dishing the dirt now I can see myself leaving this place in a pine box.'

'Okay, Dom,' she whispered. 'I hear what you're saying. But just tell me one thing, will you – and you don't have to say anything – just nod or shake your head. Do you think Carl got that lethal dose of drugs from one of the prison officers in here?'

'I can answer that,' he nodded. 'And I can tell you this: there are at least half a dozen screws bringing gear into this place on a regular basis. They want paying in cash from the outside. Carl didn't have anyone on the outside to do that for him. Not any more. In the beginning, when I first met him, he had a pal – someone he used to deal for – who owed him a few favours and made sure he got supplies. But a couple of months after I got here he told me his pal had been shot in some turf war. Bit of a silver lining in that, 'cos it helped him kick the habit, not having a regular supplier any more. Not sure he would've got himself clean if it hadn't been for that.'

'What about that girlfriend you told me about? Could she have been getting hold of drugs or money for him?'

'I doubt it.'

'Why? Did he talk about her? Did he tell you why she'd decided to hook up with someone like him?'

He shook his head. 'He didn't tell me that much about her. I know she had big plans for when he got out, though.' His face creased into frown lines. 'I was chuffed for him and all that but it surprised me, because she hadn't been coming to see him for very long. And she wasn't the usual type you get writing to guys in prison, you know? They tend to be older and, well, sadder, if you get my meaning.'

'But this girl was young and attractive, you say?'

'She was, yes. But Carl was a good-looking guy as well. I guess they just clicked. And why would she have been so keen if she knew he was back on drugs? Why would she want to set up home with a smackhead?'

'Hmm.' Megan considered this for a moment. 'What about that other thing you told me – about the guy he killed in a fight over drugs?'

'That was a long time ago. More than fifteen years, I think he said. It's like the thing in the laundry – why wait that long for revenge?'

'What if someone's been biding their time? Maybe a mate of the dead man who's been in prison and only just got out? Did he ever say the name of the person he killed?'

Dom screwed his face up. 'He did, yeah. It was something weird out of the Bible. Let me think… Noah, or Ezekiel or something…' He scratched his head. 'No, I've got it: Moses – that was it. Moses Smith.'

The sun was setting as Megan walked away from the prison. It set the shinier gravestones in St Mary's churchyard ablaze with colour. There were some huge, elaborate memorials; towering angels with chipped wings and noses, harking back to a time when this was a prosperous, respectable area of Birmingham.

She was searching for the last resting place of Moses Smith. There was no particularly good reason for this. But she had to pass through the graveyard anyway and she felt impelled to find something, anything, that connected to Carl Kelly's past. She had felt the same about the Birmingham prostitutes whose killer she had brought to justice just over a year ago. Like Carl, they were vulnerable people on the fringes of society. And – also like him – they were regarded by the tabloid-reading public as deserving whatever gruesome fate befell them. One thing that had struck her during the many post-mortems she had attended was that in death, everyone is equal. If some rock star or politician had been found dead from strychnine poisoning the press would be howling for an explanation. In her view, Carl Kelly was no less important.

It took longer than she expected to find the grave. The stone was smaller than average and the inscription was almost obscured by a stand of rose bay willow herb that had seeded itself directly in front of the black granite slab. All that was visible was "RIP Mos". She bent down to push the pink-headed stalks aside. Now she could read it all. There wasn't much: "RIP Moses 'Mo' Smith, 13.1.60 – 14.3.91."

As she straightened up she noticed something else. There was a rectangular patch of bare earth at the centre of the grave. All around the grass grew thick and coarse, but in the middle of Moses Smith's plot, the ground had been disturbed. She stood staring at it in the fading light. Had someone else been buried here recently? His wife, perhaps? It seemed unlikely that burials would still be taking place when the church itself was derelict. And anyway, the patch looked too small for that. It was barely three feet long and only a couple of feet wide. Not even big enough for the wooden caskets they put people's ashes in. So what had happened? Had someone deliberately interfered with the grave? And if so, why? Could it have something to do with Carl Kelly's death?

She shivered as the dying rays of the sun lit up the clods of earth at her feet. The police would have to be told about this. And if they wouldn't listen she would come back here tomorrow with a camera. And a trowel.

Chapter 5

There wasn't time to go home. Megan was due to meet her
friend Delva Lobelo for drinks at one of the bars overlooking
the canal basin. She'd planned to shower and change, to
wash the vile smell of the prison from her skin and her hair.
But she'd spent longer than she intended with Dom Wilde.

The walk back from the prison took her to the rear entrance
of Heartland University's Department of Investigative
Psychology. She paused when she reached the reserved space
where her car was parked. Glancing up at the windows of
the building she noticed that there were still a few students
in the library. What was the betting one of them was Nathan
MacNamara? She knew that part of the reason she didn't
want to go back to her office to check the phone messages
and emails that had no doubt piled up during her afternoon
at the prison was because of him. It was getting ridiculous.
It was as if he could sense her presence in the building. She
was going to have to ask the admin people to intercept him
if they saw him coming along the corridor. With a heavy
sigh she climbed into the car. She would just have to put off
checking the emails until she got back home.

But there was one thing she wouldn't put off. Before
driving out of the car park she punched out the number
of West Midlands Police on her mobile. She was halfway
across the city before the switchboard managed to locate DS
Willis.

'A disturbed grave? At St Mary's?'

She could tell from the inflection in his voice that he

had her down as a timewaster. The unkempt graveyard of a derelict church was a prime target for local louts. Why should what Megan had spotted be anything other than a random act of vandalism? The fact of the grave being that of Carl Kelly's alleged victim failed to impress him. Kelly had never been convicted of murder and he wasn't interested in what he obviously regarded as tale-telling by a fellow inmate.

With a grunt Megan ended the call. Put that way, it did sound pretty flimsy. But there was something about the way the grave had been disturbed; it was all so...*neat*. Why would some bored teenager bother to dig a perfect rectangle on the top of someone's grave? Far more effective, surely, to spray graffiti on a tombstone or knock the head off an angel. She could almost imagine kids exhuming a body for a gruesome prank, but they couldn't possibly have got a coffin out of a hole that size. She frowned as she searched for a parking space along the canal basin. It didn't add up. There had to be an explanation, but it wasn't going to come to her tonight.

There was a large mirror at the entrance to the bar and she winced at the site of her reflection. Her long black hair was windswept and her olive skin looked sallow in the fluorescent light. She darted into the ladies and rummaged in her bag for one of the many lipsticks that lurked at the bottom. Her fingers closed round the silver tube of a Body Shop number called Pink Ginger. It did an instant brightening job on her face. Glancing down, she adjusted the long silk scarf that had slipped into two unequal tails on the walk from the prison. Great things, scarves, she thought, for hiding a bulging tum.

Pulling a wry face at herself in the mirror, she reached for the door. She'd long since stopped worrying about what she looked like next to Delva, who was a statuesque West African with Naomi Campbell cheekbones. The last time the two of them had been out together they'd been called 'an exotic pair'. The comment had come from an elderly man who was somewhat the worse for drink and he had incorrectly guessed that Megan was Brazilian. People usually had her down as southern European. Her mixed Welsh/Indian heritage was an unusual one and she liked the way it kept people guessing.

She walked through to the bar and immediately caught sight of Delva's braided hair, which twisted round her head like a sculpture. She was chatting to the barman, who was beaming at her, no doubt revelling in the kudos of serving someone he'd seen on the telly. Delva was anchorwoman on the local news channel and she had just finished her shift. In a red linen pencil skirt and cropped jacket, she looked as if she'd just stepped off the catwalk. No matter how hectic her day had been, Delva's clothes were always immaculate. Megan wasn't sure how she did it. She supposed that being on camera every day made her ultra-conscious of her appearance.

But Delva's personality was the total opposite of the model-girl image. Off screen, when she opened her mouth the first thing you were likely to hear was her amazing, throaty laugh. It was so loud and so deep that it took people by surprise. It was the kind of laugh that made it almost impossible for those who heard it to keep a straight face. Megan heard it now, booming across the room as Delva caught sight of her.

'Hiya –what you having? He's making me a Pink Lady!' Delva guffawed at the barman, who grinned back as he poured a lurid-coloured liquid into a silver cocktail shaker.

'Well, I er…' Megan hesitated. She felt like a drink to loosen her up after the prison visit. 'I think I'll have a small Pinot Grigio.'

'Oh come on! It's Happy Hour!' Delva batted her on the bottom with her Louis Vuitton handbag.

'Oh, go on then!' Megan sank onto a bar stool, suddenly aware of how tired she felt. But a few sips of Pink Lady seemed to have a remarkable effect on her state of mind. She and Delva moved to one of the little booths at the far side of the bar where they could chat without being overheard. Delva started regaling her with tales of the latest shenanigans in the newsroom and Megan found herself almost crying with laughter. It was like listening to an episode of *Drop The Dead Donkey*.

'Anyway,' Delva said, downing the last of her cocktail, 'tell me about Jonathan. How's it going?'

'Well,' Megan said, rolling her eyes, 'he's in Australia at the moment as an expert witness in a murder trial. And the week before that he was in Bosnia, so I haven't seen much of him lately.'

'Bosnia? What was he doing there?'

'He was with a team of forensic anthropologists, trying to identify victims found in a mass grave. It's an ongoing thing – he's supposed to be going back there as soon as the trial in Australia's over and done with.'

'Ugh – rather him than me.' Delva shuddered. 'It must be awful. '

Megan nodded. She had started seeing Jonathan Andrews while they were both working on a murder case in Wales. As one of only two professors of forensic dentistry in the world, he was in great demand. He was based in Cardiff, so getting together wasn't easy. He also had a teenage daughter from his marriage, which had ended when the girl was three years old. Juggling his job and seeing his child left little time for a relationship.

'I'm beginning to understand why his marriage broke up.' Megan stared at the pink liquid in her glass. 'It's impossible to plan anything because he seems to live his life out of a suitcase. We haven't had a weekend together for about two months. The best we've managed was a night at my place when he was en route to a court case in Jamaica – and the only reason he came over then was because the flights from Cardiff and Bristol were booked up.'

Delva wiggled her eyebrows. 'Oh, come on! I'm sure that wasn't the *only* reason!'

'Well, it wasn't exactly romantic,' Megan shrugged. 'He had to be up at five the next morning to get to the airport.'

'So when are you seeing him again?'

'I don't know. Next weekend maybe – if Laura doesn't have plans for him, that is.' When they'd first got together, Megan had thought Jonathan was the perfect partner. They got on well, had loads in common and laughed at the same things. The fact that he already had a child had seemed a big plus. Megan had been told at the age of twenty-five that she would be unable to have children. It was one of the big regrets of her life, not least because it was her own fault. A botched abortion as a student had damaged her fallopian tubes. It was a mistake that had dogged her throughout her adult life, scuppering her marriage and her last long-term relationship. Both her ex-husband and her previous lover had got other women pregnant while they were still with her. It had nearly destroyed her faith in men but meeting Jonathan had changed that. Here, she thought, was a man for whom having children was not a priority. And it was true: Jonathan didn't want any more kids. What Megan hadn't realised was that she would be competing with the one he already had.

'What is it about men, eh? I think I'm going to get myself a dog instead.' Delva let out a snort of a laugh that had heads turning in their direction. Megan couldn't help laughing with her. Delva's record with men was nearly as disastrous as her own. In her case it was being famous that caused problems. She never knew if men were interested in her for herself or because she was a face on TV.

'Come on, let's have another drink,' Delva said. 'Then you can give me the lowdown on Balsall Gate – we've been trying to get inside that dump for years!' Over a second Pink Lady, Delva told Megan that BTV had been trying to get permission to make a documentary about the prison. 'Governor's as tight as a duck's arse, though, isn't he? We've had to resort to subterfuge. One of our researchers has started writing to a prisoner. She's young and very innocent-looking. Once she's buttered him up she's going to try smuggling a camera in. You can get really tiny ones now and the searches in that place are supposed to be pretty lax.'

'Tell me about it.' Megan shook her head slowly. 'Listen,' she said, 'I don't want this to go any further at the moment, but as far your documentary's concerned, it's absolute dynamite.'

Delva's eyes widened as Megan told her about Carl Kelly's death. 'Strychnine? Where the hell would you get hold of something like that?'

'No idea. But it's not the sort of thing that would go unnoticed, is it? If there was a batch of it cut with heroin, I mean.'

Delva shook her head and her braids shuddered. 'If it had happened to anyone outside the prison we'd have known about it. I mean, you don't get many stiffs with a grin on their faces, do you?' Her own mouth curved down as if she had tasted something nasty.

'No,' Megan replied. 'That's why I think it was deliberate.'

Delva blinked. 'You think someone murdered him?'

'I think someone smuggled that dodgy heroin in – probably via one of the screws – to settle some score.' She told Delva about the grave in St Mary's churchyard; about the patch of disturbed earth.

'What did the police think?' Delva asked.

'They weren't interested.' Megan sat back in her chair, folding her arms. 'It really pisses me off. Carl Kelly was in jail when he died, and his death involved drugs: the subtext of every conversation I've had with them is that he's not worth bothering with '

'So what are you going to do?'

'Dig.' Megan raised her eyebrows. 'Figuratively and literally.'

Delva's eyes narrowed. 'Is that legal?'

'Strictly speaking, no. That's why I'm going very early tomorrow morning – as soon as it's light. There won't be anyone about so if it turns out to be nothing, I'll bugger off and no one will be any the wiser.'

'What if you find something? I mean, what do you think might be there?'

'I've really no idea. It's just a hunch.' Megan closed her eyes and shook her head, searching for a better way of explaining what she felt. 'I just feel I have to do it. Not just for Carl Kelly but for all the other blokes in that god-forsaken jail. I've got a horrible feeling that if I don't get to the bottom of what's happened someone else could be at risk.' She didn't say his name. In fact she had deliberately withheld it when telling Delva about the events of the past few days. She was afraid that her friend would see it in her face; would suss out that there was something more than concern for a confidante in her mind.

The way she felt about Dom Wilde was turning into something she hardly dared admit to herself, let alone to anyone else.

'What time will you be getting to St Mary's?' Delva asked.

'About half-five.' Megan shot her a quizzical glance. 'Why?'

'Can I come with you?'

Chapter 6

Birmingham was still sleeping when they reached the churchyard. The tombstones looked eerie in the grey light of dawn and the dew-covered grass clung to the women's legs as they made their way to Moses Smith's grave. A trio of crows eyed them malevolently from a broken fence post.

'What do you think?' Megan asked as Delva peered at the disturbed patch of earth.

'It's weird, isn't it?' Delva knelt beside the grave. She looked very different from last night, clad in khaki cargo pants with a rip in the left thigh that exposed her ebony flesh. The hood of her top was up, covering her hair, and it flopped forward as she bent closer to the earth. 'Did you bring your trowel?'

Megan nodded. Without a word she started scraping away the soil nearest to the tombstone. Delva did the same at the other end of the rectangle. There had been no rain for the past few days, so although the topsoil was damp with dew, the earth beneath it was dry and easy to move. The air had an early morning chill about it but a bead of sweat trickled down the back of Megan's neck. Her heart was pounding in her chest. It felt very wrong, disturbing a grave. She wondered if the person whose handiwork they were examining had felt the same.

For a while they worked away in silence. Both were using a light scraping technique – the way an archaeologist might work – for fear of damaging anything that might lie beneath the surface. Suddenly Delva let out a little cry.

'What is it?'

'Something hard…a corner of something.' Delva was panting for breath. 'A box, I think.'

As they both scraped away at the surface, lettering appeared. An E and a K. Then and I and an N.

'*Nike*!' Delva sank back onto her calves, her arms flopping to her sides.

Megan stared at the familiar logo. It was a shoebox. A cardboard shoebox. What could be inside it? Someone's dead cat? Some sort of time capsule buried by kids for a laugh?

Nothing could have prepared her for what she saw when she lifted the lid. At first she thought she was looking at the face of a doll; a very old, very damaged doll. It was wrapped in blue fabric that turned out to be a pillow case. It was only when Megan pulled the fabric aside that her fingers told her this was no doll. There were tiny hairs protruding from its brown, leathery arms.

'It's a baby.' She looked at Delva, who was kneeling, open-mouthed at the head end of the box.

'But it's…' Delva shook her head. 'It's all…'

'I know.' Megan bit her lip, filled with a sudden, overwhelming sadness. 'I think it's been dead for a very long time. So long that the body's mummified.'

'Mummified?' Delva stared at her in disbelief. 'I thought that kind of thing only happened in hot countries?'

'It does,' Megan nodded. 'But it can happen in cool climates if a body is stored somewhere warm and dry for a long time' She let her eyes travel back up the tiny body from the feet to the face. She was thankful that its eyes were closed and the eyelids still intact. She had seen many dead people but his was the first time she had seen a dead child. She swallowed hard. 'What's clear,' she said, 'is that this body has been brought here quite recently.' She listened to herself speaking, as if she was outside her own body. She knew she sounded as if she was giving a lecture but she couldn't help it. It was the only way to stem the rising tide of emotion that the sight of the baby had released. 'This couldn't have happened here,' she went on. 'The body wouldn't have been preserved in this way in these conditions.' She glanced about her. The crows were still eyeing her from their perch on the fence post. One of them hopped down and edged towards the grave. With a flap of her hand she shooed it away.

'So someone has brought the baby here and buried it.' Delva nodded her head slowly. 'It can't have been long ago. I mean, look at the box – it's hardly rotted at all and the print's still quite clear.' She glanced at the baby's face and looked away. 'Why would someone do that?'

'I don't know.' A wave of nausea swept up from her stomach. She coughed and swallowed in a bid to suppress it. Then, a little unsteadily, she got to her feet, wrapping her arms round her middle as she straightened up. 'I don't know what I expected to find here.' She said the words softly, almost to herself. 'But it certainly wasn't this.'

'What do you think we should do?'

Megan shook her head, her eyes on the gravestone. 'We're going to have to report it to the police.'

'But what if it's something completely innocent? Unrelated to what happened at the prison, I mean.'

'Delva, it can't be innocent, can it? Someone has concealed a dead baby for – I don't know – years and years, maybe decades, and now they've buried it in someone else's grave with no marker of any kind…'

'Yes, I see what you mean.' Delva rubbed her chin, crumbs of soil sticking to her skin. 'We'll have to put one hell of a positive spin on it, though, won't we?'

* * *

An hour later a procession of police boots had beaten a path through the grass and weeds to the grave. DS Willis was obviously less than impressed by Megan's maverick approach. Predictably, he was more concerned about what she'd done to the burial ground than what had been found in it.

'You do know that it's an offence to interfere with a grave, don't you?' He stared at her, his eyebrows arched.

Megan opened her mouth to reply but Delva got in first. 'Oh come on, Detective Sergeant,' she said, 'Do you honestly expect us to believe that anything would have been done if Doctor Rhys hadn't taken the initiative?' Before Willis had a chance to respond, she let fly with a second round: 'It'd make a great story on tonight's evening news, wouldn't it? Body of a baby found by BTV after police refused to investigate...' She paused, her eyes blazing.

'We didn't refuse to investigate, Ms Lobelo, we simply hadn't got the manpower...'

'Whatever,' Delva spread her hands, palms up. 'But I don't think it would do you any favours at this point to start criticising what Dr Rhys has done.'

Willis' eyes narrowed. 'Are you threatening me?'

'Of course not, Detective Sergeant,' she replied, a tight smile stretching her generous lips, 'I'm just deciding how to word the story.'

With a grunt Willis turned away, wandering across the grass to greet the photographer who had come to record the body *in situ*.

'Well done,' Megan breathed, squeezing her friend's arm. 'You handled that far better than I would have done.'

'Yeah – power of the media can be a wonderful thing sometimes, can't it?' Delva winked at she glanced at her watch. 'I'm going to have to go and get ready for work. You coming? We could grab a quick coffee – I'm gasping for one.'

'So am I,' Megan nodded, 'but I want to wait for the pathologist. Do you mind? I'll call you as soon as I get back to the office.'

Alistair Hodge arrived a few minutes after Delva had gone. His hair was sticking up in grey tufts and he was unshaven. Apparently he had rolled out of bed and driven straight over. He knelt beside the shoebox, his face devoid of expression. Slowly and deliberately he pulled the fabric away from the tiny corpse so that the whole body was exposed. It was a while before he spoke. 'A boy,' he said without looking up. 'Looks to be newborn. Umbilical stump still in evidence but the flesh is dessicated. I've seen it once before – a few years ago now. Case of a baby that was hidden under floorboards by the mother.' He shook his head. 'She was only thirteen. Terrified of disgracing her parents.' He glanced up at Megan. 'It's the most common form of mummification in temperate climates, you know?'

'Common?' Megan gave him a puzzled frown.

'Put it this way,' the pathologist replied, 'You're much more likely to find a mummified baby in this country than a mummified adult. It's all dependent on the rate of cooling. The body of a newborn infant will cool and dry much more quickly than that of a man or a woman ' He leaned closer to the shoebox. Taking a magnifying glass from his pocket he held it close to the baby's sunken ribcage. 'Hmm…thought so,' he muttered.

'What?'

'Looks like moth holes. Do you see?' He passed the magnifying glass to Megan. She hesitated a moment, struggling with the fact that this was a baby. She had learned to suppress her feelings when dealing with the corpses of adults. She must do the same now, otherwise she would be of no use at all. Angling the magnifying glass towards her, she moved it back and forth until she had a clear view of the pitted skin.

'I didn't know moths were attracted to corpses.' She managed to keep her voice steady as she passed the magnifying glass back to him.

'They're not, usually. But dessicated flesh is like fabric. The Brown House Moth is the usual candidate – we'll check it out in the lab'

'How long ago do you think he died?' It felt strange, calling the little thing in the box 'he'. It made the baby real. Where was the woman who had given birth to him, she wondered? Was she still alive?

'Could be five years, could be fifty,' the pathologist shrugged. 'Very hard to estimate when the body's been removed from the conditions in which mummification occurred.'

'I suppose there's very little hope of identifying someone so young?'

Hodge shook his head. 'Almost no chance, I'm afraid. No dental records, obviously. Unless someone sees it on TV and comes forward...' He tailed off, pulling the blue shroud back over the shrunken body.

'Why would someone do this?' Megan was thinking aloud now. She didn't expect Alistair Hodge to venture an opinion on the motive. But to her surprise, he did.

'Could be a house move,' he said. 'Someone conceals a baby, lives in the house for many years, then moves on. They're afraid the body will be discovered by the new owners, so they move it before they go.'

'But why bury it here?'

'Nearest graveyard, I'd guess. Mother has some sort of religious belief and wants her child laid to rest in consecrated ground.' He glanced around at the overgrown tombstones. 'This place is ideal, isn't it? Church no longer in use. No one keeping an eye on the graves.'

She nodded. 'But why this grave?' She told him about the connection with Carl Kelly.

'Hmm,' he rubbed his bristly chin. 'That's one hell of a coincidence.'

'But what does it mean?' She blinked as the sun came out from behind a cloud. 'Let's just assume for a moment that Carl Kelly was murdered. And let's also assume it was some sort of revenge for the death of this man.' She nodded at Moses Smith's tombstone. 'How does a long-dead baby connect with that?'

'And was the baby put here before or after Carl Kelly died?'

'Exactly.'

'Well, that's something we might be able to find out in the lab,' Hodge said. 'We can run tests on the box, check local weather conditions over the past few weeks.' He reached for the cardboard lid, studying the logo. 'Don't think it'll tell us a lot more, though. See this bare strip?' He pointed to a place on the lid where the print was missing. 'Someone's ripped off a sticker – probably a serial number. That would have told us where and when the shoes were sold and might even have given us the name of the person who bought them.'

'I doubt that's going to matter much.' Detective Sergeant Willis' voice startled Megan. He had walked noiselessly across the grass and was peering over her left shoulder.

'Why do you say that?' She stepped sideways, uncomfortable about having him so close.

'A TV appeal should do the trick. I've spoken to Ms Lobelo's boss at BTV.' The tone of his voice made it clear that the intention was to pre-empt any plans Megan and Delva might have made about the handling of the story. 'We'll get something on air by lunchtime. I wouldn't be surprised if someone comes out of the woodwork by this time tomorrow.'

'What – you think the person who did this is going to turn themselves in – just like that?' Megan and the pathologist exchanged glances.

'I didn't say that, did I?' DS Willis frowned at her. 'It's usually a neighbour or a friend from way back when. It's rare for the perpetrators of this type of crime not to confide in someone somewhere along the line.'

'Oh? You've come across cases like this before, have you?' Megan tried not to let her dislike of the man creep into her voice.

'Well, not personally, no,' he replied, 'but it stands to reason, doesn't it?'

Megan blinked. There was no point arguing the toss: clearly he'd decided there was only one way to take this forward and he was sticking to it. She hoped Delva would be able to persuade her editor to keep her name out of any news reports. Otherwise she could kiss goodbye to any further assistance from Dom Wilde. Gathering up her jacket and bag from the grass she said goodbye to the pathologist and gave a curt nod to DS Willis. She took a last look at the shoebox before turning away from the grave. The thought of the tiny, stiff body inside made her stomach lurch.

Moses Smith. The name on the gravestone echoed through her mind as she drove away from the churchyard. He was the only link; the only clue to this mystery. She would start by finding his death certificate. It shouldn't be difficult; a quick trawl of the internet should do it. Someone must have buried him. Someone had paid for that that tombstone. And her instincts told her that whoever it was would also know something about the baby.

Chapter 7

Delva Lobelo allowed herself to smile as the red light went off. She had managed to get the whole thing on air without dropping Megan in it. The editor had given her a hard time about that but she had fought her corner and won. She had told him she had a duty to protect her sources and had hinted that if she did, there would be more to come. And he was as keen as she was to dish the dirt on Balsall Gate nick, so he knew it was in everyone's interests to keep schtum.

'Can I get you a coffee?'

It was Natalie, one of the researchers. Nice kid. Not like some of the arrogant little shits BTV attracted. Natalie was bright but she had respect. You didn't get the feeling she was counting your wrinkles and marking off the days till she could step into your shoes.

'Thanks.' Delva switched off her laptop and gathered up the hard copy version of the news she had just read out.

'I'm going to Balsall Gate Prison this afternoon.' Natalie spoke quietly, as if she was reluctant to push herself forward.

'Are you?' Delva raised one eyebrow. 'Who are you visiting?'

'A lifer called Dominic Wilde. I've told him I'm a sociology student. He seems quite…well, you know…quite well educated. For a…' she tailed off with a shrug, as if she was afraid that she was not being politically correct.

'Is this your first visit?'

Natalie shook her head. 'I've been writing to another one

as well. I went to visit him but it was no good. He was only interested in… you know.' She flushed and looked at her feet.

'Yes, I can imagine,' Delva said. Natalie was a pretty little thing. She wondered why the producer had chosen her to write to the prisoners in Balsall Gate. It would take a tough cookie to put up with the sort of crap she was likely to get from the inmates. 'How do you find it, going there?' she asked. 'Must be a bit of an ordeal.'

'Oh no,' the girl smiled brightly. 'I love it. It's absolutely fascinating. And I don't really feel like me because I wear a wig.'

'Really?' Delva laughed. 'How do you get the names of the guys you write to?'

'From court, initially,' Natalie said. 'That's how I got the first one – I sat in on his trial and when he was sent down I asked the court usher which prison he'd be going to.' She flicked a strand of dark hair away from her face. 'I didn't have to go to court for this one though.'

'Oh? How come?'

'We've got this new guy on the team – Tim – have you met him?'

Delva shook her head.

'He's an ex-copper. Knows how to access Home Office records.' She smiled and her cheeks went pink again. She muttered something else about him but she said it to her feet so Delva couldn't quite make it out.

'Well,' Delva said, 'you could find yourself slap in the middle of a very big story – so keep your antennae up, eh?'

'Actually, I was going to ask you,' Natalie looked up, her face earnest. 'How do you think I should play it? Should I ask outright about Carl Kelly? Say I saw it on the news?'

'Hmm,' Delva rubbed her chin as she considered this. 'Yes, if you're fairly subtle about it. You could say something like: "Wasn't it awful about that baby in the churchyard? Is it true what they were suggesting on the news? That the grave belonged to a victim of a prisoner who died in here the other day?" Then you can sit back and see what he says. I mean, he might clam up, but I don't think it would make him suspicious in any way.'

Natalie nodded. 'Great – thanks.' She scuttled off to fetch the coffee. When she came back she put it down without a word.

'Thanks, Natalie,' Delva smiled. 'And good luck for later.' She watched her disappear through the studio door. It was a shame someone more senior wasn't going in her place. It was unlikely this timid girl was going to get the kind of scoop they needed to take the story further. Delva wished she could go herself. She laughed as she visualised the lengths she'd have to go to to disguise her identity. No, she thought, she was going to have to rely on Megan for the information she needed.

Megan had locked herself in her office with strict instructions to the admin staff to keep Nathan MacNamara away. If anyone else wanted to see her they would have to phone first. The subsequent lack of interruptions allowed her to find out quite a lot about Moses Smith. She had called up his death certificate, which stated that the cause of his demise was blood loss due to stab wounds. She had also found a short newspaper article from the *Birmingham Evening Mail* dated 16th March 1991, which stated that Moses Smith, a father of one, had been stabbed to death. His partner – rather confusingly, as they were not married – was named Sonia Smith. She was quoted as saying that the murder had been carried out by a gang of three masked men who had broken into the flat while the family were asleep. Her age at the time of the murder was nineteen. The name and age of the child were not given. The article ended with an appeal for information. Apparently Moses and Sonia Smith had not known the identity of any of the men.

There was no address given for the Smiths, other than the fact that they lived in the Balsall Gate area of the city. Megan tried the electoral roll for 1990, but drew a blank. If Moses Smith was into drugs he was probably the type to move from one place to another without ever getting onto the voters' register. She wondered where Sonia Smith was. She would be thirty-six or thirty-seven by now. And the child would be at least seventeen. She did a search of birth certificates with father's name Moses Smith, but found nothing. Could that child be the baby she had found in Moses Smith's grave? A child whose birth was never registered? Alistair Hodge had said he thought it was a newborn. Perhaps it had been only days old when the murder took place and had died soon after its father. But how? And why would the mother have hidden its body?

She needed to find Sonia Smith. Her only chance with a name as common as that was the burial records. Someone must own that plot in St Mary's churchyard and the chances were it was Moses Smith's partner.

A couple of phone calls revealed that the records had been transferred to the City Library. She would have to go in person to look the records up, but it was only half a mile from her office. She was about to go out of the door when Delva phoned.

'You will let me know if you find anything, won't you?' Delva said when she heard where Megan was off to.

'Of course I will – but don't hold your breath,' Megan replied. 'With a name like Smith the only real chance of finding her is if she's stayed at the same address since the burial.'

'Hmm, I s'pose that's pretty unlikely, isn't it? It's what? Seventeen years ago?'

'That's right. And I don't think I'd want to carry on living in the place where my partner had been murdered, would you?'

'God, no,' Delva said. 'Have you got any other ideas?'

'Not really. I'm going to the post-mortem on the baby later this afternoon, though. I'll be interested to know how old he really is – both his age when he died and the length of time he's been dead.' Megan paused for a moment then said: 'You didn't mention my name on the news, did you?'

'No – I promised I wouldn't, didn't I?' There was a trace of irritation in Delva's voice, as if she was cross with Megan for not trusting her.

'And you didn't say anything about the strychnine?'

'No.' There was a definite sigh this time. 'All I said was that the baby was found in the grave of a man who was murdered more than a decade ago and that one of his alleged killers died yesterday, in Balsall Gate prison, of a suspected drugs overdose.'

'What about Willis' appeal? He didn't say anything about me, did he?'

'No. It was a straightforward thirty-second soundbite of him asking for anyone who might know something about the baby to come forward.'

'Okay – thanks,' Megan said. 'I'll call you if I get anything. Promise.'

It took her less time than she'd thought it would to get her hands on the burial records. Not that she had her hands on them, strictly speaking. She had to wear white gloves to examine the big leather-bound book that had been removed from St Mary's when the building was deconsecrated. Even though the last entries were only fifteen years old the book smelt musty. The dates on the first few pages were from the nineteen-fifties, which gave an indicaton of how few burials had taken place there over the last decades of the twentieth century. Balsall Gate had once been a thriving community but slum clearance programmes and tower blocks had put paid to that. For as long as Megan could remember, Balsall Gate had been the kind of district you would only live in if you were desperate.

She found what she was looking for, her gloved finger moving down a page headed 'March 1991'. There he was: Moses Smith. Interred on March 28th. Plot owned by Sonia Smith of Flat 29, Coniston House, Hartley Street, Balsall Gate.

With a sigh, Megan shut the book. She remembered Coniston House. It was one of three tower blocks that had been blown up five years ago after the council finally admitted that the flats were uninhabitable. They were riddled with damp and structurally unsafe. She had watched, fascinated, from her office window as they crumbled to dust.

As she walked out of the library she felt a sudden urge to go and talk it all over with Dominic Wilde. There wasn't any need, she told herself. Why should he be able to cast any more light on what had happened? As far as she was aware, he had told her everything he knew. She blinked as the realisation came. That she wanted to see him, full stop.

She told herself that she mustn't. That it would be madness to stoke this spark of…what? Lust? It didn't feel like lust. More like a yearning for a kindred spirit. *Jonathan's coming to see you this weekend*, she reprimanded herself. *But he might not come*, a voice in her head hissed back.

Dom Wilde's face hovered before her eyes as she crossed the street. And instead of turning right to go back to her office, she took a left. She knew she was abusing the power the Ministry of Justice had granted her: the right to visit the prison for her research without any prior warning. But she put this to the back of her mind, overpowered by the need to see him, to hear his voice. Ten minutes later she was walking through the churchyard, past the grave of Moses Smith with its border of police tape fluttering in the breeze. And five minutes after that she heard the huge wooden door of Balsall Gate jail bang shut behind her.

Chapter 8

Dom Wilde didn't smile when he was escorted into the room. When they were left alone he sat staring at the floor, avoiding eye contact.

'Hi Dom,' Megan ventured. 'How are you?'

'Okay.' Still he didn't look up. They sat in silence for a few seconds before the penny dropped. He must have seen the report on the television. He had put two and two together: guessed that she was the source of the story. A wave of panic swept through her.

'Dom,' she began, 'what you saw on the news…'

'*Heard*, actually,' he interrupted her, eyes still fixed on the floor. 'Radio in my cell.' It sounded like an accusation, as if he had expected to hear it from her first. All the warmth in him had gone. Clearly he felt she had betrayed his trust. This she couldn't bear.

'You think I was wrong to go to the grave, then?' She tried to keep her voice steady.

'I didn't say that.'

'But you don't like the fact that everyone knows what Carl did?'

She heard him draw in his breath. 'I don't know. I suppose it doesn't matter now he's dead.' There was a pause. Finally he looked at her. 'You could have told me. Warned me.'

She was mesmerised by his eyes. Liquid grey, like the deepest wells; full of emotions she couldn't fathom. And looking into them her guilt and fear were shot through with elation, excitement. 'I'm sorry, Dom: really I am. I don't

know what made me go looking for Moses Smith's grave.
But I never expected to find...' She bit her lip, knowing it
sounded lame.

To her surprise he put out his hand and grasped hers. 'It
must have been a shock, finding...what you found. *I'm* sorry
– I shouldn't have come in here accusing you like that.'

Her eyes stung. She felt inexplicably close to tears. He
thought this show of emotion was about finding the baby. He
had no idea just how upset that had made her. But it wasn't
that now: it was the fact that he was disappointed with her;
that she'd taken advantage of him.

'No, you're right,' she said, 'I should have warned you.'
She could feel the warmth of his fingers squeezing hers. She
knew she should pull her hand away. 'I saw the ground had
been disturbed but it was getting dark, so I went back next
morning, very early.' She told him about meeting Delva;
about swearing her to secrecy about Carl's death. And all
the time he kept hold of her hand.

'But when you found the baby there was no way of keeping
quiet about Carl,' he nodded. 'I see that now.' For a long
moment he gazed into her eyes. He had lost that accusing
look. She gazed back like someone paralysed. The longer it
went on, the more compromised she would be. Never had
she overstepped the mark like this. In all the prisons, all the
one-to-one sessions with inmates she had held over the years,
she had always behaved with absolute propriety. What was it
about this man that was making her so reckless?

'Dom,' she said, smiling as she unwound his fingers from
hers, 'you're going to get me into trouble.' She patted his
hand before crossing her arms and leaning back in her seat.
He smiled and shrugged, his movements mirroring hers. To
her relief he seemed untroubled by her pulling away. But she
felt as if she'd touched a live, bare wire.

'What did you think when you heard about the baby?'

Her voice sounded high and unnatural. She coughed and tried again. 'Had Carl ever mentioned a child?'

He shook his head. 'All he ever told me was his victim's name and the fact that he was buried in St Mary's. I got the impression he didn't really know him from Adam. He was just some guy who pushed his luck too far and had to be sorted.'

'Did he mention if there were others involved in the murder?' She watched his expression for tell-tale signs. An awful thought had crossed her mind. Something quite at odds with the way she felt about him. Dom Wilde was in jail because he'd killed a man. So what if it was him? He had, by his own admission, been the last person to see Carl alive. What if he was feeding her this stuff to divert attention from himself? And the hand-holding – had that been part of some plan to soften her up?

He gave her a blank look. 'No,' he said. 'Were there?'

She nodded, her eyes fixed on his face. 'According to the newspaper report there were three of them. There was also a partner in the flat when they broke in. Apparently they left her alone.' She paused. His expression hadn't changed from that look of blank puzzlement. The voices in her head were subsiding. She wanted to believe he was being straight with her, wanted it with a ferocity that scared her. 'They had a child too,' she said.

'Not the baby...' he tailed off, his eyes wide with alarm.

'Who knows?' she replied. 'The newspaper article didn't say how old the child was and I've drawn a complete blank with tracing the partner. But who ever the baby belonged to, why was he put on top of Moses Smith's grave?'

'And was he put there before or after Carl died?'

Megan told him what the pathologist had said about having the box analysed. 'If you hadn't told me about Moses Smith I doubt the baby would ever have been discovered. If someone wanted to draw attention to the link between Carl and Moses they could have made it a lot more obvious.'

Dom frowned as he weighed this up. 'It doesn't make any sense at all, does it?'

'No, it doesn't.'

'The newspaper article you found – what was the date on it?'

'The sixteenth of March 1991. Why?'

'That explains why I never got to hear about it. Carl never told me exactly when it happened. And I thought I'd remember a name like Moses Smith – if I'd read about it in the paper at the time. But I wasn't living in Brum in '91'

She searched his eyes, wondering how he was going to react to what she was about to ask. 'I need to find out where that dodgy heroin came from, Dom.' Silence. But he didn't look away. 'I want to talk to Carl's girlfriend,' she persisted. 'There's just a chance he might have said something to her; told her more than he told you.'

There was a small sigh before he responded. 'Well,' he said, 'you know I can't help you with the first thing, but I have got this.' He reached into the pocket of his denim shirt: 'It's one of his girlfriend's letters: it's got her address on it.' He leaned forward, his head inches from hers. She thought he was going to touch her again and her insides went into meltdown. But whatever he intended was interrupted by the rattle of keys. Megan stuffed the letter into her pocket as the face of Fergus appeared round the door.

'You've got another visitor,' he winked at Dom. 'Popular today, aren't we?'

Megan thought she saw a flicker of confusion in Dom's eyes as he rose to leave. She wondered who this visitor was. He hadn't talked about anyone on the outside; no one who mattered, other than his daughter.

* * *

Megan didn't leave Balsall Gate straight away. She asked to see the governor, Malcolm Meredith, who was dunking a digestive biscuit into a pint-sized mug of tea when she was shown into his office. As she sat down he carried on without a hint of embarrassment. Nor did he attempt to conceal the newspaper that was spread on the desk in front of him, open at the crossword, which he had half-finished.

'I've come about Carl Kelly.' She said it baldly, with no preamble. She was damned if she was going to be polite when he didn't even have the manners to offer her a cup of tea. Before he could gulp down his soggy biscuit she went on: 'Someone gave him those drugs and I think you should start searching the staff. They should all be checked when they arrive for work. Bags, wallets – even their lunchboxes.'

Meredith eyed her over his rimless bifocals, which were steamed up from the tea. She knew he didn't like her; that he resented her being foisted on him by the Ministry. He'd made his views about psychologists quite clear at their initial meeting. As far as he was concerned she was a namby-pamby academic looking to boost her own reputation by brown-nosing the likes of Dom Wilde.

'Dr Rhys, am I labouring under some kind of mis-apprehension?' She glared back at him. What did he mean by that? She kept silent. 'I was under the impression that you were here to research the Listener service,' he went on, his lips barely moving as he enunciated the words. 'Is this some new brief from the Ministry? Something I haven't been informed of? Because unless I'm very much mistaken, you've come marching in here trying to tell me how to run my own prison.' She held his gaze, refusing to be fazed by this accusation. But she remained silent, a trick she had learned long ago when interviewing prisoners. It confused them. Gave you the psychological advantage. Meredith's eyebrows knotted as he waited for a reply. 'Well?' His voice was shriller and his face was going red. 'I don't think searching the staff would do a great deal for the atmosphere in here, do you?'

'I don't expect it to.' Her own voice was deadpan. 'But if Carl Kelly died because one of your staff is bent I think we need to know, don't you?'

He gave her a look that reminded her of the iguanas in the window of a pet shop she passed on her way to work; a narrowing of the eyes that could pass for a smile but was actually a prelude to gulping down some unsuspecting locust. 'But what about the visitors?' he said. 'They're a much likelier source of illicit drugs.'

'Equally likely, I'd say.' She stared back at him, unblinking. 'I think it's something you should seriously consider.'

'Well, I'll *consider* it, yes.' Meredith was a lazy bastard; that much was obvious. He wasn't going to institute staff searches – it was far too much hassle. So she tried another tack, something that would cost him no effort whatsoever; something he'd be tempted to say yes to in a bid to get her off his back: 'I'd like to look at Carl Kelly's records,' she said. 'He was using the Listener service. Using it fairly regularly, as it turns out. So I think my interest in him is quite legitimate from a research perspective.' She paused as he took this in. The silence was broken by a soft 'plop' as the end of his biscuit fell into his mug. 'I'd like to establish whether he had any visitors other than the girlfriend Dominic Wilde told me about. And I have an address for her that I'd like to check out.'

He nodded slowly as he fished around his mug with his spoon, trying to locate the lost lump of biscuit. 'Shouldn't the police be doing that?'

'Of course they should, but as you know, they've shown very little interest in the case.' She pulled the plate of biscuits towards her and took the last one, crunching it loudly before she swallowed. 'I think inmates – even dead ones – deserve some respect, don't you?'

Without looking at her he reached across the desk for a slip of headed paper. Scribbling on it he said: 'Well, thanks for the Thought For The Day – I'll bear it in mind for my retirement speech.' He shoved the paper towards her. 'Now perhaps you'll allow me to get on?'

Balsall Gate's office manager proved to be a lot more helpful than the governor. Once Megan had handed over Meredith's hastily-written consent, it took only a couple of minutes for the records to arrive. She looked at the photograph in the top right hand corner of the file. So this was what Carl Kelly had looked like in life. Dom was right. He was a striking man who looked younger than his thirty-six years. The photo had been taken when he first entered the jail, but even so, he could have passed for someone in his mid-twenties.

She took out the letter Dominic had given her. The signature at the bottom was Jodie. Her surname was Shepherd. She was listed as visiting the prison the day before Carl Kelly died. A quick search revealed that she had made two other visits during the previous two months. Megan asked the office manager if there had been any calls from the girlfriend since the news of Carl's death broke. Apparently there hadn't, which Megan found odd. All the more reason to find her and talk to her, she thought.

The only other visitor Kelly had received during that time was an Anthony Greaves. Apparently he was one of the duty solicitors and a frequent visitor to the jail. Megan made a note of his office telephone number. It was not unknown for solicitors to smuggle drugs in for their clients.

When she left the main office she had to pass through the visiting room. To her surprise Dom Wilde was sitting

opposite a petite, pretty girl with long, white-blonde hair.
She was smiling at him and he was laughing. Megan
felt a stab of jealousy. Who was she? She looked about
twenty-five. Too old to be his long lost daughter. Was she
a girlfriend? She certainly didn't look like a lawyer or a
probation officer. With a frown Megan checked herself. She
was stereotyping the girl on the basis of physical appearance
– something that irritated her intensely when it was done to
her. Megan's nose stud and her dark skin had led to all kinds
of misunderstandings. She simply didn't conform to most
people's preconceptions of what an academic looked like.
Now, it seemed, she was operating the same prejudices as
they were. Why should blonde locks and a pretty face equal
no brain?

With a click of her tongue she told herself that it didn't
matter who Dom Wilde's visitor was; that it was none of her
business. But the bile of jealousy refused to subside.

As she reached the door a loud bell signalled the end of
visiting time. She was suddenly at the centre of a throng of
people, all pushing their way towards the gate. The smell of
prison was swept away on a tide of perfume. The visitors
were mostly women; mothers, wives and girlfriends. And
they had obviously made a huge effort for their men. Some
had small children with them. A toddler in a pushchair
was screaming at the top of its voice; hungry, tired, bored
or simply confused at being taken to see a father who was
little more than a stranger. It must be difficult for Dom,
she thought, seeing these children. They must be a painful
reminder of his own daughter. He hadn't said whether he
had anything to remember her by. Probably not, if he hadn't
seen her since the day she was born. Megan wondered what
he had done to cause the mother to cut him out of her life so
completely.

She was shaken out of this speculation by the sight of the

blonde-haired girl. She was a few feet from Megan and about to pass through the gate; somehow she had managed to worm her way to the front of the queue. Soon she disappeared from view. Where was she going? And what had been the purpose of her visit? For God's sake, Megan whispered to herself, you don't *own* him!

She left the clusters of visitors who were waiting outside the prison for buses or taxis and made her way to the churchyard. She tried to push Dom's visitor out of her mind, focusing instead on the girl who had been to see Carl. *She was what the lads in here would call very fit.* Those were the words Dom had used to describe her – as if he himself wasn't in a position to judge such things. What had he meant by that, she wondered? Was it possible that he was jealous of Carl's girlfriend but trying to cover up the fact? Perching on the end of a cracked stone bench she pulled the letter from her jacket pocket and unfolded it. It was very short; more of a note, really:

> *Dear Carl,*
>
> *It was great to see you yesterday. I wish we could have had longer together. I feel as if we've got so much to talk about.*
>
> *I've never met anyone like you before. You make me feel so special with the things you say.*
>
> *Please don't worry yourself about what I'll be doing while I'm on holiday with Mum and Dad. You have to believe that I'm not interested in anyone else since I met you. All I want is for us to be together and I'm counting the days until you are free.*
>
>

Love you babe
Jodie xxx

So the girl was on holiday. That explained why she hadn't responded to the news of his death. Megan wondered how long she'd gone away for. She scanned the large, neat handwriting. The spelling was perfect. Not what she would have expected from someone writing to a prisoner. In her experience there were two kinds of women who corresponded with inmates they had not previously met. There were the better-educated liberals who took on prisoners as a good cause and then there were the very desperate, who tended to be at the lower end of the social scale and had given up on meeting men through normal channels. The former sometimes ended up falling in love with the men they campaigned for but it was not nearly as common as the tabloids liked to make out.

Megan stared at the signature. Dom had summed it up quite accurately with his comment that the women who courted prisoners tended to be older and sadder than the writer of this letter. Her eyes moved back up the page to the address: Linden House, Fitton Street, Bordesley Green, Birmingham. Bordesley Green was only a mile or so from the university. Linden House...her eyes narrowed as she stared at the name. Then she remembered: Linden House was one of the student halls of residence. A *student* writing to a convicted drug dealer? Why would a student want to form a relationship with a man like Carl Kelly?

There was no point going to Linden House if the girl had gone on holiday. There must be a mobile number, though: perhaps Carl had written it down somewhere. Dom would know where to look. She glanced at her watch. Too late to go back there now – Alistair Hodge was expecting her at the mortuary. Punching out the number of the prison on her phone she left a message for Dom with the office manager.

She rose from the bench with a shiver. The stone had made her buttocks and thighs go numb. She set off across the churchyard, unable to help taking a backwards glance at Moses Smith's grave. As she did so something registered on the periphery of her vision. It moved in and out of sight so quickly she couldn't even be sure she had really seen it. But she was left with the abiding impression that something bright and shiny had emerged from behind one of the stone angels. When she turned to look there was nothing there. She blinked, wondering if what she had seen was an after-image of the sun. It had been yellowy-white; not round, like a disc, though – more like a ghostly curtain swishing out. She frowned as she turned away. This place was making her imagination work overtime: just like poor Carl Kelly.

Chapter 9

The mortuary was housed in the basement of the university's teaching hospital. To reach it Megan had to pass through a narrow corridor whose shelves were lined with large glass jars bearing some of the most grotesque remains she had ever seen.

Most of them were foetuses. Deformed or grossly abnormal, they had been pickled in formaldehyde and put on display for the benefit of successive generations of medical students. Megan always found it an ordeal to walk past them. She couldn't help being reminded of the baby she had allowed to be destroyed. She wondered if the mothers of these poor creatures had any idea of their fate. Presumably they had miscarried while in hospital. She had a disturbing mental image of a doctor, shocked by what he saw yet secretly gleeful at the prospect of showing some bizarre new specimen to his colleagues. The foetus would be spirited off while the distraught mother was distracted with platitudes about Nature's way.

And what of the medical students who were led down to the basement to see these sad relics of women's hopes and dreams? To them it was little more than a freak show – something to giggle over in the Union bar after the lecture was over.

Megan thought about the mummified child she was about to see. Some might accuse her of the same questionable motives as the students; would say that there was no good reason for her to be here in person; that she was simply

74

gratifying some distasteful urge for the sensational. But anyone who had ever attended a post-mortem would know that the reality of it was so grim that no one in their right mind would attend one out of choice.

She swallowed hard at the thought of what was to come. There would be no smell, at least, with this corpse; the mummification would have dried everything out. And the face was so changed it looked more like a doll than a human baby. But the knowledge that this was a child, a child whose life had been snuffed out before it had begun, was going to make this more traumatic than any post-mortem she had ever attended.

She had to be there, though. Had to watch Alistair Hodge's every move. There was no good reason to doubt him; he was a professional of many years' standing. But to him, this baby was just another lump of dead flesh. Confronted on a daily basis with the worst that human beings could do to each other, he was inured to it. And her fear was that it might just make him miss something.

If she were to tell him her thoughts he would say she was being overly sentimental; that empathising with the victim had nothing to do with performing a thorough job. But she would never tell him, because then she would have to give the reason why the sight of this dead child stirred up such a maelstrom of emotion. And that was something she would never tell a living soul.

When she opened the door to the mortuary Hodge was already gloved up. He hovered over the corpse of the baby boy, which was still zipped up in a body bag. It was a forlorn sight; a small bump in a black plastic shroud designed for a larger, adult body.

'We've checked out the pillow case,' he said, nodding at her by way of a greeting. 'No moth holes.'

'Oh,' she said, frowning as she took this in. 'So that means he wasn't wrapped in it when he was concealed?'

'No, he wasn't, which is a shame: we could have dated the fabric by analysing the fibres. That might have given us a better idea of the time of death.' He unzipped the body bag and called 'Ready!' A thin young man with lank black hair and a Meatloaf tattoo on his forearm appeared from behind a screen. There was a camera slung round his neck, and at Hodge's command, he began photographing the body from every possible angle

'Where's Sergeant Willis?' Megan glanced at the door.

'Oh, he's been and gone.' Hodge glanced up at Megan as he began taking swabs from the baby's dessicated flesh. 'Said he thought his time would be better spent in the incident room. Seems he's banking on someone coming forward.'

'Hmm. He'll be waiting for bloody Godot in that case.'

The pathologist gave her a wry smile. He had been around police officers even longer than Megan and had seen the good, the bad, and, like this detective sergeant, the purely indifferent.

'There must be something about the body that can give us some clue, mustn't there?' She stepped sideways as the photographer pulled out a chair and stood on it to get a bird's eye view of the corpse.

'Well, there might be fibres stuck to the body. Remnants of whatever it was wrapped in originally. It's unusual for these babies to be concealed naked. I'll swab him all over, just in case. Shouldn't take long.'

'And what about the cardboard shoebox? Any progress on that?'

'Well,' Hodge said, pushing his glasses up his nose, 'We've had one of the driest winters on record, haven't we? We haven't had really heavy rain since the middle part of January – the sort that would make the cardboard begin to disintegrate, I mean.'

'So the box could have been buried any time during the last – what – ten or eleven weeks?'

'I would say so, yes. It's hard to be more precise than that. Oh…' He stopped suddenly, one hand on the baby's left leg, a swab held aloft in his right. 'What's this?'

Megan and the photographer moved towards the body from opposite sides of the metal trolley, their heads almost touching as they leaned forward to see what Alistair Hodge was looking at. The flash bulb lit up a tiny fragment of something thin and yellow stuck to the lower part of a shrivelled thigh that was no thicker than a chicken drumstick.

'I'll have to turn him over.' The pathologist picked up the tiny body and laid it face down on the table. The child looked even less human from this angle, his buttocks flattened by years of pressure from the surface he had been laid on and the flesh marked with creases from whatever he had been wrapped in at the time of his death. Megan blinked as the flash went off again. Then she saw what Alistair Hodge had noticed. It was a strip of what looked like newspaper, stuck to the back of the thigh like a second skin. She could make out letters, faded to a pale grey against the yellowed paper.

'Hang on, I'll get my magnifying glass,' Hodge said.

Megan moved round the table as the pathologist retrieved it from his bag. The writing looked upside down. It was in capitals, like a headline. Her eyes narrowed as she strained to make them out. Then, as the magnifying glass glided over them, the letters jumped out : 'M 6 FREE'. She said it aloud, slowly. Then again, looking from Hodge to the photographer. 'M 6 FREE?'

'Hmm,' the pathologist pursed his lips. 'Not much to go on, is it?' He moved the magnifying glass this way and that, searching for other clues on the torn strip of newsprint. But there was nothing. No other lettering and certainly no date.

They were all staring at it, Megan racking her brains for any news story she could remember about the M6 motorway.

'Could it be something to do with the toll road?' Hodge frowned. 'When did that come in? Only about five years ago, wasn't it?'

'Less than that,' the photographer shrugged. '2004 wasn't it?'

'I'm going to make a quick phone call,' Megan said. 'I haven't got a clue what that headline's about, but I know someone who might.'

She paced the corridor outside the mortuary with her mobile to her ear, waiting for Delva to return to her desk after reading the afternoon news bulletin. Megan kept her eyes firmly on the floor, avoiding the sight of the foetuses, whose liquid graves were lit orange by the rays of sun that pierced the basement's high, barred windows. She was suddenly reminded of the jail. Images of the prisoners collided with those of the jars on the shelves. She blinked, sickened by the thought that the inmates of Balsall Gate were like the dead creatures that surrounded her; some, like Carl Kelly dead in reality; others dead inside. Dom Wilde was one of the very few who seemed to have bucked the system. Somehow he had managed to escape the pickling process. How had he done it? Was it through immersing himself in a degree programme? Or was it the Buddhism with its hours of meditation?

Her train of thought was brought to an abrupt halt by the sound of Delva's laugh. She could hear her coming towards her office phone. There was a clunk as she picked up the receiver: 'Hi Meg, any news?'

In a few sentences Megan explained what the post-mortem had turned up. 'We were wondering if it was something to do with the motorway – the toll road or something?'

'Hmm,' Delva said, 'It might be. Tell me something,

though – was there a gap between the letter M and the number six?'

'Er, yes, I think there was. Why?'

'Well, if there is, it might be nothing to do with the motorway. If it was a story about the M6 you'd expect the letters to be bang up against each other – no gap.'

'Right. I'll go and check.' She darted back into the mortuary and grabbed the magnifying glass from the instrument table.

'What are you doing?' Hodge hissed.

'I'll tell you in a minute,' she replied, the phone still pressed to her ear as she angled the magnifying glass against the newsprint. 'Yes, there's definitely a gap,' she said into the phone. 'That's bad, isn't it? If it's not the motorway, the M must be the end of some other word. That's going to make it much harder to identify.'

'Not necessarily,' Delva said. 'Hang on.' There was a pause. 'I'm just writing it down. I think… yes, I think it could be…'

'Could be what?' Megan's knuckles went white as she pressed the phone hard against her ear. The pathologist and the photographer were staring at her intently.

'BIRMINGHAM 6 FREE.' Delva said the words as if she was reading the news to an audience of thousands. 'It was March 1991,' she went on, her voice hesitant now, but excited. 'It was the first big story I got to cover when I started at BTV. That was the date, wasn't it? The date on Moses Smith's headstone.'

'God, yes, it was!' Megan made a thumbs-up sign at Hodge and the photographer. 'I don't suppose you can remember the exact date, can you?'

'I'll check it out and call you back.'

Less than five minutes later Delva was back on the phone. 'It was March the fourteenth,' she said. 'I looked up the

Evening Mail's archives on the web: it was on the front page
– the verdict came through that day.'

'March the fourteenth,' Megan flicked through the pages
of her notebook. 'That was the actual day Moses Smith
died.' She heard Alistair Hodge draw in his breath. 'Can we
get hold of a copy of the original newspaper? Compare it to
what we've found, just to be certain?'

'Should be no problem,' Delva said. 'We've probably got
a copy in our own archives. Shall I bring it down? I'm off
shift now.'

When Delva arrived at the mortuary any remaining doubts
about the fragment of newsprint were dispelled. The letters
were exactly the same size and style as the photocopy she
had taken.

'Of course, it doesn't prove the baby died on the same
day as Moses Smith,' the pathologist said as he peeled off his
rubber gloves. 'The newspaper could've been lying around
the house for months – years even. It doesn't actually help
us with time of death.'

'But it's too much of a coincidence to ignore, surely?'
Megan frowned. 'I mean, to wrap a baby in newspaper
suggests no premeditation. It implies to me that the body was
disposed of in a hurry by someone who simply grabbed the
first thing that came to hand to wrap it in. A newspaper lying
on a bedside table would be an obvious choice; something
that nobody else in the house would miss: not like using
a towel or a piece of clothing. Which suggests it was that
day's paper, or possibly the day before.'

Alistair Hodge nodded. 'Yes, I think you're probably
right. I'm thinking about that teenage girl I told you about –
the one whose parents were very religious. She wrapped her
baby in newspaper before she put it under the floorboards.'

'You don't think there could be some link, do you?' It
was Delva who spoke. She was staring at the piece of paper

in her hand.

'What do you mean?' Megan asked.

'With the Birmingham Six.' Delva's eyes narrowed. 'I mean, this guy dies the day they get out of jail. And a baby dies the same day or day after. Could we be looking at some sort of revenge thing?'

Megan blinked. 'But Carl Kelly told one of the other inmates he'd killed Moses Smith in a row over money he was owed for drugs.'

'How do you know he was telling the truth?' Delva looked at her, her eyes gleaming like a dog scenting a fox. 'How do you know the guy you spoke to wasn't lying?'

Chapter 10

'So you're saying, what?' Megan spread her hands, palms up, on the table in front of her. She and Delva were back in the canal-side bar, but this time all either of them could face was black coffee. 'You think Moses Smith's death was something to do with a miscarriage of justice that happened thirty-odd years ago?' She couldn't stomach the idea that Dom Wilde had lied to her. She was trying to reason this out in a logical way. But it wasn't easy to conceal the panic she felt inside. She consulted her notebook. 'Moses was born in 1960. When were the Birmingham Six arrested – early seventies, wasn't it?'

Delva rummaged in her bag for the newspaper article. '1974,' she said.

'So he'd have been fourteen.' Megan pursed her lips. 'A bit young, don't you think?'

'Could have been his father, then, couldn't it?'

'His father?'

Delva nodded eagerly. 'What if Moses Smith's father was one of the cops who beat the Birmingham Six up when they were arrested? What if he died while they were inside so they took revenge on the son instead? Or…' she paused, wagging her finger at Megan, 'what if they thought that killing his son – and his grandson – would be more fitting revenge than killing the cop himself?'

Megan took a gulp of coffee, piecing together the implications of what Delva was suggesting. 'Okay, she said. 'Let's just assume for a moment that you're right. It would mean that two of the Birmingham Six – accompanied by Carl Kelly – went straight round to Moses Smith's place after being let out of prison. They killed Moses and his newborn baby, but left his girlfriend alive.' She looked askance at Delva. 'You were part of that media storm that engulfed them the minute they walked out of court. Do you really believe they'd have had the inclination – or more importantly, the opportunity – to go and murder somebody?'

'Well, I s'pose it does sound a bit far-fetched when you put it like that,' Delva frowned. 'But they could have sent someone to do it for them, couldn't they? Carl Kelly and some of his mates, I mean.'

'It's possible, yes. But why wait till you get out of jail to do that? If you've got someone on the outside who's willing to kill one of your enemies, you could make it happen anytime.' She rubbed her chin with the heel of her hand. 'I remember seeing those men on television when they came out. They were absolutely broken. The idea that any one of them could've ordered something as brutal as the killing of a baby is unimaginable. But let's suppose they had: why would they hide him away, then rebury him seventeen years later in his father's grave?'

'I don't know,' Delva shrugged. 'Guilt?'

'But none of it explains why Carl Kelly was killed, does it?'

'I suppose not.' Delva fiddled with the handle of her coffee cup.

'I'm not sure we should rule out some sort of link, though, even if it's not direct.' Megan took another sip of coffee. 'There could have been some old friend or supporter, who, unknown to them, wanted revenge. Perhaps it had lain dormant in that person's mind, but the sight of them all being released triggered something: some lynch-mob mentality.'

Delva drained the last of the coffee from her cup. 'It'd be

interesting to know if Carl Kelly had any connection with the Birmingham Six. Could he have been a schoolfriend of a son or daughter of one the men? Or a drinking pal, or something.' She leaned back in her chair. 'I interviewed several members of the men's families when they got out. I've still got the numbers, although I know some of them have moved away.'

'What would you say, though?' Megan frowned. 'I mean, if there was some direct link with Moses Smith's murder, they're hardly likely to tell you, are they?'

'I know,' Delva shook her head. 'I'd have to come up with something innocent-sounding.' She stared at the table, her lips pressed together in concentration.

'I think it might be better if we came at it from a different angle,' Megan said. 'We could try finding out if Moses Smith's father or any other male relative was in the Serious Crime Squad at that time. If so, we've got a possible motive.

'You're right,' Delva nodded slowly. 'I could get some of the research team at BTV onto it if you like. One of them's an ex-copper – he should have some connections we can use.'

It was dark by the time they left the bar. Megan drove home on automatic pilot. She was thinking about Dom Wilde. He hadn't responded to the message she'd left at the prison office. Was he avoiding her now because, as Delva had suggested, he'd lied about Carl Kelly? She knew there could be several explanations for his failure to get back to her; the most likely being that he hadn't received the message. It wouldn't be the first time the admin people had cocked up in that respect. But Delva's words echoed in her mind. 'Okay,' she said out loud, 'if he's holding something back about Carl, that implies he was involved in the murder. Either he gave Carl that lethal dose or he turned a blind eye while someone else did it.' She ran this scenario through her mind. It meant Dom had some link with whoever wanted revenge on Carl – or that the revenge was his. 'Hang on, though,' she said. 'If that was the case, why would he have told me Carl had given up drugs?' She nodded as she thought it through. It would have been so much more convenient for him to make out that Carl was a regular drug user: his death would have seemed unremarkable. No, she reasoned, it was counter-intuitive for Dom to flag up the man's abstinence if he was anything other than innocent.

She heaved a sigh of relief, her thoughts turning to the baby lying in the mortuary. The post-mortem had bought them no closer to establishing the little boy's identity. Alistair Hodge had talked about extracting DNA from the tissue but he wasn't confident that any would have survived the process of dessication. And even if it had, Megan reflected, what would you compare it with? Unless someone came forward with information about the child's family, the DNA would be useless.

The idea that the baby had been murdered as an act of revenge was hard to stomach. The post-mortem had revealed no marks on the body but in its mummified state only the grossest injury would have been apparent. The child could easily have been suffocated with a pillow over his face, but the tell-tale signs of such a death would have been erased as the body dried out.

He could have been stillborn or died within hours of his birth, but if that was the case, why would the mother have concealed her baby boy instead of giving him a proper burial? The other alternative was that the mother had killed him herself. Megan tried to imagine that scenario. Had the mother been a teenager, terrified of her parents finding out, as Alistair Hodge had suggested, or an older woman with a different reason for wanting to dispose of her child? It was hardly surprising no one had come forward: even if the baby was stillborn, concealing it was still a criminal offence punishable by two years in jail. Typical of the legal system to be so outdated and so condemning, she thought. Ethically, concealing a stillbirth was no different from opting for an abortion. Her hands tightened on the steering wheel as the familiar feeling of regret welled up inside her. This was all getting too close.

Her mind was in a whirl as she drew up to the house. Annoyingly someone had parked right outside her front door. Other cars were parked nose to tail all along the terrace, so there was no option but to drive round the block until she found a space. She stomped back towards the house, wishing she hadn't stuffed so much into her briefcase. Suddenly her body tensed. There was a flicker of something in the pool of lamplight to her left; someone in the car outside her door. A man or a woman? She couldn't tell. She didn't recognise the car. A wave of irrational fear engulfed her. Who was waiting for her at this time of night? A mugger? A stalker? A rapist? She quickened her pace, berating herself for getting paranoid. As she grasped the catch on the gate she heard the click of a car door opening. She wanted to run but she was rooted to the spot.

'Meg! At last!'

She spun round. 'For fuck's sake, Jonathan! You frightened me to death! Why aren't you in Sydney?'

'And I love you too, darling!' he grinned back. 'The trial finished early. I wanted to surprise you – and I certainly seem to have done that!' From behind his back he produced a bunch of flowers.

She bashed him on the leg with her briefcase, her lips sliding into an unwilling smile. 'Sod it! Why can I never be cross with you for more than thirty seconds?' She punctuated her words with more jabs of the briefcase.

'Ow!' He darted past her, through the gate. 'Aren't you going to invite me in?'

'I suppose I'm going to have to,' she tutted. 'Can't let you loose on a decent neighbourhood at this time of night!'

The hall light revealed that his flowers were wilting at the edges. The large yellow sticker and bar code betrayed a hasty purchase from a garage forecourt.

'All the way from Australia, are they?' She curled her lip at the withered bouquet as she plonked it down on the kitchen table.

'Got you this as well.' He turned his big puppy dog eyes on her.

'What is it?' She peered into the red, white and blue British Airways bag.

'It's DKNY *Be Delicious*.' He wiggled his eyebrows at her. 'Very fruity, it said in the in-flight sales blurb – but we'll have to find out, won't we?'

'Hmm.' She dodged away as his hand went round her waist. 'It's a nice thought,' she said, reaching for the kettle. 'Can I try it in the morning? I'm knackered and I'm wearing Eau de Morgue at the moment.'

'Oh.' He pressed against her as she turned on the tap. 'Only trouble is, I'm going to have to be off pretty early tomorrow.'

'How early?'

He nibbled her ear. 'Crack of dawn, I'm afraid. I've got to get the hire car back to Cardiff by nine and I need to see Laura.'

She pulled away from him, ramming the kettle back on its stand. 'Oh, I see! That's why you've come on a Thursday night, is it? Wanted a quick shag before you go off to see your darling daughter?' She'd never spoken to him like this before. She'd tried so hard not to criticise; not to nag. But she was tired and she was mad and she was fed up with playing second fiddle. No: *third* fiddle, actually. It was his work first, then his daughter, then her.

'Meg, I'm sorry.' He took her hand in both of his. 'I know we planned to make this a weekend for us. But Laura's having a really hard time at the moment. She's being bullied at school. She needs me and I can't let her down.'

She pushed him away. 'But you're not bothered about letting me down!' Even as she said the words she knew she was being unreasonable. How could she put her own needs above those of a kid who was suffering in that way? But despite the voice of reason inside her head, she folded her arms across her chest and glared at him.

'She's only fourteen, Meg. I feel I've already failed her by walking out on her mum. I don't want her to feel that all I ever do is abandon her.'

Megan's eyes dropped to the floor. How could she argue with that? He was right, of course. But it was like torture, having him here for a few brief hours. There was no time for anything…she struggled to find the right word. For anything of *substance*.

'I'm sorry,' he said again. 'You've had a hard day and now I've made things even worse.'

'Oh, it's not your fault.' She shook her head slowly. 'It's just that I sometimes wonder if it's all really worth it.'

He reached out, placing a hand on each side of her face. 'It *is* worth it – at least for me.' She could feel his warm breath on her skin. 'It's not about sex, Meg. I know that's how it might look but it's not true.'

'So what is it about then?'

'Companionship. Friendship…' he hesitated, searching her eyes. 'Love?' He reached past her and flicked the switch of the kettle. 'Come on,' he said. 'Put your feet up while I make a coffee, then you can tell me about your day.'

'Are you sure you want to listen to this?' She paused in the middle of describing the post-mortem on the baby. 'You must be absolutely shattered yourself; how long was the flight?'

'Twenty-one hours,' he shrugged. 'Don't worry – I'm used to it. And anyway,' he leaned forward to top up her coffee, 'I want to know more. Have they run a DNA test yet?'

She shook her head. 'I was about to tell you: they're not sure they'll be able to extract any.'

'Why not?'

'They think the flesh is too dessicated.'

'What about the teeth?'

'What teeth? It was a newborn baby.'

'Ah,' he nodded, 'No teeth visible, but they'd have been developing in the gums and you could still get DNA from them.'

'Really?' Her eyes widened. 'That would never have occurred to me.'

He gave her a wry smile. 'Glad to hear I'm not completely bloody useless!'

She poked him in the ribs. 'Not *completely*. But there's something else, *Professor Andrews*,' she sat back, eyeing him over the rim of her mug. 'We've got the DNA – what do we do with it?'

'What do you mean?'

'Well, we've got nothing to compare it with, have we? We don't have any relatives. It's been on the telly, in the papers, but no one's come forward. Not a dickie bird.'

He looked at her askance. 'Are you winding me up?'

'No,' she frowned. 'Why would I?'

'Well, isn't it obvious? You've got a *body*.'

'A body? You mean the baby?'

'No: the one in the grave where the baby was found. You can get his DNA and see if there's a match.'

She blinked. 'You're talking about an exhumation?'

'It's common practice,' he shrugged. 'All you need is a court order from a magistrate.'

'Hmm,' she looked him up and down, nodding slowly. 'You're right: you do have your uses – I'm just glad I don't have to pay for your professional services.' A smile creased the corners of her eyes.

'Not in money…' he arched his eyebrows. 'But I don't come cheap…' he slid his arm around her waist. She flinched momentarily as his fingers found the flesh between her blouse and the waistband of her trousers. Sensing her discomfort he pulled away. 'Shall we have a good long soak in the bath?' He gathered up the mugs. 'Why don't you go and run it and I'll get us some wine. Have you got any of that Chablis?'

'Yes,' she replied, glad of the chance to take things slowly. 'There should be a bottle already open in the fridge.'

Later she slid into bed and waited for him to emerge from the bathroom. She was more relaxed in body but still troubled in mind. Sex with Jonathan had always been fantastic, something she had looked forward to. So why had she recoiled when he touched her? She couldn't explain the way it had made her feel but she knew it had felt wrong; uncomfortable. The only analogy she could come up with was that of a caterpillar spinning a cocoon. It was as if she was retreating into some inner part of herself, building a protective case that had not yet had enough time to harden off.

Turning onto her stomach she buried her face in the pillow. She wanted to want Jonathan but something had definitely changed. She wasn't sure exactly what, though she knew it had something to do with Dominic Wilde. How could someone she'd spent so little time with have such a powerful impact on her? Why couldn't she get him out of her head?

Jonathan wandered in and she twisted her head round to see that he had a towel tucked decorously round his waist. 'Have you got any of that coconut oil?' he asked.

'Er… yes, I think so. Why?'

'I thought you might like a massage.' He sank down onto the bed beside her, stroking her shoulder.

'Okay. Thanks.' She turned her face back to the pillow, knowing there would probably have been more warmth in her voice if she'd been addressing some white-coated stranger in a health spa. Perhaps a massage would do the trick, though; make her feel how she was supposed to feel. Her body tightened as he splashed the oil onto her back. She tried to relax as he began to knead her shoulders. Then she felt the weight of him as he leaned across her to flick off the light. She was glad of the darkness. It made what followed easier. She might have fooled him, but she wasn't fooling herself: in her head she was making love to someone else.

Chapter 11

Delva was in the newsroom early the next morning. The need for caffeine was overpowering. She headed for the broom cupboard that passed as a kitchen for her first fix of the day. The aroma wafting down the corridor towards her suggested that someone was even more eager than herself. As she pushed the door open she caught a sudden movement. What had appeared at first glance to be one person now became two. It was Tim and Natalie, two of the researchers, and they were obviously a lot closer than she had realised.

'Good morning!' She grinned at their reddening faces. 'Nice to see you taking our corporate bonding policy so seriously!'

Tim, who towered over the petite Natalie, gave Delva a rueful smile. 'It may not look like it, but we were actually discussing some serious issues – work-related, that is.'

'Oh, really?' Delva looked enquiringly at him. 'Anything I should know about?'

'Not sure yet.' He leaned one long arm on the worktop, raising the other to adjust the brown ponytail that hung down his back. Delva noticed a small silver Celtic knot stud in his left ear. For an ex-cop, she thought, you're rebelling big-time.

'So there might be something then?' She looked at Natalie, whose cheeks were still glowing. 'Is this to do with your visit to the prison yesterday?'

'Well, yes, it is,' Natalie frowned.

'You saw him then? I've forgotten his name – Dominic

something, wasn't it?'

'Dominic Wilde,' she nodded.

'What did he say?'

'Very little, really,' Natalie shrugged. 'He was good as far as information about prison conditions went; in fact he was extremely articulate. But I couldn't get a squeak out of him about Carl Kelly.' She glanced at Tim. 'We were just saying, weren't we, does that mean he really knows nothing or is he just trying to cover something up?'

'Hmm,' Delva reached for the kettle and switched it on. 'What was your gut instinct?'

'Well, he was surprisingly charming and urbane – for a prisoner, I mean. He was very upfront about why he was a lifer: he told me all about the murder he'd committed.' Her eyes darted towards Tim again. 'The victim was a policeman – he killed him during a robbery that went wrong. But he seemed genuinely remorseful.' She hesitated. 'So at one level he seemed absolutely convincing, but when I mentioned Carl Kelly he changed completely. He said he knew him, but not particularly well. I got the distinct impression he was lying, or at least holding something back.'

'Well, I don't think you should give up on him just yet.' Delva reached up to the cupboard, past the communal jar of instant coffee to her personal supply of *Rombouts* filters. 'I wouldn't have expected him to be all that forthcoming on your first visit. Maybe he'll loosen up a bit next time.' She balanced the plastic holder on top of her mug and poured in the steaming water. 'There is something we can do in the meantime, though,' she said, breathing in the heady scent now rising from the filter. She described the discovery of the newspaper fragment at the post-mortem on the baby; of her theory about a link between Carl Kelly's victim and the release of the Birmingham Six. By the time she had finished they were both staring at her, open-mouthed. 'What we need to do,' she continued, looking at Natalie, 'is to find out whether Moses Smith had any links with the Serious Crime Squad.' She saw a look of uncertainty in the girl's eyes. 'You know about them, do you? The things they were accused of?'

'Well, sort of,' she said. 'I know about the Birmingham Six thing…' she tailed off, obviously unwilling to show her ignorance. Delva sighed. No reason why she should know, really. She would have only been about three when the squad was disbanded.

'They were accused of getting a whole raft of convictions through false confessions,' Delva explained. 'And according to their victims, they went in for torture. Plastic bagging was one of their favourite techniques, allegedly.'

'Plastic bagging?' Natalie looked from Delva to Tim, who turned away and stared at the floor.

'It's a way of forcing suspects to sign confessions without actually marking them,' Delva nodded. 'You put a plastic bag over their head until they're on the point of suffocating.' Delva watched the colour drain from Natalie's face. 'They also made up the statements they got people to sign. But this new forensic technique – the ESDA test – was developed just before the Birmingham Six appeal. It proved the confessions had been fabricated. The problem was, despite all that evidence, only a handful of the squad were ever prosecuted. Anyway,' she said, topping up the water in the filter, 'Moses Smith wouldn't have been old enough to be in the force himself but his father might have been. Can you go on the internet for me? Get hold of his birth certificate?'

'Well, yes, of course I can,' Natalie nodded, 'but with a name like Smith…'

'I know,' Delva replied, 'but it's not just going to give you a name – it should give the father's occupation as well.' She turned to Tim. 'You were in the West Midlands force, weren't you? Can you get me names of all the guys in the Serious Crime Squad at the time the Birmingham Six went down?'

He blinked at her before replying. 'Well, I'll do my best but it's still a very touchy issue for the force, you know.' His eyes narrowed. 'There are people out there who are keen to keep all that dead and buried.'

Delva held his gaze, wondering how much he already knew but wasn't prepared to let on. 'You're just going to have to tread carefully, then, aren't you?' Grabbing her coffee, she tossed the filter into the bin. 'Keep me in the loop,' she said as she squeezed past them on her way to the door.

Megan was barely conscious when Jonathan said goodbye. She was in the shower, washing away the traces of him when the phone rang. By the time she got to it, it had stopped. Cursing, she dialled 1471. The number she got was Jonathan's mobile. She replaced the receiver, relieved that she hadn't had to speak to him. She was still cross with him for wrecking her weekend. If he'd told her in advance about his need to see his daughter she could have arranged something else, like a trip to Wales to see her sister and the kids, which she'd been promising for ages. But it was too late now; too short notice for Ceri, who didn't like surprise visitors.

She was fed up with the way Jonathan just expected her to drop everything if he happened to be around. But it wasn't just that. She was angry with herself, too. For letting him stay last night when her heart wasn't in it. She would call him – but it wouldn't be today.

She padded down the stairs in her dressing gown and slippers to make coffee. She was halfway down when she noticed a pink envelope lying on the doormat. She headed towards it, puzzled. It was too early for the postman. And she was sure there'd been nothing there when she let herself in last night. She would have noticed something as bright as that.

When she bent down to pick it up she noticed that the envelope had landed face up. There was no address and no stamp. Just her first name in large, curlicued letters with a small heart drawn where the stamp should have been. Perhaps it had fallen off the bouquet of flowers Jonathan had given her last night? It didn't look like his writing, though. She ripped the flap and pulled out a card that looked expensive and handmade. It had a red appliqué heart on a black background with gold thread sewn into the edges. Inside was a message that looked as if it had been written with the kind of gold rollerball pen she sometimes bought for doing her Christmas cards:

'Missed you today. Can't bear it when you're not around. Can I take you for lunch sometime?'

Her heart sank as she saw the signature: Nathan. And three kisses. *Oh bloody hell, Nathan, what are you playing at, you silly boy!* She hissed the words at the letterbox, wondering when he'd pushed the card through the door. She realised with a sudden shock that he could be standing out there now, waiting for her to come out. Turning away she bounded up the stairs to the spare room, which overlooked the street. Edging along the wall she peered round the curtains, taking care not to show herself. There was no one there. She didn't know if Nathan MacNamara owned a car, but if he did he wasn't lying in wait inside it. She had a clear view of all the cars parked alongside the pavement as far as the end of the terrace and all of them were empty. Still, she thought, it wasn't good that he knew where she lived. She wondered how he'd found out, short of following her home. She was going to have to put a stop to this. What had started out as something mildly irritating was turning into something quite inappropriate. Nathan was going to have to be told in no uncertain terms that his degree was on the line unless he backed off.

She dressed hurriedly, gulped down a quick coffee and took a banana from the fruit bowl to eat when she got to the office. She wondered if Nathan's card had arrived before Jonathan had left the house. If it had, he would have been bound to notice it. What would he have made of it? Perhaps he had picked it up and laid it down face up to indicate that he had seen it. She could just imagine him putting two and two together and making five. Was that why he'd phoned her earlier?

As she drove to work she forced those questions out of her mind, concentrating instead on the new line of inquiry Jonathan had suggested. She wondered how she could persuade DS Willis to go for an exhumation. He had made it crystal clear that he was in charge and he was going to handle things in his own way, without any interference from her. She reminded herself that she shouldn't really be playing detective at all. That she was allowing Carl Kelly's death to hijack the time she was supposed to be spending on research into prison suicides. She knew she should be devoting more hours to analysing spreadsheets; to comparing national statistics with local ones. But at this moment that seemed less important than getting to the truth of what had happened at Balsall Gate. She had no faith whatsoever in Willis' ability. It seemed the only way to get the police to take this case seriously was for her to prove that Kelly's death was murder. Then Willis would be replaced by a more senior and – hopefully – a more able officer.

She scanned the lobby as she pushed open the glass doors of the Psychology building. No sign of Nathan. She did the same thing when she stepped out of the lift, glancing down the corridor before she made her way to her office. She would deal with him later. First she must tackle the sergeant.

'DS Willis.' He was the only man she knew who could make his own name sound like a grumble. When she announced herself he interrupted her mid-sentence. 'No news. No one's come forward. Okay?' His tone was dismissive.

'Well, no, actually,' she replied, her voice as polite as she could make it. She was well aware that if she was going to win him over she was going to have to be less confrontational than she'd been thus far. 'There's something else that might throw a bit of light on things.' She told him about the possibility of extracting DNA from the baby's teeth and made the case for the exhumation of Moses Smith.

'Let's get this straight,' he said, with an air of weary resignation, 'You want me to get a body dug up on the off-chance that its DNA might match that baby's?'

'Yes, I do,' she replied, forcing her lips into a smile in an effort not to snap back at him, 'because at the moment there's nothing else to go on.'

'Have you any idea of the amount of red tape involved in getting a body exhumed? It's a hell of a lot of work for what's actually a very minor offence. I mean, even if we find the mother, chances are it'll never go to court.'

'But it's not about that, is it?' she persisted. 'I'm not after nailing some poor woman for concealing her dead child; I'm looking for hard evidence to track down Carl Kelly's killer.'

His response was icily polite. 'May I remind you that at this stage we have no reason to treat that incident as a murder inquiry?'

'Oh, have there been other cases of strychnine poisoning then? I hadn't heard.' She was being disingenuous, but she wasn't going to let him off the hook.

'Er… Well, no. Not as yet. We're waiting for developments

on that front, though.'

'I see. But how long are you prepared to wait? Another week? A month? I'm just worried that if there's any possibility of it being murder, the trail is going to go cold.' There was silence at the other end of the line. She tried another tack: 'Of course, the other problem is that the TV people are running out of patience.'

'What do you mean?'

'Well, they've been onto me already this morning,' she lied. 'Apparently some anonymous source at the prison leaked the results of the toxicology report. That makes it a much bigger story and they want to take it forward. I think what they're planning is to ask for a live interview with you – probably they'll make out it's just a catch-up on the appeal for information about the baby – then they'll slip in the big question when you're off your guard: they'll ask you *why* you're not treating Kelly's death as a murder inquiry.'

She heard what sounded like a groan at the other end of the line and she fisted the air, knowing she'd rattled him. 'If I was you I'd get in there first; show that you're being proactive. What have you got to lose by getting Moses Smith's body exhumed?' It shouldn't take more than half an hour of paperwork, and it'll get the media off your back.'

'Okay.' His tone was grudging but it had lost that aggressive edge. 'But do me a favour will you? Get onto that TV woman and tell her no interviews until we get it okayed by the magistrate. Tell her I'll put out a press release – I don't want them bugging me over the weekend.'

'Consider it done,' Megan replied, baring her teeth at the receiver in a parody of a smile.

No sooner had she put the phone down than it rang again.

'Meg, it's Dom.' The sound of his voice quickened her pulse. 'Sorry, I only just got your message. Meg – you still there?'

'Yes.' The images flashing through her mind flustered her; images of last night, when she'd conjured Dom's face as Jonathan made love to her. 'I… er…' She cleared her throat; tried to sound businesslike: 'It was about Carl's girlfriend.'

'What about her? Did you find her?'

'No – I mean I haven't tried the address yet because the letter said she was going on holiday. I was wondering if there was a mobile number. Would Carl have left it written down somewhere, do you think?'

'Hmm.' There was a pause. 'I don't know, is the answer. He wasn't much of a one for writing things down. Only time I ever saw him write anything was on the back of his hand.'

'So he didn't write letters to her? To Jodie?'

'I don't think so. See, he never really learned to read and write at school; sort of slipped through the net, like a lot of the lads in here. Any mail he got, I read it out to him.'

'So he would have phoned her then?'

'Yes. He told me that he phoned her whenever he could. Spent most of his wages on phonecards.'

'So she must have a mobile then,' Megan said. 'The address on the letter was one of the student halls of residence – they only have payphones.'

'Well, he must have memorised the number,' Dom replied. 'You say she's a student?'

She detected a note of doubt in his voice. 'Yes. Why?'

'Carl said she worked in a café.'

'Oh.' Megan considered this. Perhaps Carl had spared details like that when confiding in Dom. It seemed unlikely, though, given the intimate facts he *had* disclosed. 'Lots of students have part-time jobs,' she said. 'Did he say which one?'

'No.' She heard what sounded like a small sigh at the other end of the phone. 'I'm a bit surprised he never mentioned it

– that she was a student, I mean.'

'Well, I need to track her down, anyway,' Megan said. 'She might have given the admin people her mobile number. They should have all her details. I'll pop in this afternoon and check. We can have a quick chat if it's okay with you.' She held her breath, worried that she was making it too obvious. The desire to see him had been heightened by what she had imagined last night.

'Yes, that'd be great.' She could hear the warmth in his voice. 'I've had a hell of a night. It'll be great to have a normal conversation, so please, even if it's just for five minutes, do come.'

She felt a thrill of anticipation as she replaced the receiver. 'My God, are you mad?' she said aloud. Her voice sounded loud in the quiet of her office, the words bouncing back at her from the book-lined walls. Yes, this *was* madness. It was both foolish and naïve to contemplate a relationship with someone like Dominic Wilde. What was it about him? He had a physical effect on her; that was undeniable, but it was more than that. She admired him. Respected him in a way that she had rarely respected any man. He had faced his demons and conquered them in a way she never seemed able to have done herself. He had endured the most impossible circumstances and yet had emerged as a man transformed; reconciled with his past and at ease with his present. No wonder she felt unable to draw away, whatever the consequences.

Chapter 12

Before going back to Balsall Gate Megan had to deal with the knotty problem of Nathan MacNamara. The challenge lay in getting him off her back without ruining his chances academically. She wondered if there was any way of doing it without involving the Vice Chancellor. Technically, as her line manager, the matter should be reported to him. But he had a reputation for being very heavy-handed with any student he perceived as a troublemaker. Instead she wrote a letter to Nathan on headed departmental paper, warning him that his behaviour was inappropriate and that if it continued she would have no option but to refer the question of his suitability as a student to the Senior Tutor. As she sealed up the letter she turned to glance out of the window. It was sunny again. Perfect weather for a walk. She had a legitimate reason to go to Balsall Gate this afternoon but if she skipped lunch she wouldn't feel so guilty about tacking on a visit to Dom.

Her stomach was rumbling as she left the building so she stopped to pick up a double shot espresso from the Starbucks across the road. Hopefully it would fool her stomach into thinking she'd eaten something. As she was giving her order her mobile went off. 'Sorry,' she mouthed at the girl behind the counter. It was Delva, eager for news. As the coffee machine hissed into action she told her about the exhumation and how she'd had to play dirty with DS Willis to get him to agree.

'You're learning, girl!' The familiar guffaw boomed out

of the phone, so loud that she had to hold it away from her ear. 'Where are you now?' Delva asked.

'I'm on my way to the prison,' Megan replied. 'I'll check the grave as well. I hope they haven't left it unattended, but I wouldn't be surprised. Have you had any joy with the Serious Crime Squad?'

'Not yet, no, but I've got a couple of researchers on the case – including that ex-cop I told you about.'

'Good. Keep me posted, won't you?'

The espresso livened up Megan's pace. A few minutes later she was approaching the broken shell of St Mary's church. As she had suspected, there was no police presence in the graveyard. The fluttering plastic tape was the only thing that betrayed the fact that this place was a crime scene.

She stopped, glancing this way and that, looking for... what? The ghost of a waning moon hung low in the clear blue sky. In the shadowy hollows of the graveyard dew still lay on the long, unkempt grass. It sparkled where the sunshine touched it, giving the place an almost ethereal beauty. But she couldn't help imagining what it would look like in a few days time. There would be a tent erected over Moses Smith's grave; possibly arc lights if they decided to dig the body up after dark, as was often the case when graves had to be disturbed. But that was unlikely to deter the ghoulish once the story hit the news. She had to admit there was a certain macabre fascination in the idea of a corpse being dragged out of the earth after seventeen years. It made her think of something she'd picked up in a history lesson at school: about Oliver Cromwell, whose body was dug up and publicly hanged many years after his death in an act of ritual retribution.

She walked on, away from the church and the tombstones to the gloomy gates of the prison. As she passed through security her mind was still on the graveyard. She knew that what she had requested was a violation but there seemed no alternative; with so little else to go on, establishing the identity of the baby was crucial.

As she approached the jail's main office the governor appeared in the corridor ahead of her. She quickened her pace, catching up with him before he reached the door of his room.

'Mr Meredith!' she called.

He wheeled round, his arms loaded with buff-coloured files. 'Dr Rhys – what an unexpected pleasure.' His eyes had that cold, reptilian look that told her he was on his guard.

'The drug checks on the prison officers,' she said briskly. 'You said you'd consider it.' She knew what the answer would be but she wanted him to know that she wasn't going to allow him to ignore the Kelly case completely. It was obvious he wanted to slip gently into a well-paid retirement but she wasn't going to let him have an easy ride.

'To be blunt, Dr Rhys, I decided against it.' He cleared his throat. What came out next sounded like a prepared speech: 'You must appreciate that I and my colleagues operate in a challenging environment. The approach you have asked for is potentially damaging for morale. It's hard enough to retain officers as it is, without insulting them with blanket surveillance.'

Before she had time to respond to his management-speak he launched a second offensive. 'I'd be grateful if you could give me some indication – in writing – of how much longer this research of yours is going to take. It's taking up far more of everybody's time than I'd anticipated.' He gave her a barbed look before elbowing his way into his office and kicking the door shut behind him.

She stood staring at the closed door. He was probably on the phone to the Ministry of Justice right now, demanding an end to her presence in the prison. She could just imagine his reaction if he got any whiff of the fact that she was now using her research as an excuse to visit Dom Wilde. He would no doubt take great delight in denouncing her to the Ministry; of rubbishing her reputation as an academic. She had underestimated Meredith; she'd caught a glimpse of something cold and calculating lurking beneath the world-weary, *laisser faire* persona he presented to the outside world. She wasn't sure what it signified but she was going to have to be very, very careful.

With a grunt she turned back in the direction of the prison's main office. She still had the authorisation slip Meredith had given her and – to her relief – the admin people processed her request without a murmur. But the visiting order for Carl Kelly's girlfriend revealed no more information than she already knew: no mobile phone number – in fact no telephone number had been given at all when the application was made. She wondered what he had done for visitors before Jodie Shepherd came along. From her briefcase she pulled out the records she had hurriedly photocopied yesterday. According to the file Kelly's solicitor, Anthony Greaves, was the only point of contact. The sight of his name reminded her that she hadn't yet checked him out. She pulled out her mobile and tapped "Wilko" into the search facility. This brought up the number of Rex Wilkins, a man she had come to know while researching her book on sex offenders. Wilko was Birmingham's top criminal lawyer and knew all the solicitors in the area – good and bad. If anyone could give her the lowdown on Carl Kelly's brief, it was him. She tried the number but it went straight to voicemail. Hardly surprising: he was probably in court. She left a message then returned to her perusal of Kelly's file.

She stared at the large, boyish eyes looking out from the photo in the top right hand corner. Underneath the picture there was a blank space in the section marked 'Next of Kin'.

Could a man really be so devoid of links with the outside world? Did that suggest he was under some sort of threat from someone? Was he frightened of who might visit him? She remembered what Dom had said about the way Carl felt about Moses Smith: *He used to lie awake at night thinking the bloke was coming back to haunt him...* Why would such a hard man be bothered by the supernatural? Was there a darker guilt that he carried with him? Something that bothered him more than the disposal of an addict who was probably destined to die young anyway? The image of the baby's corpse leapt into her mind. She had met prisoners who had been involved in the death of children. It was something they had branded on their souls; something they could never erase unless they were complete psychopaths. Was that the source of Kelly's irrational fears?

Chapter 13

Megan's stomach gurgled as she negotiated the maze of corridors that led to the counselling room. She was being escorted this time by Ferret-face's sidekick – the other officer who had failed to show respect when Carl Kelly's body was removed from the cell. Like his mate, he hadn't bothered to introduce himself to her. So she had asked him his name. He had grunted it out and she had had to ask him to repeat it: Gerry Kirk. On the walk through the prison she tried making conversation but he responded with monosyllables. When they got to the room where Dom was waiting Kirk left her at the door without saying a word.

'Meg, you made it!' He stood up as she entered the room, his tall, powerful frame bathed in the sunlight that slanted in through the window. He looked better than he'd looked in the past few days; his eyes were bright and he had lost some of his prison pallor, although the hollowness around his cheekbones was still there. She wondered if that was down to Carl's death or the continuing pressure of being a Listener. All this went through her mind in the seconds it took to walk across the room and by the time she sat down her heart was hammering. He was leaning forward, smiling eagerly. She leaned back and folded her arms tightly across her chest, fighting the urge to reach out and take his hand.

'I've had some good news since we spoke this morning,' he said. 'I think I might have found my daughter!'

'Oh, Dom, that's fantastic!' Instinctively she dropped her arms, went to hug him, but stopped halfway, her hands flailing stupidly as she pulled back. 'What… I mean… how did you find her?'

'Well, it was the chaplain who tracked her down,' he said. 'He offered to search the electoral roll for me. I knew exactly how old she was, so that helped. It was a bit of a long shot, though, because I didn't know if she'd still be living in the Birmingham area. But she is.' His face broke into a delighted grin. 'So I've got her address and I'm going to write to her.'

'I'm so pleased for you.' She allowed herself to pat him on the shoulder. Just the once. As she pulled her hand away it felt as if her fingers were on fire. 'I never asked you – what's her name.'

'Elysha,' he replied. 'Nice, isn't it? Don't know where her mother got it from but I like it.' He reached into his pocket and pulled out a small, faded photograph. 'This is her,' he said. 'A nurse took it the day she was born.'

Megan's eyes moved from the baby, wrapped in a pink blanket, to the figure immediately behind. The only familiar thing about him was the eyes: those slate-grey irises shining with pride as he perched on the side of the hospital bed. His hair was black – not a trace of the grey that had turned completely white since he'd been inside. His face was tanned and he looked impossibly young for the scene the photograph portrayed. He had his arm around a pale-faced girl who was little more than a child herself.

'She was only seventeen,' Dom said, reading her thoughts. 'Weird to think that Elysha's older now than her mother was when she gave birth to her.'

Megan nodded. 'What are you going to say in the letter?'

'Don't know yet,' he shrugged. 'It's going to take a lot of thinking about. I don't know if she even knows I exist. And when she finds out I'm in prison, well…' he rolled his eyes.

'I mean, what would you think?'

'Hmm, it's tricky, isn't it?' she said. 'You can use my address if you like – the university one, I mean. If you put it care of the department anything she sends will come to my office and I'll bring it in to you myself.'

'That's really kind of you, Meg.' His beaming eyes held hers and she felt herself weaken.

'Oh, it's nothing,' she said, reaching into her jacket to distract herself. 'Here's my card. It's got the full address on. When you've written the letter give it to me to post, then there won't be any prison stamp across it.'

He took the card and tucked it in the pocket of his shirt along with the photograph. 'I forgot to ask you,' he said, 'Any luck with Carl's girlfriend's mobile?'

She shook her head. 'I'm going to have to try tracking her down through the university's internal email system,' she said. 'If she's away on holiday there's a chance she'll still be accessing her emails. One thing struck me, though: Carl seems to have had very little contact with the outside world. I couldn't find any name in the file under next-of-kin.'

'That's because he grew up in care,' he replied. 'He never knew his parents. And he never mentioned any brothers or sisters.'

'Was that a Birmingham children's home, do you know?'

'Oh, yes. He was a local lad.'

'What about friends? Did he ever mention anyone – apart from the girlfriend, I mean, that he was close to?'

'No,' Dom shrugged. 'He seemed like a real loner. The only person he ever mentioned before Jodie came on the scene was the bloke who used to supply him with drugs – the one who got shot.'

'Oh yes, I remember you telling me,' Megan nodded. 'Was he afraid of anyone on the outside, then, do you think?

Could he have been targeted by the same people who shot his pal?'

'I don't think so. His mate was black – part of a Yardie gang. Like I said, the shooting was about some turf war – nothing to do with Carl.' He dug his hands in the pockets of his jeans. 'I wouldn't say Carl was scared of anyone; not anyone *living*, that is.' He cocked his head towards the window. 'Remember what I told you about Moses Smith? How Carl got this idea in his head that he'd come back to haunt him?'

She nodded.

'He kept having these nightmares – especially when he was coming off the drugs. He spent hours telling me about them. He'd imagine Moses was in the cell with him, covered in blood, about to strangle him or something.' Dom sucked air between his teeth. 'Sometimes, after our talks, he'd be afraid to go back to his cell, afraid to go to sleep. A couple of times I was asked to go to him in the middle of the night, when he'd woken up from one of his nightmares screaming the place down. He didn't have a clue where he was, just kept rambling on about burning in hell for what he'd done. It shocked me how genuinely terrified he was.'

'I was thinking about that on my way here,' she said. 'About what you'd said about Carl feeling as if he was being haunted.' She told him what had occurred to her; that Carl Kelly's obsessional state might have been triggered by the something like the death of a child.

'You're thinking about the baby,' he said softly. 'Yes, I've been wondering about that, too. He never said anything, though. Never mentioned a child at all.'

'What did he say, exactly?'

'It was incoherent, mostly. He just kept going on about the blood. "Blood everywhere" – he kept repeating that like a mantra, muttering it under his breath. He reminded me of

Lady Macbeth, you know? It was like he was awake but not completely conscious when he was saying it. Then, when he came round properly, it was as if his memory had been wiped: he couldn't describe what it was he'd been seeing in the nightmares.'

'Dom…' She hesitated a moment, wondering how best to frame the question. 'Carl's surname: Kelly. Could he have had any Irish connections, do you think?'

He looked blank. 'Irish? I don't think so. Why do you ask.'

Before she'd come to see him today she'd wondered whether she should tell him about the fragment of newspaper found on the baby's body. Delva's words of caution still lingered in her mind. But looking at him now, at those wide, earnest eyes, she couldn't believe he was anything but genuine. So she told him about the discovery: about Delva's theory. 'Of course, it flies in the face of everything you've told me about Carl,' she added. 'But is it possible he was covering something like that up?' She paused, watching his face. The blank look had turned into a frown. 'You said he couldn't remember any detail about the flashbacks he was having,' she went on, 'Do you think that he was just being… well… economical with the truth?' She held her breath, not sure how he would react to the suggestion that someone he had counselled might have pulled the wool over his eyes. To her relief, he merely shook his head.

'I think it'd have come out one way or another,' he said. 'We've had lads in here with IRA connections. If he'd had links with people like that it would have been obvious; I'd have noticed.'

'Okay.' She nodded slowly. 'There's something else puzzling me. You described Carl as a loner; so how come he had a girlfriend? '

'Oh, that started off as a prank, actually – but whoever it

was ended up doing him a favour.'

'What do you mean?'

'Well, some wag – someone from in here who'd just got out, we thought – put an advert in the lonely hearts column of the Evening Mail. Carl got this letter, from Jodie Shepherd, saying she'd seen it and…' Before he could finish the sentence the door burst open.

'You're wanted.' It was Gerry Kirk, the prison officer who had escorted her to the room. He stood on the threshold, arms folded, looking expectantly at Dom. There was no word of apology for interrupting their meeting and no explanation as to what was going on.

'What is it?' Dom got to his feet.

The officer replied in the terse shorthand he had used on Megan when she had attempted to make conversation with him earlier: 'Beta wing. Bloke's brother's died.'

'I'm sorry,' Dom turned to Megan with a shake of his head. 'Are you able to wait for half an hour?'

She nodded. 'Don't worry. There are things I can do from here.' She slid her mobile out of her jacket pocket.

'Okay – I'll find out what's needed and be back as soon as I can.'

When he'd gone she used the web browser facility on her phone to access her university contacts database. After a few minutes' search on the staff intranet she found what she was looking for: an email address for Jodie Shepherd. She left a message designed to elicit a prompt reply without any clue as to why it had been sent: "The university needs to get in touch with you urgently. Please ring this number as soon as possible." The number she left was her own mobile. The girl would see her name on the email but would not recognise it. Students rarely knew the names of any lecturers outside their own department. Jodie Shepherd would just assume some admin person was trying to get hold of her.

As she winged off the email her phone bleeped to alert her to a text message coming through. It was from Rex Wilkins, the lawyer she had tried to call about Carl Kelly's solicitor. The message simply read: "Greaves is kosher. Best, Wilko." Megan grunted as she deleted it. Another possibility bites the dust, she thought. If the drugs weren't brought in by the solicitor, it had to be either a screw or Kelly's girlfriend. But Dom seemed convinced it couldn't be Jodie Shepherd. As she returned the phone to her pocket Dominic appeared at the door. His face was unreadable.

'Everything okay?' she asked, tucking her phone back in her pocket.

'Sort of,' he replied. 'Jamie Ryan – nice lad – only eighteen. He's in a hell of a state.' There was an air of resignation in the way he said it. This is his daily fodder, Megan thought. Tragedies happening all around him: men already living on the edge pushed one step further, tumbling into the abyss. 'I know we agreed that I wouldn't repeat anything from my counselling sessions, but there's something that's really bothering me.' She could hear his fingers tapping against the door frame. 'Jamie's brother was found dead in Strangeways.'

'Oh? What happened?'

'They think it was contaminated drugs.' He sat down heavily in the chair opposite her. 'Bit of a coincidence, that, isn't it?'

'Contaminated with what?'

'I don't know. They didn't say.'

Megan felt a creeping chill in her stomach.

'What are you thinking?' he asked.

'That maybe I've got this all wrong,' she said slowly. 'That if there's a dodgy batch out there, it could be the same dodgy batch that killed Carl.'

'I suppose that *is* possible, yes,' he frowned. 'But I think it's unlikely that the same dealers are supplying both prisons. If that was the case you'd expect to see a lot more victims on the streets.'

'You're right, of course. But it's odd, isn't it, that the person who died had a connection with this place...' she paused, thinking it through. 'Do you know anything about the Ryan family?'

'Not a lot, apart from the fact they're all Brummies.'

'Do you know what the brother was in Strangeways for?'

'No idea. I only know his name: Patrick. Jamie Ryan hasn't been in here long. I've not spoken to him before today.'

'I've got a friend who works at Strangeways,' Megan said. 'Someone I was at university with. She's the deputy governor.'

He gave her a wry smile. 'Friends in high places, eh?'

'Well, it's worth a try.' She took out her mobile, scrolling down the contacts until she found the name she was looking for. Dom settled into a chair as she waited for the ring tone.

'Veronica Burns.' The familiar voice sounded breathless.

'Ronnie, it's Megan.' A pause. No response. 'Megan Rhys.'

'Oh, Megan! Sorry. I was expecting someone else. How are you?'

'Look, I've probably caught you at a bad time, so I'll keep it brief. I'm at Balsall Gate. You've had a death from contaminated drugs – so have we. I'm trying to find out if there's a link. Do you know what the drugs were cut with?'

'Er... no. We're waiting for the toxicology report.'

'Did you see the guy who died?' Megan persisted. 'Was there anything unusual about the way he looked when they found him?"

'Well, yes, there was, actually,' Ronnie replied. 'His

face…' she tailed off as if the effort of remembering was too much for her.

'What about his face?' Megan could feel the blood surging through the artery in her neck, making her face hot.

'It was horrible. I've never seen anything like it. He had this awful, evil grin.'

Chapter 14

At five o'clock that afternoon Megan boarded a train bound for Manchester Piccadilly. Ronnie had invited her to stay the night, promising her dinner and a look at Patrick Ryan's file. The train was packed, and as she squeezed into one of the few remaining seats the ring tone of her mobile sounded. She scrabbled to retrieve it from her bag but by the time she'd located it the ringing had stopped. She looked in 'Missed Calls'. Damn. Private number. She wondered if it had been Carl Kelly's girlfriend. She could have picked up that email by now. If she was in a hotel abroad somewhere she'd be calling through a router, so nothing would show up.

A couple of minutes later she heard the beep of a voicemail message coming through. It wasn't Jodie Shepherd: it was Jonathan. He had tried to call her from his office, whose switchboard always withheld its number. His message was short and businesslike. He thanked her for last night in the kind of voice he might have used to thank a waitress for bringing him a meal. There was no warmth; no intimacy. Perhaps there were other people around when he sent it, she thought. But if that was the case, why had he mentioned last night at all? She thought about Nathan's card lying face up on the doormat. Was that the reason for Jonathan's frostiness? Or had he simply picked up the vibes she was giving out?

Although she felt guilty about the way she'd been with Jonathan she couldn't help contrasting his voice message with the affectionate way Dominic had said goodbye a couple of hours ago: he had laid his hand gently on the bare skin above her wrist as he wished her luck. It was as if he sensed the loneliness that hovered beneath the surface of a life that was so full of other people. This thought stayed with her as she drifted into a doze, lulled by the heat of the carriage and the motion of the train. In the chaotic dreams that followed, the central character was Dominic. Scenes from the prison, the university and her past were all jumbled together but he was always there in the background, a soothing, guiding presence: guiding her to what she didn't know.

She awoke with a start as her mobile beeped again. It was a text from Delva: "Mo's dad's name is Ron," the message read. "Middle name Aaron. Birth cert gives job as army. That was 1960 so he cd hv joined cops l8r – will check."

"Thanx Del," she texted back. "Am on my way to M'chester 2 check poss linked death. Spk soon, Meg." Pressing send, she glanced out of the window and spotted the floodlights of Old Trafford in the distance. She thought about Delva's theory. Patrick Ryan: that was a very Irish-sounding name. What if he was one of the others? One of the three who had gone to take revenge on Moses Smith?

The train slowed but even before it came to a stop people were scrambling to get off. The man wedged into the seat next to her plonked his size eleven boot on her toe as he struggled to get out. 'Sorry,' he muttered, 'these carriages are like bloody cattle trucks.' She was about to echo the sentiment when her phone went off again.

'Damn!' She scrabbled in her bag, trying to get it before the voicemail cut in. How many times had she promised herself she'd sort out the junk she lugged around with her? And why did they make phones so small these days, anyway? 'Hello,' she barked, expecting to be too late.

'Meg?' It was Delva's voice. 'Can you talk? You sound a bit hassled.'

'It's okay – I'm just getting off the train.' She squeezed into the space between her carriage and the next one, flattening herself against the door to the toilet as a tall girl hauled a huge rucksack onto her back, oblivious of those behind her.

'Come on, tell me more, then.' She could hear the excitement in Delva's voice. 'What's this about another death?'

She wondered if Delva could hear the hubbub going on around her. 'To be honest, I don't know much more than I said in the text – can I call you back in ten minutes?'

It took longer than that to get a taxi. By the time she got through the ticket barrier there was a queue snaking all along the front of the station. Three-quarters of an hour later she was finally out of earshot, safe behind the glass partition of a black cab, on her way to the hotel where she'd arranged to meet Ronnie. But Delva's phone was switched off. Megan glanced at her watch. She was probably on air. She sent a message giving what little information she knew, with a promise to call back as soon as she'd found out more.

She flicked down the cover of the phone and leaned across to open the window. It was good to feel the cool night air after the stifling heat of the train. As the taxi pulled up at traffic lights she glanced into the window of a house a few feet from the pavement. The light was on and she could see a man and a woman, about her age, sitting at a table, eating. There was a bottle of wine between them and as she watched she saw the man raise his glass, as if in a toast, smiling at the woman as he spoke. She felt a twinge of something in that fleeting moment before the taxi pulled away. Envy? No – it wasn't that. To her surprise she realised that what she'd experienced was a sense of relief; that she would be spending the evening with Ronnie rather than Jonathan.

If someone had told her a few days ago that she would feel this way, she wouldn't have believed them. At the beginning of the week she had been looking forward to spending the weekend with Jonathan; planning what they might do. But last night had changed everything. It would have been almost unbearable if he had stayed longer; if she had had to go through the motions of a relationship that was…what? *Stillborn*. The word jumped into her mind. With a shudder she shut the window. Where had that come from? Her thoughts switched immediately to the baby in the mortuary. But it was true: that word exactly described her relationship with Jonathan. So much promise at the start but starved of the vital elements it needed to thrive.

It wasn't that she blamed him for spending the weekend with his daughter or for having a job that took him all over the world; but those two things together, coupled with the fact that he and she lived more than a hundred miles apart meant there simply wasn't enough *time* for the relationship to develop. With Laura at school in Cardiff Jonathan wasn't likely to want to relocate to Birmingham, even if his university would allow it. And, as a head of department, for *her* to move to Wales was out of the question.

You're talking yourself out of it, aren't you? That was her mother's voice. If only you were here, Mum, she thought. So many times over the past three years Megan had wished she could pick up the phone and talk things over with her mother. When she was in her twenties it had never occurred to her that she would lose both parents before she turned thirty-four. What on earth would Mum make of the dilemma she was in now?

The taxi drew up outside *The Midland*, forcing her back to the present. As she stepped onto the pavement she glanced up at the hotel's Edwardian façade, impressive in the early evening light. It was a welcome sight. It felt good to be away from home, if only for twenty-four hours. She was glad that tonight she would not be sleeping in her own bed; on sheets that would still smell faintly of Jonathan. Tomorrow she would change the bed; would think about returning his call; would face up to what she had to do.

As she reached the entrance to the hotel she spotted Ronnie waiting in the lobby, a briefcase at her side. Patrick Ryan's file would be in there. Megan was desperate to know what it might contain. But she hadn't seen her friend for more than two years. To launch straight in would be plain rude.

On seeing Megan, Ronnie rose to her feet and greeted her with a kiss on both cheeks. 'You're looking great, Meg,' she said approvingly.

Megan rolled her eyes. 'D'you think so? I must have put on two stone since I last saw you. It's giving up the fags – I'm starting to look like a little Buddha.'

'Don't be daft,' Ronnie laughed. 'And anyway, I hope you're not thinking of dieting tonight – I've booked us a table at a Spanish tapas place on Deansgate for later. I don't know about you, but after the day I've had I could eat a horse – didn't even have time for one of those shrivelled sandwiches from the canteen.'

With a shock Megan realised that nothing bar a Starbucks double espresso had passed her lips since the banana she'd grabbed from the fruit bowl for breakfast. Surprisingly, she didn't feel all that hungry – even the packet of prunes in her bag had remained untouched. Perhaps her body was finally learning to do with less food. 'Well, I must admit I avoided the British Rail catering on the way up,' she laughed. 'The damn train was so packed I didn't dare leave my seat. But how about a couple of Margaritas to warm us up? Do you think you can still handle it?'

'Oh, I don't know about that. I haven't quite got the staying power I used to have. So perhaps something non-alcoholic to start?'

As Megan followed the sober-suited Ronnie to the bar she

smiled at the thought of her friend, the legendary university party animal, becoming the abstemious deputy governor of one of Britain's biggest jails. They'd both been high octane as students: she remembered the time they went on a whim to get their noses pierced after downing a bottle of tequila the day their finals ended. Ronnie had let hers heal up; she had toned herself down a lot since those carefree college days. As well as losing the nose stud she had let her hair – once dyed a vivid magenta – return to its natural brown. The style she wore it in now was a short, no-fuss cut. As a woman working in a men's prison it didn't do to stand out in anyway. Megan had learnt that lesson a long time ago.

As the Margaritas arrived – one alcohol free – Ronnie beamed at Megan across the table. 'I'm really glad we've been able to get together tonight – even though it's not for a very nice reason – because I've just had some really good news.'

'Oh? What's that?'

There was a brief pause. Ronnie, still smiling, was blushing.

'Come on,' said Megan, 'What is it? You look like the cat who got the cream. Don't tell me you're going to be a governor at thirty-seven?'

'No, much better than that – I'm pregnant.'

'God, Ronnie…' Megan was suddenly lost for words. This was the last thing she'd expected. She'd always had Ronnie down as the archetypal career woman – someone who was determined to make her mark in what was still a man's world. She distinctly remembered a conversation they'd had as students, when Ronnie had forcefully made the point that women having it all was a fallacy. She had cited her own mother as a perfect example: an Oxford law graduate trying to combine a career as a barrister with raising three children. In the end she had given up, Ronnie said, because she couldn't bear the fact that if they were ill or upset they called for the nanny, not her.

'Well, aren't you pleased for me?' Ronnie's voice brought her back to the present.

'Sorry, of course I am.' Megan made herself smile. She *was* pleased but she was also as envious as hell. 'I'm just a bit shocked, that's all,' she said, swallowing hard.

'Don't worry – so was I! I never thought it was going to happen for us.'

'When… er… when's the baby due?'

'The beginning of October, according to the scan.' Her face suddenly changed, as if she'd read Megan's thoughts. 'Anyway,' she said briskly, 'enough of me for the moment – what about you? Anything happening on the romance front?'

Megan grunted. 'No one that you might describe as a "significant other".'

'Ah!' Ronnie gave her a sideways look. 'So there is someone, then?'

'Well, there *was*. I'm not sure the present tense is still appropriate.'

'You've dumped him?'

'Kind of.'

'What do you mean, "kind of"? You either have or you haven't, I would have thought.'

'I suppose I have in my head,' Megan shrugged. 'I think I've only just realised myself that there's no future in it – it's kind of complicated.' She wasn't going to tell Ronnie how complicated, or confess to her feelings for Dom Wilde. She could imagine Ronnie's reaction if she knew she was even contemplating breaking one of the cardinal rules of prison ethics.

'He's married?'

'Let's just say he's not available, full stop. So there you

have it – my boring but tangled life,' she said with a wry smile. She drained her glass. 'God, that cocktail's gone straight to my head. I'd better have a look at that stuff you brought before I get I get completely ratted.'

'Sure.' Ronnie glanced at her watch. 'We've got another ten minutes before the table's booked.' From her briefcase she pulled the standard-issue buff-coloured inmate file and handed it over. 'I've taken a look myself but I didn't see anything unusual or particularly interesting. 'You said on the phone you thought the look on his face could have been caused by strychnine but our doctor said tetanus causes that.'

Megan nodded. 'That's what they thought at Balsall Gate until the toxicology report came through.'

'Hmm.' Ronnie rubbed the stem of her glass between her finger and thumb. 'Well, I think whoever brought the drugs in must have been a visitor – we've had a big clampdown in the last couple of months on screws bringing stuff in.'

'What sort of visitors,' Megan asked as she opened the file.

'Quite a few, actually in the last few days before he died, but most of them were official: his solicitor, a probation officer and the chaplain. He didn't get many personal visitors.'

Megan was confronted by an aggressive-looking face framed with a shaggy mop of red hair. The photograph of Patrick Ryan didn't do him any favours. He had small, mean-looking eyes and a clutch of freckles spreading from the middle of a snub nose. She would have guessed that he was in his mid-to-late forties, but she was wrong about that: his date of birth was down as the third of June 1967 – which made him a couple of months short of forty-one when he died – four years older than Carl Kelly.

Her eyes moved down the page to Ryan's conviction details. 'Oh,' she said suddenly, bending her head closer to the page to make certain she'd read the words correctly.

'What?' Ronnie peered over her shoulder.

'Well, I might be wrong, but...' Megan dived into her briefcase, pulling out the copy of Kelly's file and lining it up on the table alongside Patrick Ryan's. 'These are the conviction details of the guy who died at Balsall Gate. Look,' she said, jabbing her finger at the paper. 'Same court. Same offence. Same date.'

Chapter 15

It was difficult to talk above the hubbub of the tapas bar in Deansgate. It was only when they got back to Ronnie's house that Megan was able to properly explain about Carl Kelly's death; about the discovery of strychnine in his body and the almost simultaneous discovery of a long-dead baby in his victim's grave.

'I was convinced it was some kind of revenge killing,' Megan said, cradling the glass of whisky Ronnie's husband had poured her before tactfully retiring to bed. 'Then when I heard about what had happened here, my first thought was that the police were right: that it *was* a batch of contaminated drugs and my theory was way off beam. But now I've seen the file…' She gazed at the face of Patrick Ryan as it had looked on the day he entered Strangeways. Then her eyes ranged over the photographs spread out on the coffee table; photographs that Ronnie had been unable to show her in public. They had been taken in the mortuary where Ryan's body now lay. The close-up of the face was truly grotesque. Megan pitied whoever had had the grim task of identifying him. 'Who was it that found him?' she asked.

'One of his cell mates,' Ronnie replied. 'They were all on association, but he'd stayed behind. He'd told them he didn't feel well and wanted a lie down. They came back an hour later and found him dead on the bed with the syringe on the floor beside him. So they knew straight away it was drugs and they assumed it was an overdose.'

'That's pretty much what happened with Carl Kelly,

except he still had the syringe in his leg.'

Ronnie's mouth turned down at the edges as she pictured the scene. 'So if our guy was poisoned as well, it could be some kind of vendetta, couldn't it? Maybe some drug baron that Patrick Ryan and Carl Kelly rubbed up the wrong way?'

'Well, it certainly looks as if they could have been members of the same gang,' Megan agreed. 'I'll need to check the court records; find out if they were both involved in the same case. It could be that they happened to be in court on the same day for completely unrelated offences.'

'Unlikely, though, isn't it?'

Megan nodded. 'There is another possibility, although there's no hard evidence to back it up so far.' She told Ronnie about the sliver of newspaper stuck to the body of the baby in the mortuary; about Delva's idea of a link between Carl Kelly's victim and the Birmingham Six .

'Well, Patrick Ryan's an Irish-sounding name,' Ronnie said, 'but he was in here for a drugs offence, so that seems to back up what your contact at Balsall Gate said, doesn't it? We don't know if Patrick Ryan was in on that murder, do we? All we know is that he and Carl Kelly got banged up on the same day more than a decade later. If someone's killed them both, the Moses Smith thing could be completely coincidental. Their deaths could be revenge killings, but for something else; something related to drug trafficking, I mean.'

'But what about the baby?' Megan asked. 'How do you explain that happening within a matter of weeks of Carl Kelly's death? It's too much of a coincidence.'

'Yes, I suppose it is.' Ronnie shook her head. 'Poor little thing – it makes me shudder to think about it. It must have been a horrible thing to find.'

Megan nodded. She didn't want to dwell on how it had

made her feel, especially with Ronnie being pregnant. 'I think what I really need to see is the list of visitors Ryan had over the past month or so,' she said briskly. 'Any chance of nipping into the prison tomorrow?'

'Yes, of course we can. The office won't be open but I've got keys'

'And we need to get that toxicology report as soon as possible – make certain that it actually *was* strychnine. When do you think you'll get it?'

'Well,' Ronnie said, taking a sip from her steaming mug of cocoa, 'he said Monday, but I could try phoning him in the morning – he's often in the lab at the weekend.' She began to yawn and clapped her hand over her mouth. 'Sorry Meg – I'm totally knackered. I didn't realise you could get this tired so early on in a pregnancy.'

'It's okay. Don't apologise. I'm a bit wiped out myself.' She didn't feel like explaining why: that she'd been up till God knows what time having sex with the man she'd just told Ronnie she was finished with. She shooed her friend up the stairs with her cocoa and sat for a while on the sofa, finishing her whisky. When the noises from the bathroom had ceased, she tiptoed up to the spare room.

She stood looking at the bed for a few moments before getting under the covers. Although she was glad to be away for the night, it felt strange, climbing into a bed she had shared so many times with Tony during the years they were married. Tony had got on well with Ronnie's husband; one of those rare situations when the partners of friends become really good friends themselves. Part of the reason she hadn't been to visit Ronnie for so long was that she felt such a gooseberry without Tony there as well. And now there was a baby on the way... Megan sighed as she switched off the light. It would probably feel even weirder next time she paid them a visit. But she was just going to have to come to terms with that. If she started crossing people off her Christmas list just because they'd sprogged, she'd end up with no friends left at all. Funny how she'd never felt like that with Ceri, though: when her sister had had the first baby she'd accepted it quite calmly, because at that point she'd just been promoted to head of department. It seemed fair. Ceri was having children and giving up full-time work while she was powering up the career ladder. But in the past couple of years it hadn't felt quite the same. Somehow the career was no longer enough.

'Stop being such a bloody misery,' she whispered to herself in the dark. Closing her eyes, she searched her mind for something to distract her from the subject of babies; what was it the TV shrinks said? Oh yes: "Focus on something exciting; something you would really like to have. This will release endorphins, giving you an instant lift." The only thing she could think of was Dom Wilde.

Megan was woken at just after six o'clock the next morning by the sound of Ronnie throwing up in the bathroom. She got out of bed and pulled on her jeans. They were newly washed and she had to lie back down to do them up, they were so tight. She glared at herself in the mirror, pinching the roll of fat that bulged over the top of the waistband. It seemed cruelly ironic that Ronnie was stick thin and three months' gone while she didn't even have the excuse of being pregnant. She was going to have to do something: snacking on prunes was obviously not enough – she needed to go on a proper diet and do some pretty serious exercise.

With a sigh she went downstairs to make a cup of tea. There was a packet of Vanilla Cream Hobnobs in the cupboard beside the teabags and she ate two to cheer herself up. No point starting the new regime while she was away, and by the sound of things, Ronnie wasn't going to want them.

A few minutes later Ronnie appeared round the kitchen door looking like a ghost. 'I'm sorry, Meg. Did I wake you up?'

'It's okay. I was awake anyway,' she lied. 'Can I get you a cup of tea.'

Ronnie held up her hands as if fending off anything related to food or drink. 'No thanks,' she mumbled. Clapping her hands over her mouth she rushed back upstairs.

It was after nine when Ronnie came down again. She had dressed and put on make-up, but the bronzer on her cheeks couldn't disguise her pallor.

'Are you sure you should be up?' Megan studied her friend's face, concerned at how drawn she looked. 'I feel awful, hijacking your weekend like this.'

'No, honestly, I'd rather be doing something,' Ronnie said. 'I've been getting it every morning for about a week now, but it usually goes by mid-morning.' She reached for the phone. 'If I sat in bed thinking about it I'd feel even worse.' She punched out a number. 'The toxicologist,' she mouthed at Megan as she waited for it to answer. 'He should be in by now... Hello – Chris? It's Ronnie. Any news?'

Megan listened intently to Ronnie's conversation. It sounded as if the results hadn't come through yet. After a couple of minutes Ronnie put her hand over the receiver and said: 'They've ruled out tetanus but they can't say for sure yet that it's strychnine. He hopes to know by this afternoon. Would you like a word with him?'

Megan took the phone. There was plenty she wanted to ask this man, even without the results. She explained what had happened at Balsall Gate. 'Do you mind if I pick your brains?' she asked. 'Only I need to know a bit more about the cutting of strychnine with heroin. I know it's unusual but could someone have done this by accident? And if so, how could they make such a mistake?'

'I doubt very much if it would be a mistake,' he replied in broad Mancunian. 'It's bloody hard to get hold of and anyone who did would know that you could kill someone with a very small dose.'

'So you think it was probably deliberate, then? Not a dodgy batch?'

'Yes, I do. A batch like that would have the mortuaries in Brum bursting at the seams. The heroin trade these days is production line stuff. The dealers that supply prisons are doing it all across the country.

'That's what I suspected,' she said, 'but when I first heard about the Strangeways case I thought I'd somehow got it wrong.'

There was a look of triumph on her face when she put down the phone. 'He agrees with me,' she said, in answer to Ronnie's questioning look. 'So assuming it *is* strychnine – and I don't really see how it could be anything else now the tetanus angle's been ruled out – we've got two guys from Birmingham, probably members of the same drugs gang, who died in the same manner in separate jails within a few days of each other.'

'It's all starting to stack up, isn't it?'

She nodded. 'Can we go and take a look at those visitor lists?'

Megan had been to Strangeways several times before. Its architecture was very different to that of Balsall Gate: imposing, impressive, even. But if she'd closed her eyes it could have been the same place. It was the smell: that distinctive mix of sweat, cigarettes and institutional food that assaulted the nostrils the minute you got through the gates. It was a very male smell, quite intimidating to the uninitiated. Like a simmering cauldron of testosterone. Women's prisons were different. The greasy cooking and the fags were still there, but overlaid with a suffocating mix of deodorants, perfumes and body sprays.

Ronnie led the way to the main office. It didn't take long to locate the visitors' record for the week leading up to Patrick Ryan's death. Megan scanned the list, looking for names with his prison number recorded alongside them.

'That's his solicitor,' Ronnie, said, pointing at one of the entries. 'And his probation officer came later the same day.'

'Hmm.' Megan noted that the solicitor had a different name from the one who had been visiting Carl Kelly. She didn't recognise the name of the probation officer, either, although she knew plenty of people from the Birmingham team. 'Who's this?' she asked, pointing to a name further down the list.

'Rebecca Jordan.' Ronnie read it out loud. 'Girlfriend, I think.'

'Would she be from Birmingham, then?'

'Probably. Hang on a second, I'll find the form she filled in when she applied for the visiting order.' Ronnie went across to the other side of the office and unlocked a filing cabinet. After a short search she pulled out a piece of paper with Rebecca Jordan's details on it. 'Yes. She is from Birmingham.' She handed the form over. The address was near the top of the sheet of paper. Megan gasped as she read the first line.

'What is it?' Ronnie frowned.

'Linden House.' Megan scanned the rest of the address to be sure she wasn't mistaken. 'It's a student hall of residence at Heartland,' she said, blinking in disbelief. 'The *same* hall of residence that Carl Kelly's girlfriend lives in.'

Chapter 16

'Why would a student be in a relationship with a man who's been inside for three years?' Ronnie was incredulous. 'These girls would be first years, probably, wouldn't they, if they're in a hall of residence? So they'd be… what… about fifteen years old when these guys were sent down.'

'I know,' Megan said, 'But Carl's girlfriend only started seeing him a few weeks back. One of the other inmates told me they met through a lonely hearts column in the local paper.'

'A lonely hearts column?' Ronnie's eyebrows disappeared beneath her fringe.

'That's what he said. He reckoned it was a prank by someone who'd just got out and thought he'd set Carl up. When he told me, it didn't strike me as being anything malicious. Now I'm not so sure.'

'What if these girls are acting as mules? They could be bringing the drugs in for someone else.' Ronnie's eyes narrowed. 'They might not even know that it's something deadly.'

'That would make sense,' Megan nodded. 'It's the kind of thing you could imagine a student doing for money, if they were desperate. Whoever's behind it probably placed the lonely hearts ad as well.'

'What, you mean they used the ad as way of getting to Carl Kelly without him realising it?'

'It's possible, isn't it? Bloody clever way of hoodwinking a guy in prison: make him think some good-looking girl on the outside fancies him; a couple of visits and he's hooked. She offers to bring him drugs as well and he thinks he's really landed on his feet.'

'Well, that's one hell of a scam, if it's true.'

'There's a number here,' Megan pointed at the form Rebecca Jordan had filled out. 'It's a mobile.' She looked at Ronnie. 'Would this girl have been informed of Patrick Ryan's death, or is it just the next of kin that know?'

'Just next of kin,' Ronnie nodded. 'There's only the brother, the one in Balsall Gate. We don't have the names of his parents or any other relative. You get that a lot with the men in this place – you know, disjointed families; people whose relatives have either disowned them or just disappeared.'

'It'd be interesting to find out how she'd react to the news, then, wouldn't it?' Megan said. 'If it was her who brought the drugs in, and she knew what was in them, it would be no surprise. But then I'd be very surprised if that phone number was genuine, wouldn't you? Why would she give it if she knew she was likely to be traced?'

'You're right.' Ronnie frowned, thinking it through. 'Even if she thought she was just acting as a mule you wouldn't expect her to give her real number, would you? It'd probably be some stolen mobile she used for as long as she needed it, then chucked it away.'

'Hmm. If that's the case, she'd only answer this number if she was innocent: if she really *was* Patrick's girlfriend and had nothing to do with the drugs.' Megan took her phone out and stared at it, wondering what to do.

'What will you say if she answers?'

Megan shook her head, shoving the phone back into her pocket. 'I'm not going to risk it,' she said. 'I need to find her: talk to her face-to-face. I haven't been able to contact Carl Kelly's girlfriend – her last letter to him said she was going on holiday – but I'm worried now.'

'Worried? Why?'

'I'm wondering whether whoever's behind this might have got to her; decided she was dispensable once she'd done her job in Balsall Gate.'

'And you think the same thing might happen to this Rebecca Jordan?' Ronnie frowned.

'It's possible, isn't it? What if she's still got the phone? Hasn't got rid of it because she doesn't expect to be rumbled for what she thinks was a routine drugs run? She might do this sort of thing all the time and get away with it – I don't mean murdering people; I mean smuggling heroin into prisons. So if she gets a phone call from me she might tell her boss, who would realise someone was onto him.' With a shrug, she spread her hands in front of her. 'She's the weakest link, so it's goodbye Rebecca.'

Ronnie considered this. 'You could leave a message. Something that won't arouse her suspicions.'

'I could, but I think it'd be best just to go to the hall of residence. Catch her by surprise.'

'You'll still have to come up with something pretty convincing to say, won't you?'

Megan nodded. 'I'll have to pretend to be a welfare officer or something. Say I've been told she's having financial problems and I've come to offer some advice.'

'Yes, that could work – but what happens after that?'

'I'll have to play it by ear, I think,' Megan replied. 'Once I know what she looks like I might have to do some tailing; see if she'll lead me to the person who's masterminding this – if there is such a person.'

'Okay, but I hope you're not thinking of doing this on your own? You *are* going to get the police involved, aren't you? I mean, the kind of people you're likely to run up against wouldn't think twice about disposing of you if they thought you posed a threat. You can get a hit man around here for five hundred quid. Life is cheap. Don't risk it.'

'I know what you're saying and I promise I haven't got a death wish but, so far, the police haven't shown the slightest interest. I will be careful though.'

'You make sure that you are.'

The Saturday afternoon train was much quieter than the one she'd caught yesterday. A few minutes into the journey she dipped into her bag for the packet of prunes. There was only one left so she decided to visit the buffet car. It was a relief to be able to wander along the carriages without fear of losing her seat. Before she reached it the smell of grilling bacon wafted towards her. Saliva trickled under her tongue. Her stomach felt empty – all she had eaten since the Hobnobs first thing that morning were two pieces of dry toast: one hers, and one that Ronnie had been unable to eat more than a corner of. If she'd been eating toast at home she would have smothered it with a thick layer of easy-spread butter and a dollop of Manuka honey (the pricey honey was her token attempt at eating something with health benefits). But seeing poor Ronnie's face when she opened the fridge had made it next to impossible to eat a proper breakfast. Despite her friend's protests, she'd decided that a bit of sisterly solidarity was called for. So dry toast it was – and that had been six hours ago.

There was only one other person in the buffet car, a ruddy-faced, pot-bellied man in a suit, and the bacon was for him. She watched him smother it in brown sauce as he waited for the woman behind the counter to whizz up a cappuccino topped with squirty cream. She wasn't sure if it was the sight of the sauce oozing from the corners of his mouth or the smell of his armpits as he raised the sandwich from the plate, but suddenly she felt quite nauseous. By the time the woman glanced round to take her order, all she could face was a cup of black coffee.

She took it back to her seat, taking deep breaths as she put a good distance between herself and the sauce-dribbler. As soon as she took a sip of coffee her stomach began to rumble. Damn, she thought, I can't go back there now: I should have at least bought a packet of crisps or a biscuit. The gurgling from her insides was getting so loud she was sure the other people in the carriage must be able to hear. So for once it was a relief when the shrill notes of her mobile drowned her out.

'Megan, can you talk?' It was Delva. 'I've got some news about the Serious Crime Squad.'

'Oh, what?' Megan grabbed her coffee and walked as fast as she could down the carriage. She propped herself against a wall outside the toilet. With the sliding doors to the carriages on either side shut, she was confident no one would overhear her conversation. 'Have you found Moses Smith's father?'

'Well, not exactly,' Delva said. 'His name's not among the list of the men who were prosecuted, but that doesn't necessarily mean anything.'

'Why not?'

'Well, only a few men were ever punished for what they did,' Delva replied. 'A lot were accused, but in the end just seven men were convicted – for fairly minor offences. What we've found out, though, is that the names of all the officers involved first came to light around the time that Moses Smith was murdered: it was between 1989 and 1991 that the information was passed to the Crown Prosecution Service.'

'Right,' Megan nodded as she took this in. 'So anyone with links to the CPS could have found out the names of all the men who'd been accused?'

'Exactly. It brought the whole thing into the public domain

for the first time.'

'So you think Smith senior could have been one of the ones who got away with it?'

'It's possible, yes, but we still haven't got any firm evidence that Ron Smith was a copper at all. Tim tried to do some more digging yesterday. He asked the CPS for the list of names to see if Ron's was on it but they blew him out. Said the records were only accessible to authorised personnel.'

'Hmm. Hardly surprising, I suppose.'

'I know. He tried stinging them with a Freedom of Information request but you can imagine how that went down. I think the official line was that any approach for information would be turned down in the interests of the security and safety of the people on the list.'

'Well, yes, that's understandable.'

'To his credit, he didn't give up, though. He tried sounding out a few of his mates in the force to see if he could get them to go to the CPS on his behalf. No one was keen – they were all worried about jeopardising their careers – but one of them did tell him about a letter the force received at the time the Serious Crime Squad scandal broke.'

'What kind of letter?'

'The sort that threatened severe retribution. Tim managed to get his hands on a copy. It was addressed to "The Bastards of West Midlands Police, Torturers of Free Irishmen".'

'Not pulling any punches, then.' Megan's tongue clicked against the back of her teeth. 'Any clues as to who sent it?'

'No, it was anonymous. Tim reckons, though, that the higher echelons of the IRA made it clear at the time that they would hold individuals accountable for the actions of the Squad'.

'So the crucial thing now is to find out if Ron Smith's name is on that list. Has Tim got any more ideas?'

'He's supposed to be phoning me later on this afternoon,'

Delva replied. 'He said there was one possibility but he didn't want to say any more until he was sure it was a "goer", as he so quaintly puts it.'

There was a rush of sound as another train hurtled past the window. Delva was saying something but Megan couldn't make out what it was.

'I said you haven't told me what's been happening at your end,' Delva repeated. 'Where are you, anyway? Sounds bloody noisy.'

'I'm on the train – should be back into New Street in about forty minutes.' Megan gave her a shorthand account of what had unfolded in Manchester.

'So you're going there tonight? To Linden House?'

'Yes. I want to catch Rebecca Jordan when she's likely to be up and about. No point waiting till tomorrow – most of the students I know don't surface before mid-afternoon on a Sunday.'

'Can I come along?'

'Well, yes…' Megan hesitated. She hadn't planned to take anyone with her. But she thought about what Ronnie had said to her before she'd left Manchester: it probably wasn't sensible to go alone. 'Are you sure you want to, though? I'd have thought you'd have far better things to do on a Saturday night.'

'Well if I get a better offer I'll let you know,' Delva chuckled, 'but otherwise it's a takeaway on my lap in front of *Strictly Come Dancing*. Anyway, what about you? I thought the red hot lover was on his way back from Oz for the weekend.'

'Sore point,' Megan replied, grimacing at her reflection in the train window. 'He's blown me out for a younger model. More than twenty years younger, actually.'

'His daughter, huh?'

'You got it in one. It's brought things to a bit of a head,

as it happens. I'll tell you later.' Keen to change the subject, Megan asked Delva if she knew where Linden House was. She didn't, so Megan offered to pick her up. They lived just a few streets away from each other in almost identical Victorian houses. Like her place, Delva's was a nightmare as far as parking was concerned. 'I'll be there at seven and I'll pip my horn,' she said. 'Make sure you're ready, won't you? Otherwise I'll probably get lynched by that neighbour who told me off for blocking his drive.'

'Don't worry, he's on holiday,' Delva replied. 'But I will be ready. I'm looking forward to it.'

'God, you're even sadder than me!' Megan laughed. 'Okay, see you later. Oh, and by the way, you'd better wear sunglasses and something frumpy – we don't want anyone recognising you.'

'Cheeky cow! I don't own anything frumpy! But I'll do my best…'

The phone beeped as Megan pressed the 'end call' button. A few minutes later it beeped again as a text message came through. It was Ronnie this time, with the news that the toxicology report had come through. So it *was* strychnine. No real surprise, but seeing the word spelt out suddenly brought home how potentially dangerous the situation was becoming. She was glad that she wasn't going to be venturing out alone tonight.

As the train rumbled through the green fields of north Staffordshire Megan's mind turned to the murder of Moses Smith. The IRA thing was something they were going to have to keep an open mind about until Tim could make some headway with those records. Perhaps the story Carl Kelly had told Dom was just that: a fictionalised version of the real reason behind the attack. If Kelly had had sympathies with the IRA there was no reason why he couldn't have been recruited by someone hellbent on revenge. That didn't mean he wasn't a drug dealer back then, nor would it have stopped him carrying on being a drug dealer. He and his mates could possibly have been offered a lot of money by someone who knew that Moses Smith trusted them and would let them into his home.

The face of Patrick Ryan lying on the mortuary slab in Manchester flashed in front of her. If Ryan was a second member of the gang that had killed Moses – and at the moment it was still a very big 'if' – who was the third? If revenge for Moses' death was the motive for the poisoning of Kelly and Ryan, that third man could be in mortal danger. She needed access to the court records of the case Kelly and Ryan were sent down for: there was just a chance that all three had remained part of the same gang and if that was the case, that third man could have appeared in court alongside them.

She cursed the fact that it was the weekend; that there was nothing she could do about it until the court office opened on Monday. Perhaps by then, though, she might have a lot more to go on. She muttered a silent prayer for Rebecca Jordan to be there when she and Delva arrived at Linden House.

The hall of residence was a series of interconnected grey rectangles, typical of the brutalist architecture of the 1960s. The steps outside the main block had been colonised by a group of smokers. Some were sitting, some leaning against the wall and most had a can or a bottle in the hand that wasn't holding a cigarette. The girls were clad in their flimsy Saturday night finery, cleavages heaving as they dragged on low tar Marlboro's, belly bars glinting in the dying rays of the sun

Megan noticed heads turn as she and Delva threaded their way through. Delva had not heeded the advice to dress down:

in fact dressed *up* would be a better description of the way she looked. She had wound a brightly coloured scarf round her braids, its vibrant red and orange hues echoed in the African-style robe that swathed her body. The outfit seemed to add at least six inches to her height. No wonder the students were staring: they must look a very odd couple.

Leaving the smokers behind, they found themselves in the relatively deserted lobby of the building. The smell of battered fish lay heavy on the air and the distant clatter of plates and cutlery could be heard. Evidently they had arrived just as the evening meal was being cleared away. Directly in front of them was a honeycomb of pigeonholes, each with a letter of the alphabet above it. Megan glanced across at the reception area. A middle aged, bespectacled woman wearing a yellow polo shirt with the university crest on it was handing a key to a girl in sports kit who had a hockey stick in her hand. From what she could make out the girl had locked herself out of her room. An amiable but involved discussion seemed to be taking place and Megan decided to take advantage of this. 'Stay here a minute, will you?' she whispered to Delva.

'Where are you going?' Delva hissed back.

Megan jerked her head towards the row of boxes. She headed for the one marked 'S'. She was well aware of the privacy guidelines for students' correspondence but she needed to see if there was any mail for Jodie Shepherd. If she really was on holiday there ought to be at least junk mail waiting for her. As she took out the letters she heard Delva come up behind her.

'What are you doing?'

'Delva! I'm trying to sneak a look at the post!' Megan gave her an exasperated look. Go back to the door – please! You might as well have a neon sign above your head saying "Look at us!"'

'But what are you looking for?' Delva persisted.

'Anything for Jodie Shepherd.' Megan stepped sideways, away from Delva, hiding the bundle of letters inside her jacket.

Suddenly a voice boomed across the lobby. 'Good evening. Can I help you?' They wheeled round. A tall, slim man who looked barely older than the students was coming towards them. His black hair was brushed back behind his ears revealing an angular but handsome face, quite in keeping with the resonant voice. He was looking at Delva. Megan stepped between them. 'Sorry.' She offered him her hand almost in a reflex action. 'Dr Rhys – Department of Investigative Psychology. I've just come to enquire about a student.'

'Dr Rhys!' His lips parted in a wide smile. 'Delighted to meet you in person. I don't know if you remember, but we spoke on the phone a few months ago about my PhD thesis.' She looked blankly at him. 'Oh, sorry, I didn't introduce myself: David Dunn – Department of International Politics. I'm the warden here.'

'Oh, David, yes, I remember,' she said, relieved that she was suddenly able to place him. 'Your doctorate was on post-conflict stress, wasn't it? I gather it was rather well-received.'

'That's very kind of you to say so,' he replied, two spots of pink colouring his cheeks. 'What you told me really helped. Perhaps I can repay the favour. What can I do to help?'

'I… er… I need to speak to a couple of students.' She hesitated, not wanting to give too much away. She certainly didn't want to spell out the real reason she was there – not at this stage, anyway. 'They haven't been replying to emails and I'm a bit concerned. My friend and I were just passing so I thought I'd pop in on the off-chance.'

'Have you got their student numbers?'

'Not on me, no.'

'Oh well, no problem. What are their names?'

'Well, one of them is Rebecca Jordan. The other is called Jodie Shepherd.'

'Jodie Shepherd?' He looked at her, slightly bemused. 'But she hasn't been here for months.'

'Oh? Why not?'

'She was involved in a car crash the week after she arrived here. It was terrible – hit and run. She was in a coma – still is, as far as I know.'

Chapter 17

Megan's mind was racing ahead as he led them through to his office. A stolen identity: someone had used this accident victim as a cover. It was ideal – a student legitimately registered, with postal and email addresses set up, but no longer in a position to collect or respond to any letters or correspondence. When the visiting order was sent from Balsall Gate prison the imposter would simply do what Megan herself had done: choose a suitable moment to take whatever mail had arrived.

Megan and Delva perched on a low-backed brown leather sofa while the warden tapped the keyboard of his desktop computer. 'Here it is.' A printer whirred into life somewhere in the direction of his feet and he bent down to retrieve the sheet of paper. 'Rebecca Jordan – she dropped out just before Christmas. Says here that she vacated her room on the seventeenth of December.'

'Does it say why?' Megan asked.

'Should do.' He flipped the paper over. 'Yes, here it is: "Reason for departure: Dissatisfied with the course. Taking time out to travel before returning to new course next year."' He looked up. 'Can I ask why you're particularly interested in Rebecca Jordan and Jodie Shepherd? They were both outside of your faculty, weren't they?'

'I should have told you before.' Gingerly, she took the bundle of envelopes from her jacket and handed them over. 'Before I came here this evening I wasn't sure what I was going to find, but now I'm pretty certain that both Rebecca and Jodie are victims of identity theft. ' She gave him the bare bones of the story, telling him that girls using the students' names were suspected of having smuggled drugs into prisons. She didn't mention the poisonings or the location of the prisons involved. She had a good reason for holding information back: whoever had stolen those identities would need to have the confidence to be able to blend in and return to the lobby time and time again to check for mail. That person was either going to be a student or someone else closely connected with the hall of residence. She glanced at the young man standing in front of her. It could be him. Just because he was being so co-operative didn't mean he wasn't implicated in some way. In fact his very willingness to assist might disguise an involvement. She had to be careful not to give too much away.

'Well, I'm truly shocked.' Dr. Dunn raked his fingers through his hair, disturbing its slicked-back elegance. 'These are very serious allegations. Do you think other students could be at risk?'

'I'm not sure,' she shrugged, 'but what I'm wondering is whether one of the students has actually perpetrated this. Have you seen anyone acting suspiciously? Possibly someone loitering around reception when the post is normally delivered.'

He shook his head. 'I can't say I've seen anyone. I will ask the porters – they're more likely to have seen anything like that. I have to say, though, we have tightened our security a lot in the last couple of months. We've had quite a number of thefts of laptops from the bedrooms, so we've been much more vigilant about people coming in and out of the building.'

'I don't suppose you've got CCTV?' Delva piped up.

'Unfortunately not.' He gave a small sigh. 'It's something I've been nagging the Director of Estates about, but as you know, Dr Rhys, university finances are very tight at the moment.'

There was something about his voice, Megan thought. That honeyed tone never varied, even when he was talking about something negative. 'Okay,' she said. 'Let me know what the porters say, won't you?' She reached into her bag, pulling out a card with the institutional logo on it. 'That's got my mobile number on it.' She handed the card to him.

'I'll get onto it straight away,' he replied, tucking the card into the pocket of his crisply ironed chinos. 'The porters aren't all on duty over the weekend, so it might be Monday before I'm able to give you the full picture.'

'Just one other thing before we go,' she said. 'Could I have the contact details for Rebecca Jordan's family? I'd like to make absolutely sure that she wasn't involved in this; that she really is travelling overseas.'

'Of course,' he nodded. 'You might as well take this, actually.' He handed her the sheet of paper he'd printed off the computer. 'Her home address and telephone number are at the bottom.'

'Thanks.' She shook his hand. 'It was nice to meet you, David. I'm sorry it was in such unfortunate circumstances.' She held his gaze for a moment, watching for a flicker in his eyes. Her years of interviewing prisoners had taught her to recognise the signs. She could usually tell when something was being held back. But he simply smiled back her, his eyes unblinking.

As she left the building Megan was acutely aware that any of the young people lounging on the steps could be tied up in all of this. How on earth could she make any headway with so many potential suspects? Of course, the letter purporting to be from Jodie Shepherd might yield fingerprints – she must get that checked out. But that would also mean fingerprinting the entire hall of residence. How was that going to go down with the university authorities?

She and Delva mulled this over in Megan's favourite Thai restaurant on the Bristol Road. 'What do you think's behind it all?' Delva asked, dipping a corner of prawn toast into a pool of sweet chilli sauce. 'I mean, is it the Irish connection? Is it drug smuggling? Or is it just plain revenge for a very old murder? It's all getting so complicated, isn't it?'

'I know.' Megan slid a chunk of chicken satay off its wooden skewer. 'In all the other cases I've worked on the options have closed down the further in you get. But this time it's almost the opposite: there are so many possibilities it's hard to know what to focus on. I suppose there's no more news on Ron Smith, is there?'

Delva shook her head. 'I'm hoping there might be by tomorrow, though. Tim said he was going to pay his parents a visit tonight – he didn't tell me before but it turns out his dad was in the force during the period when the Birmingham Six were arrested.'

'What? You mean Tim's dad was in the Serious Crime Squad?'

'No, nothing like that, just a lowly PC, according to Tim. But he would have heard the talk going round at the time. Tim reckons he might be able to throw some light on it.'

'Good.' Megan nodded as the waiter brought two bottles of Tiger beer.

'What did you think of that bloke in the hall of residence?' Delva said when the waiter had gone. 'Bit smarmy, wasn't he?'

'I suppose he was a bit full of himself,' Megan nodded. 'But he's very well thought of in academic circles.'

'You didn't like him, though, did you?' Delva grimaced.

'He was very helpful.' She lifted her glass and took a good mouthful of beer. 'But let's just say I'm keeping an open mind about him.' From somewhere in the depths of her bag she heard the trill of her mobile phone. 'Sorry,' she hissed, as she bent down to locate it, 'I'd better get it – it might be him.'

But it wasn't David Dunn, it was Dom Wilde, calling from the prison with his phonecard. 'I haven't got much juice left on this,' he said. 'Just wanted to know how you got on at Strangeways.'

The sound of his voice had the usual effect on her insides. She felt as if the lump of chicken she had just swallowed had got stuck on its way to her stomach. She coughed with her hand over the phone, glancing around at the other diners. It was a few seconds before she gave him a reply. 'Sorry,' she said, 'I'm in a restaurant. Can't go into detail, really: it was the same as Carl, though. I'll come in first thing Monday, okay?'

'Don't worry. I understand. Take care, Meg, won't you?'

'Bye Dom. You take care too.'

'Who was it?' Delva eyed her curiously.

'One of the prisoners from Balsall Gate,' Megan could feel herself blushing. She hadn't meant to say his name. If she tried to be evasive Delva was bound to guess she was hiding something. 'He's what they call a Listener,' she said, concentrating hard on prising another piece of chicken off the skewer. 'He counsels other inmates when they're having problems. He spent a lot of time with Carl Kelly. It was through him I found out about the Strangeways case.'

'And his name's Dom? Not Dom Wilde?'

Megan was taken by surprise, the chunk of meat halfway between the plate and her mouth. 'How did you know?'

'He's the inmate our researcher's been visiting,' Delva replied. 'She went to see him yesterday, actually. She was quite taken with him, I think, but she said he wasn't very forthcoming about Carl Kelly.'

'Oh?' So that was who she'd seen in the visiting room

talking so intimately with him. 'What's you researcher's name?'

'Natalie. Natalie Steadman.'

Suddenly Megan was on the defensive: 'Why should he have told her anything? He probably saw straight through her. He's a bright man.' She could feel the blush spreading from her face to her chest. Delva's eyebrows lifted an inch. Realising that she was giving herself away, Megan tried to backtrack. 'I'm just worried that if one of your people rubs him up the wrong way it might blow things for me,' she said. 'I've invested a lot of time in gaining his trust.'

'But you know that's putting me in a very difficult position.' Delva was looking directly at her. 'I don't have the power to pull someone off a documentary – even if I thought it was the right thing to do.'

'Couldn't you just have a quiet word with her though? Ask her to take things easy for a while until we've worked out where all this is going?'

'I suppose so.' Delva held her gaze. 'Meg, is there something you're not telling me about this guy?'

Megan felt her face burning under this close scrutiny. It was as if Delva was reading her mind. How could she justify her feelings for Dominic? How could she explain that the idea of some girl a dozen years her junior getting close to him had her seething with jealousy? It would sound ridiculous. Delva would be incredulous. No – she couldn't possibly tell her. Not ever.

Megan had a disturbed night. She woke at least twice while it was still dark, her mind fogged with half-remembered dreams. The only one she could properly recall was about a baby. A woman she didn't recognise had brought it to her in a cardboard box. It was sitting up on a pale blue blanket and all she could see at first was the back of its head. Then, when the box was turned round, the baby reached up to her and she saw that it had no arms, just hands attached to the sides of its body. She lifted the child out and it buried its face in her neck. The woman said: "You have him. I don't want him."

Megan thought about the dream as she sat in bed sipping a mug of tea. Fairly obvious what had prompted it: the baby found in the Nike box in Moses Smith's grave. And then there had been Ronnie's news: a baby that she would no doubt see quite regularly over the years to come; whose development she would watch with more than a twinge of envy. She wondered if her subconscious was trying to give her a message; that if she couldn't have a baby of her own she should think about adopting one.

With a big sigh she threw back the duvet and swung her legs out of the bed. This was no time to be thinking about babies or the lack of them: she had work to do. Glancing at the clock on the bedside table she saw that it was only eight-fifteen. Too early to make that phone call to Rebecca Jordan's parents. Time for some breakfast first. Her stomach was rumbling despite last night's Thai feast, but when she opened the fridge, all she found was a withered piece of ginger and a yoghurt that was past its sell-by date. God, she thought, I can't even look after myself properly, let alone a baby.

She'd planned to have a bath and wash her hair before getting dressed but she was too hungry for that. Pulling on jeans and a sweatshirt she headed for the car. There was a corner shop in the next street but if she went there she'd end up buying a load of stodge. If she was going to be serious about losing weight she needed to stock up on some healthy stuff.

Her car was parked right outside the house. For once there had been a space just big enough for her Mazda MX5 when she had arrived back from dropping Delva off last night. The car was a new toy, purchased only two months ago as a birthday present to herself, so it came as something of a shock when she turned the key in the ignition and the engine died. Several more attempts at turning the engine failed. 'Sod it!' She brought the palm of her hand down hard on the steering wheel. She scanned the dashboard, wondering if she'd accidentally touched something she shouldn't have. But it all appeared normal. She got up and stood in the road, looking for anything obvious that might be wrong with it. But again, everything looked to be in its proper place. There was no point trying to push-start it: she'd never get it out of the tight space it was parked in. There was no option but to call the AA.

She was promised a quick response: an estimate of thirty to forty minutes. Enough time for her to do something constructive. Returning to the house she decided to try the Jordans' number while watching through the window for the recovery man.

The conversation with Rebecca's mother was brief: yes, she was travelling in Australia at the moment, working in a bar near Bondi Beach. She'd been away since November and no, she hadn't been in the UK since that time. No doubt, then, Megan thought as she replaced the receiver. Both Rebecca and Jodie had been used as a cover. She wondered if Carl Kelly and Patrick Ryan had been murdered by the same person: one woman posing as both of the students. She needed a good description of the two visitors. She would quiz Dominic tomorrow but she needed Ronnie on the case as well.

Rather than disturb her friend on a Sunday morning, she decided to wing off an email. The laptop was in its case in the hall and she glanced out of the window before darting to retrieve it. She perched on the arm of a chair as she tapped out the message, her stomach complaining loudly about the lack of food inside it.

The AA man arrived just as she clicked the computer shut. Fifteen minutes later, having checked all the obvious potential causes, he stood in the road rubbing his fingers on a rag, no nearer to finding the source of the trouble.

'Can I get you a cup of tea or coffee?' Megan offered.

'I'd love a coffee, please – milk, no sugar,' he replied. 'They're normally quite straightforward, Mazdas, but this one's got me stumped.' Walking to the rear of the car he dropped to a squatting position. 'I'll just see if there's anything leaking out of the exhaust.'

'Okay.' She let herself back through the gate, wondering if she might be able to find anything in the house to go with the coffee. She hadn't expected it to take this long – she was now so hungry she was starting to get the shakes. Searching the kitchen cupboards for anything resembling a biscuit, she spotted what looked like a packet of Jaffa Cakes wedged between a bottle of olive oil and a bag of brown sugar. Gleeful at the prospect of some nourishment, she grabbed it.

'Shit!' she hissed. It was empty. Emily must have scoffed them all on her last visit. Her four-year-old niece had the appetite of a baby elephant. Why did kids always put things back in cupboards and fridges when they were empty?

The kettle boiled and she spooned coffee into mugs, salivating at the smell of it. She put the mugs on a tray, balancing it on the palm of her left hand as she turned the catch on the front door with her right. What she saw when the door opened almost made her drop the lot.

Chapter 18

The rescue man was standing right outside the door with something dangling from his hand. She couldn't make out what it was but she could smell it over the oil that caked his fingers. It was something dead and rotting and it turned her stomach.

'You been rallying recently?' he said.

'What? Her eyes flicked up from the dark object hanging at his side. She looked at him, bemused. 'No... I... of course I haven't... What *is* that? What have you found?'

Slowly and deliberately, he lifted his hand so that the object was directly in her view.

'Ugh!' she took a step back. 'It's a dead rat!'

'Not a rat, no,' he replied. 'I'm no expert, mind, but I can see that it's got no tail, so in my book, that makes it a mole.'

'A mole? Where did you find it?'

'Rammed up your exhaust pipe.'

'How the hell did it get there?'

He shrugged. 'Well, they're not known for their athletic qualities, aren't moles, so unless this one's been crossed with a flying squirrel, I'd say someone's shoved it up there.' He cocked his head to one side. 'You got any in your garden? Neighbours can get very narked about that kind of thing.' He smiled at her blank face. 'Don't worry – it won't have caused any lasting damage to the engine. It should start first time. Want to give it a try?'

Megan followed him through the gate on automatic pilot.

Her eyes were fixed on the dead creature swaying in time with his steps. Her back garden was walled and gravelled, like most of the neighbours' gardens. Other than the odd cat, she had never seen anything vaguely resembling a mammal out there. This could be no coincidence. Alistair Hodge had told her that a mole was the one and only animal in this country still being controlled with strychnine. Was someone trying to warn her off?

She sat behind the wheel, her limbs heavy and numb. The engine purred into action. The AA man brought her something on a clipboard and she signed it with a mumbled word of thanks.

'You okay?' he asked.

'Oh, er, fine,' she said. 'Just a bit tired, that's all.'

'I'll take this away with me, then, shall I?' The snout was protruding from the top pocket of his overalls.

'Yes. Yes, please.' She watched him retreat in the wing mirror. When he'd driven off she ran into the house and slumped on the sofa. She no longer felt hungry – just sick. Someone had watched her; followed her car. While she was asleep last night that someone had been outside her house stuffing that thing into her exhaust pipe. She thought of the hall of residence: the last place she had been yesterday. It would have been so easy to tail her from there. Or perhaps her address had been traced through some other means. Either way, someone very dangerous knew exactly where she lived. Suddenly she thought of Nathan MacNamara. *He* knew where she lived. What if he'd been blabbing about it? He didn't live in Linden House but he might hang around with people who did… 'Oh, God!' she moaned, burying her face in her hands.

She wished there was someone else in the house with her; not just to make her feel safer but to help her make sense of this increasingly complex web of evidence. She thought about Dominic. He had a good ear and a good mind – the sort of person that could be relied on in a crisis. It seemed ridiculous that he was banged up in jail on the other side of the city when he no longer posed any threat to society. She closed her eyes in an attempt to conjure up his soothing presence. Was it so crazy to imagine him sitting beside her in this room? In a year or so he'd be out. It was not unknown for women – professional women – to form lasting relationships with prison inmates they had met through their work: she had heard of one or two such cases over the years. It was possible; anything was possible. Whether or not it was sensible no longer seemed important.

She was snatched back to reality by the shrill notes of her home telephone. She ran into the hall to pick it up, then hesitated, worried about who might be on the other end. What if it was the person who'd interfered with her car? After five rings the answering machine cut in. She held her breath, waiting to see if there would be a message.

'Hi, it's Delva.' Megan let out an audible sigh of relief. 'I've got something important to tell you. Can you ring me back when you get this?'

Half an hour later, Delva was sitting at the kitchen table, a mug of tea in her hand. 'I'm sorry I couldn't explain over the phone,' she said. 'It's the sort of thing I felt I had to tell you face-to-face.'

'What's happened?'

'I met up with Natalie and Tim earlier. I wanted to know how the meeting with Tim's dad had gone. Evidently he's on the pensions committee and has access to records of every former member of the force who's drawn a pension in the past forty years. If Ronald Smith had ever been a policeman his name would have been on file. There were a few Ron Smiths, but no one with the middle name Aaron.'

'So that's it, then.' Megan pursed her lips. 'That knocks

the Birmingham Six revenge theory on the head, doesn't it?'

'Well, yes, it does.' Delva took a deep breath. 'But there's something else.' She looked away from Megan, her eyes fixed on the carpet. 'It's about Dominic Wilde,' she said. 'I thought you ought to know.' The words filled Megan with a horrible sense of foreboding. Less than an hour ago she'd been imagining this man sharing her life. Whatever Delva was about to say, it wasn't going to be good: it was going to blow that fantasy right out of the water. 'Before he went to prison Dom spent time in the SAS,' Delva went on. 'Tim's dad said that when he came out of the forces he became one of the most feared men in Birmingham's criminal underworld – a man not to be messed with – not averse to enforcing respect through extreme physical violence.'

Megan swallowed hard, struggling to rein in her emotions. 'But that was then,' she said. 'He's held his hands up to the murder he committed. He's a different man now.'

'But it wasn't just one murder Meg – not according to Tim's father. He reckoned Dom was responsible for a number of gangland killings that were never solved. None of them involved weapons: in each case the killer used his bare hands. All the victims died of a broken neck – a classic unarmed combat technique. At the time the police suspected it was Dom Wilde but there were never any witnesses or forensic evidence.'

Megan stared at Delva. In her mind she was dissecting all that Dom had ever said about himself. Had she totally misjudged him? Had her overwhelming desire to believe in his redemption blinded her to the reality that he could have played some part in Carl's death?

'Meg, are you alright?'

'Yes... I... I'm...' Megan shot to her feet, clapping her hand over her mouth. She raced upstairs and flung open the bathroom door. There wasn't time to close it: she only hoped Delva wouldn't hear as she kneeled over the toilet, retching.

'I'm so sorry,' she said, when she came back downstairs. 'It's just that I haven't eaten yet today. Things have been a bit traumatic.' She told Delva about the dead mole; about her fears that someone from the hall of residence had followed her home.

'God, Meg, that's bloody scary,' Delva said, her braids quivering as she shook her head. 'You should have told me on the phone; the last you needed was me coming round banging on about Dominic Wilde.'

'No, I'm glad you told me, honestly.' Megan sat down a little unsteadily on the sofa. Her legs felt like jelly and her stomach muscles ached like hell. 'I needed to know. I've been relying on him for information and if he's not to be trusted, well…' She bit her lip, not trusting herself to say any more.

'Well, you're not staying here on your own tonight, that's for sure,' Delva said, rising to her feet. 'I'm going to take you to the supermarket, stock up on a load of goodies and cook you something special. We'll call round at mine on the way home and get my stuff. I'm on a late shift tomorrow so I can stay till you leave for work, okay?'

'Delva, you don't have to…'

'Yes, I do,' Delva interrupted. 'I know you'd do the same for me.'

Megan nodded limply. She felt as if she'd been kicked all over.

It was a strange evening. Delva insisted on unplugging the phone and switching off Megan's mobile as well as her own. They ate beef stir-fry and fresh mango with Greek yoghurt,

washed down with a bottle of Australian Shiraz. With the
television tuned to Paramount Comedy, they watched back-
to-back episodes of Monty Python until Megan dozed off on
the sofa and eventually crawled up the stairs to bed, lulled
by the sound of Delva's gentle snoring coming through the
open door of the spare room.

The next morning Delva went to the car with her and sat in
it as she started the engine. It seemed fine but Delva insisted
on searching all round it before she would let her drive off.
'Call me when you get to Balsall Gate, won't you?' she said.
'Let me know everything's okay.'

'I will,' Megan nodded.

'I'll get Tim and Natalie to pull up the court files this
morning – try and get a bit more background on Carl Kelly
and Patrick Ryan and any third man that might have appeared
with them. And while they're doing that I'll find out exactly
where you go to get a well-hung mole round these parts!'
She gave Megan a wry grin and waved as the car pulled
away. It had been good, having Delva to stay. Megan had
always prided herself on her independence, on her ability to
deal with unpleasant things on her own. But yesterday had
served up a double whammy. She felt more vulnerable than
she had ever felt in her life.

When she arrived at the prison she was greeted by Al, the
prison officer with the ferrety eyes. "Greeted" was not the
right word. He looked her up and down like a piece of meat
and kept her waiting while he went through all the checks
– something that hadn't happened since her first visit to the
jail. It was a complete waste of time and she was sure he was
doing it just to wind her up. While she stood there another
officer appeared, one she hadn't seen before.

'Want a bacon sandwich, Al? ' he called. 'I'm just on my

way to the kitchen.'

'Oh yeah,' Al shouted back.

'You want sauce on it?'

'Yes, please. Brown. Did you get that? *Brown*.' He glanced at Megan as he repeated the word. She knew exactly what this was: a blatant reference to heroin. He knew perfectly well that she was aware of the smuggling going on in this place. He had as good as told her he was one of the main culprits. He also knew that the governor wasn't prepared to do a damned thing about it.

With a sneer, he unlocked the gate and let her through. Suddenly it struck her that he could be the one trying to scare her off. That *he* had put that thing in her exhaust pipe. The thought of him lurking outside her house while she was asleep made her stomach lurch.

By the time she reached the room where Dominic was waiting her face was so taut that it was impossible for him not to notice that something was seriously wrong.

'Megan, what's the matter? What's happened?' He jumped out of his seat.

'I need to sit down,' she said, avoiding his eyes. She sank into the chair, grabbing the arms to stop her hands from trembling. 'I can't wrap this up in any soft words,' she began. 'I've heard things about you, Dom: things that you've never told me. Terrible things.' A crushing silence descended on the room. Still she couldn't look at him. She stared at the floor, willing him to say something in his defence.

At last he spoke. 'Meg, I'm not going to insult you by trying to deny anything. I don't know what you've heard, or where it came from, but whatever it is, it's probably true.'

She dug her nails into the palms of her hands. She wanted to scream at him, make him feel her anguish. 'Why didn't you tell me?' Her voice was low but full of venom. 'You made out that the murder you committed was a one-off;

something done in the heat of the moment. But there were others, weren't there? Murders you planned in cold blood.'

'Megan, look at me, please,' he implored.

She glanced up and saw that there were tears in his eyes. Determinedly, she turned her face away. If he thought he was going to soften her up with a trick like that he was on a hiding to nothing.

'What difference would it have made?' His voice was barely more than a whisper. 'That person no longer exists, Meg, haven't I proved that to you? Don't you realise that if I was still that man I could have had a far easier time in a place like this?'

She pursed her lips. There was no denying that. 'But why didn't you tell me?' She raised her head, looking straight at him for the first time since she had entered the room. 'Can't you see that finding it out from someone else has shaken my confidence in you? Shaken it to the core.'

'If I'd told you all that at the beginning, don't you think you'd have run a mile? Would you really have wanted to make a friend of a violent psychopath?' With a heavy sigh he bent his head, shaking it slowly. 'I don't think you realise how much it means to me, having someone like you to…' the words died as he checked himself. Megan watched him in silence, tortured by the way she felt; wanting to reach out to him but refusing to let herself do it. After what seemed like an eternity he raised his head, his deep grey eyes searching hers. 'I just couldn't face the prospect of you not coming to see me any more.'

She gazed back at him, fighting to keep control. 'Dom, don't you understand? I sought you out to help with my research because I thought I could *trust* you. The reason we got on so well was that, unlike most people in this place, I felt you were being completely open with me. How do you think that makes me feel, after what I've just heard?'

'Okay,' he said softly. 'No more holding back. You've heard about the violence. Well, there's something else about my past that I'm ashamed of. It was the reason my girlfriend left me; the reason I haven't seen my daughter since the day she was born.' He took a breath and she dug her nails into her palms, wondering what was coming. 'I treated women with contempt, Meg,' he went on. 'I couldn't be faithful to anyone. I had a different girl every week – even when my girlfriend was pregnant. I was with someone else the night she went into labour. Her mother came looking for me and someone in the pub sent her to this girl's house. So that was it. The day our daughter was born was the day she kicked me out, and that was a brave thing to do, given my reputation.' He clasped his hands together in his lap, clenching and unclenching them, as if he was afraid of their power. 'So that's the man they put away, Meg: a ruthless, selfish, womanising waste of space. You know everything now and I don't suppose you'll want anything more to do with me.'

For a moment she said nothing. She was trying to take it in. It was hard to imagine the caring, gentle man she had come to know doing the things he had just described. To mask her shock at his revelation, she slipped into her psychologist's persona. 'Why do you think you were like that, Dom? What made you so promiscuous?'

'Oh, I could trot out all kinds of excuses,' he said. 'The SAS is a good one: makes you cut yourself off from your emotions; turns you into some kind of sex-starved robot who'll shag anything in a skirt as long as there's no commitment required.' He shrugged. 'There are no excuses, though. Not really. It's just the way I was then. If I hadn't ended up in here I'm pretty certain I'd be dead by now. It sounds mad, I know, but prison probably saved my life.'

She stared at him intently. In her experience men who habitually broke the rules were the hardest to rehabilitate.

And here was a man who had confessed to not one but two of the worst patterns of behaviour – one at the extreme end of the criminal scale and the other, although anti-social rather than illegal, demonstrating a total lack of empathy and self-control. Could she really believe that such a man could change so completely? It flew in the face of all she had learned in the prison system. Was Dom Wilde's gentle, caring persona just a sham?

Chapter 19

Ronnie Burns was watching CCTV footage with one of the Strangeways warders – the one who had been on duty in the visiting room the last time Rebecca Jordan had come to see Patrick Ryan.

'That's her.' The man leaned across the desk, pointing a stubby finger at the grainy black and white image. 'Bit of a stunner, she was. I remember thinking: how's a dope like Ryan got himself a bird like that?'

'Hmm.' Ronnie clicked the tape to a halt, freezing the woman's head. 'Very long hair. Can't see much of her face, can you? It looks very light. Was she blonde?'

'She was,' the warder replied. 'Don't suppose she was a natural, though.'

'Why do you say that?'

'Well, if you look closely you can see she's got very dark eyebrows. Can I forward the tape a bit?' He pressed 'play'. The woman lurched back to life. Her hair shrouded her face as she walked through the prison gate, but as she handed over her bag, she flicked her head. He stopped the tape. 'There... see?'

Ronnie nodded, moving closer to the screen. She pressed 'rewind' and watched the sequence again. 'I think we need to talk to his cell mates, don't you?' she said. 'Find out what they know about this girl.'

Dominic Wilde unclasped his hands and laid them on his

knees. 'I'm sorry, Meg.' He slid one hand forward an inch, then pulled it back. 'I should have told you everything at the start.'

She bit her lip, wishing he wouldn't look at her like that. It made her feel like a hunter confronted by a wounded animal; made her feel as if she was the one that was in the wrong. Taking a deep breath, she folded her arms across her chest. 'Yes. You should have. But we all want to be liked, I suppose. That I can understand.' She was aware that she was trying to rationalise it all, trying to give him the benefit of the doubt. 'I suppose you needn't have told me the other stuff – about your girlfriend and the baby. It took some guts to admit to that.'

He studied his hands, saying nothing, as if he was too ashamed to acknowledge this.

'What happened to her after she left you? Do you know?'

He shook his head. 'Not really. I heard on the grapevine that she went on the game. There was a really evil bastard called Leroy Spinks pimping girls in Birmingham at the time. I think she was probably one of his girls. I was in and out of prison then, but once, when I was out, I went round the streets asking after her. Spinks came after me; chased me down the road with a bloody great machete.'

'So you didn't find her.'

He shook his head. 'Like I said, I was in and out of jail. By the time I got another chance to ask around no one had seen hide nor hair of her.'

'You must have been worried about Elysha.'

'I was, yeah. I didn't know what had happened to her: whether she was still with her mum, whether she'd been taken into care, or what. It was such a relief when the chaplain found her name on the electoral roll.' He looked at her for a long moment. 'Can we start again, Meg? If you still want to, I mean.'

'Well,' she said, her voice as neutral as she could make it. 'I think we both want to get to the bottom of what happened to Carl, don't we? There are things I need to ask you. Things I didn't realise were important until I went to Strangeways. Will you help me?'

He nodded, lowering his lids so that she was unable to catch the expression in his eyes. She wondered if he had any inkling of the feelings she was battling to conceal. She started telling him what had happened in Manchester, forcing herself into professional mode as she described the subsequent visit to Linden House. She watched his face change when she told him about Jodie Shepherd being in a coma.

'That's some scam,' he said, sucking air between his teeth.

'Yes,' she replied. 'It's very devious and very clever. I have no idea who's behind it, but at the moment all I have to go on is the appearance of the girls who visited the two men. I don't even know at this stage if it's one girl or two. So I need you to tell me everything you can remember about the one that came to see Carl. I'm going to ask for CCTV footage, obviously, but if you saw her close up, there might be things you noticed that the cameras might miss.

'Well,' he said, rubbing his fingers along his jawbone, 'She was young. A lot younger than him. She looked no more than early twenties. She had long, black hair – very straight, sort of Cleopatra-ish, if you know what I mean – and her eyes were dark too. Can't remember what colour, though.'

'Could the hair have been a wig, do you think?'

'I suppose so, yes.'

'What about her height? Was she tall? Short?'

'About average, I think. Hard to tell, really, 'cos I only saw her sitting down.'

'Anything else about her? Anything unusual, I mean?

Tattoos, that kind of thing?'

He screwed up his eyes, remembering. 'Not really, no. She never came dressed tartily, like some of the women do. Always covered herself up. So she could have had a tattoo but I never spotted one.'

'I'd better get hold of the CCTV footage and see her for myself, I think.' Her fingers went involuntarily to the ruby stud she was wearing in her nose. She rubbed it distractedly, thinking about the lengths this woman had gone to, the risks she must have taken, to get inside this place with her deadly cargo. 'I only wish I had a clearer idea of a possible motive for all this.' She fell silent for a moment. 'Dom, before this morning, before all…' she faltered, unable to spell it out a second time. 'We'd been working well as a team, hadn't we?'

'Yes.' He gave her a nervous smile. 'We made good team mates.'

'There's something else I want to ask you about but I need you to promise me it won't go any further.'

He bit on his knuckles. 'Meg, I've let you down once already, I swear I'll never do that again.'

'Okay,' she said. 'I want to tell you what I found out about Patrick Ryan. I've got a copy of his file: he and Carl were sent down on the same day, by the same court. Both were convicted of drugs offences. I think it's highly likely they were part of the same gang.' She paused, watching it register. 'I know you were inside at the time but Patrick Ryan was the same age as you. I was wondering if you ever came across him.' She opened her briefcase and took out the photocopied pages Ronnie had given her. The photograph of Ryan was black and white. 'He had red hair,' she said, 'and his address when he was arrested was Finch Road in Lozelles. Does it ring any bells?'

'No.' His tone was matter-of-fact. 'I would remember a

face like that. He must have been well down the food chain when I was doing the rounds.' She heard him draw in his breath as he studied the file. 'It could be that he was just dealing on a part-time basis. I've known lots of guys who do it every so often as a sideline to raise a bit of extra cash: combine it with their day job, so to speak.'

'But surely you wouldn't get five years for small-time stuff?'

'He might have been set up to take the rap for someone else. I've seen it happen time and time again. Of course, the other possibility, if he was friends with Carl, is that there was a bit of GBH thrown in as well. As I said, Carl was no angel when he was on the outside. Maybe Patrick was in the same mould.'

'Do you think he could have been in on the killing of Moses Smith?'

'Well, Carl never mentioned anybody else, but the golden rule in this place is not to grass anyone up, ever, unless you want a knife between your shoulder blades. And let's not forget that Patrick Ryan's brother's banged up in here. So it's quite possible, yes, and it's the only real hint of a link we've got so far, isn't it?'

She nodded. 'It's proving it, though, isn't it? What we need is hard facts.'

'Hmm.' He tucked in his chin. 'It's difficult to know where to begin – there are so many different threads to it. There's the girls – or girl – visiting the prisons; the drugs link between Patrick and Carl; and then there's the baby in the grave as well. Did you get permission for the exhumation?'

She shook her head. 'Not yet, but I'm expecting to hear something today. I put a bit of heat on that DS Willis before I went up to Manchester. It's a longshot, though, isn't it? God knows if it'll make things any clearer.'

'Well, the way things are, I think you've got to try every

avenue that's open to you.' He paused. 'I'd rather you didn't pursue all this on your own, though. If things were different I'd be doing this with you. You've seen what they're capable of, Meg. What if someone finds out you're onto them? It worries me to death to think what might happen.' His eyes met hers for a second. She caught the anguish in them and had to look away. What on earth would he say if she were to tell him about the incident with the car? But she wouldn't tell him. It wouldn't be fair. There was nothing he could do.

Chapter 20

It was hard, saying goodbye without being able to touch him. Despite everything he had told her, the feelings were still there. It was as if his fallibility had increased his magnetism. Now he seemed more like her, struggling to subdue spectres that were never very far away. With a supreme effort of will she walked to the door and, without a backward glance, strode down the corridor to the administration block.

To her relief the governor was away for the day, saving her from the annoyance of having to ask his permission to see the CCTV footage of Carl Kelly's visitor. The office manager knew her now and handed it over without any fuss. Not that it proved to be of much use. The pictures were grainy and blurred and the face so indistinct that she would have been hard-pressed to put an age to the woman with the long dark hair.

By lunchtime she was back in her office at the university. Amongst the bundle of mail she'd carried up from her pigeonhole was a pale yellow envelope. She recognised the handwriting immediately. It was from Nathan MacNamara. She felt her blood pressure soar as she ripped it open. He had sent her another card. With flowers on the front this time. A bunch of white lilies. The sort of card you might send to the relative of someone who'd died. Her throat tightened as she opened it. There was no printed verse, just more of his handwriting filling the whole of one surface:

Dear Dr Rhys,

*I am very sorry if my behaviour has offended
you in any way. I look on you as a kindred spirit
– someone I can't help wanting to be with – but
your letter made it plain that you don't share
those feelings (or if you do, you are not allowed
to show them to a student – and I can't blame you
for putting your job ahead of me). The thing is I
can't bear to be so near you but not as close as I
want to be. So I've applied to another university.
I'm going to ask for a transfer to a course in
Lancaster that's not too different from the one
at Heartland. Hopefully I'll be able to start at
the beginning of next term and in the meantime,
don't worry, I'll make myself scarce. Thank you
for being ...you.*

With my love,
Nathan xxx

Megan groaned as she laid the card face down on her
desk. She was immensely relieved that he was leaving, but
the relief was tinged with guilt. What if she had wrecked
his chances of getting a good degree? Was he likely to get
the first his tutor had predicted if he switched courses at this
stage? What if they made him retake the whole of his second
year? He'd be deeper in debt then and all because of her.

It's not your fault. Her mother's voice again. The voice
of reason. No, it *wasn't* her fault but it didn't stop her from
worrying about the boy's future. Should she reply to him?
Probably best not to. An official letter from the departmental
administrator would be more appropriate.

With a sigh she slipped the card into a drawer and turned
her attention to the emails that were waiting for her. As she
scrolled down she spotted one from Ronnie. With a stab of

her finger she brought it up:

> *Hi Meg,*
>
> *I've been watching the CCTV pix of 'Rebecca' and talking to staff and inmates about her. She had long, straight blonde hair – probably a wig – and was early twenties or thereabouts. And guess what? A cell mate of Patrick Ryan said he met her through Manchester Mates – an online dating service. As you know, the inmates aren't allowed to use the internet, so this sounds like part of the scam – possibly she pretended to have got his details from the website, with him assuming someone on the outside had posted them on there for a laugh. Anyway, I'm checking it out. We've called the police in and they want to talk to you. They're organising a case conference with people from the West Mids force for Thursday this week. I'll let you know the time and place as soon as I have details.*
>
> *Lots of love and please be careful,*
> *Ronnie x*

Megan stared at the screen. Of course, she thought. It was the perfect ruse for getting in touch with a prisoner. Write to him saying you'd seen his details on a dating site, when actually there was no advert. How would he ever know, if he had no access to the internet? Carl Kelly's Evening Mail ad had probably been a similar piece of fiction. A shame, because a real advert would have to have been paid for, leaving a trail that could be chased. But she was beginning to realise that whoever was responsible for these murders was far too clever to make an error like that.

She tapped out a hasty reply to the message and when she

pressed 'send' she noticed that a new one had come through
while she was writing, this time from Delva:

Hi Meg,

*Hope you are okay. Tim and Natalie have
been going through the court records. You were
right about Carl Kelly and Patrick Ryan – they
were sentenced for the same offences. No hint
of any third man in the court case yet, though,
but they're still looking. I found out something
interesting when I was doing a search of pest
control firms in the area – I phoned one and they
said that a new EC directive came in a couple
of months ago banning the use of strychnine
on moles. They have to use steel traps now,
which evidently means a lot more work to catch
the little blighters. I asked if anyone still uses
strychnine and they said 'not if they're legit'.
Which means we could be looking for a small-
time operator who's prepared to flout the law.
Not quite sure where this leaves us. At least
we've got the exhumation going ahead, though
– we had a press release from West Mids police
this morning. I was a bit surprised they're doing
it this evening – what did you do? Put a rocket
up Willis' arse? Anyway, let me know what
happens, won't you?*

*Do you fancy staying at my place tonight? It's
going to be on the news and I'm a bit concerned
about who might be watching when they pull out
the coffin. I'll do my mum's jerk chicken recipe
so don't bother to eat.*

Delva x

'Bloody Willis!' Megan thumped the heel of her hand on the desk. Why hadn't he told her? She grabbed the phone and dialled the BTV newsroom.

'You didn't know?' Delva was incredulous.

'Not until I got your email. Bastard's obviously more concerned about you lot than he is about the investigation. And as for putting a rocket up his arse, I think we've probably got Greater Manchester Police to thank for that.' She explained what Ronnie had told her; about the case conference due to take place between the two forces.

'Well, we're going to have to think very carefully about what to say in the programme tonight,' Delva said. 'This could be a great opportunity to put the wind up the killer, couldn't it? If we make out there's something the police are onto…some new DNA technique that's likely to turn up stuff they wouldn't have had available to them before.'

'How would you do that, though? I mean, it's not, is it? All it's going to tell them is whether the baby is related to Moses Smith.'

'*We* know that but the killer doesn't,' Delva replied. 'We could hype up the DNA angle but not be specific about what the police expect to find. We'll have cameras at the graveyard tonight. The whole place is going to be floodlit, so we can keep a careful eye on everyone who turns up for a gander.'

'Okay…' Megan was thinking ahead, wondering how she could watch those who turned up at the graveyard while simultaneously monitoring the exhumation. It wasn't going to be easy. Her next call was to the sergeant. She gritted her teeth as she waited for him to answer.

'DS Willis.' He sounded hassled. As he damn well should, she thought.

She didn't bother announcing herself, just cut to the chase: 'Why didn't you tell me about the exhumation?'

'I… er… I was going to call you when…' She could hear

him trying to think on his feet. 'When it was over,' he said, in a tone that defied contradiction.

'When it was over? What bloody good would that have been, Detective Sergeant?' She hadn't intended to swear, but he really was unbelievable.

'Now don't take that attitude, Dr Rhys,' he bristled. 'I can't see any possible reason for you being at the exhumation.'

'You do know about the Strangeways inquiry? That I'm now working with the Manchester force as well? How can I play a useful part in any case conference if you choose to keep me ignorant of the facts?'

'I'm not trying to exclude, you – not at all. I will, of course, keep you informed of the results of any tests performed on the body…'

'That's not good enough, I'm afraid.' She strove to control her rising anger. 'I want to be there when that coffin comes out of the ground.' She didn't add that she had absolutely no confidence in his ability to handle it without a cock-up, but the implication was plain.

'Really, Doctor Rhys,' he cleared his throat. 'I don't see that there's any value in your being there. I can't understand why you're hell-bent on witnessing something so…so ghoulish…'

Oh, right, she thought, he's making me out to be no better than the rubbernecks who'll be flocking to St Mary's for a freakshow. 'Listen,' she said, 'We've got no way of knowing in advance what we might find when that coffin comes up. Let's not forget that the grave is a crime scene and anything we find there is going to need careful interpretation. Who better to do that than a forensic psychologist? I need to see whatever's there before anything gets disturbed.'

She heard a slow, deliberate sigh. 'Well, I can see you're not going to be talked out of this,' Willis replied wearily. 'I still don't see the point myself but if you want to come, then come. In two staccato sentences he told her when to turn up and issued strict orders about the media. They were allowed to film the proceedings from a suitable distance but no one present at the exhumation was to talk to them. Megan wondered how Delva was going to react to this approach. If Willis thought he was going to fob her off with a few shots of a mini-digger manoeuvring about in the dark he was in for a nasty shock. Perhaps the police press office was putting someone up for the occasion: someone a lot more media-savvy than the detective sergeant.

Megan arrived early at the graveyard. There was a gap of two hours between the story breaking on the teatime news programme and the start of the exhumation. She sat in her car, watching the gates. If Delva's plan had worked, someone connected to the baby's burial was surely going to turn up. Putting herself in that person's shoes, she would want to be there sooner rather than later.

There was already a cordon around the churchyard and she could see the yellow shovel of a digger protruding from the green canvas screens shielding Moses Smith's grave. There appeared to be no police presence at the moment, which surprised her. As she watched, a group of teenage boys approached the gates, playing football with a Coke can. She wound down her window to catch their conversation. There was nothing but the odd grunt until they stuck their noses through the bars of the gates and began to wail like cartoon ghosts. When it became obvious that there was no one in the graveyard to annoy, they turned their attention back to the Coke can, kicking it at a girl who was walking past with a pushchair. It narrowly missed the plastic canopy draped over the baby inside and the mother yelled an expletive at the boys, who ran off, laughing. She shouted something else but Megan didn't catch it because at that moment her mobile phone rang out.

She groaned when she saw the caller ID. It was Jonathan. She had taken the coward's way out, putting off returning his calls. She had intended to do it on Sunday, but the incident with the mole, coupled with Delva's bombshell about Dom, had left her so emotionally drained she hadn't felt able to face the conversation she knew they had to have. There was no reason not to speak to him now. She had to do it; had to tell him.

'You're still alive, then?'

The flippant comment was tinged with warmth. It set off shockwaves of guilt. 'Jonathan,' she faltered, 'How… how are you doing?' It sounded lame. Unenthusiastic. Which just about summed up the way she felt.

'I'm fine. Had a good time with Laura – she seems better, thank goodness. And I'm sticking around for a while – in this country, I mean. The Bosnia operation's been put on hold for a couple of weeks.'

'Oh?' Bosnia. She had forgotten he was supposed to be flying there today to resume the work of identifying bodies in a mass grave.

'So, as I've got some time on my hands I decided to have a chat with old Alistair.' There was a pause. She hadn't a clue what he was talking about. 'You know, the pathologist,' he went on. 'I met him a few years back on a murder case – nasty arson attack that didn't leave much of the victim bar the teeth – anyway, I thought I'd give him a bell about this case you're working on.'

'You spoke to Alistair Hodge?' She felt a surge of irritation. What did he think he was doing, poking his nose in without consulting her first?

'Yes. I offered to do the DNA extraction on the baby. He seemed very keen when I explained it. Anyway, I said I'd collect the body tomorrow to bring back to the lab in Cardiff and I was wondering if I could come and stay – make up for rushing off the other morning.'

She was staring at a blob of bird shit that had landed on the windscreen and was sliding slowly towards the bonnet of the car. It seemed to take forever and she could hear him breathing at the other end of the phone. The symbolism was so crass it could have come from some dodgy film. But she knew she would never be able to forget this moment. The moment when she finished with him.

Chapter 21

There was no way of doing it gently – she had tried that the other night and it hadn't worked. Coward that she was, she was glad she couldn't see his face. He took it calmly enough. If he felt hurt his voice certainly didn't betray it. He was brisk. Businesslike. He thanked her for her company and said he hoped they could still be friends; said they were bound to bump into each other before too long. She came out with some vaguely assenting reply, hoping he would be wrong.

When the conversation ended she sat staring at the gates of the churchyard. So that's it, she thought: another one bites the dust. Being the one to finish it didn't make her feel any better. But she knew that the longer she had allowed it to continue, the more miserable and resentful she would have become. 'Look at you,' she muttered to herself, 'Sitting outside a graveyard in some god-awful part of Birmingham because there's no one at home to care whether you come back from work or not.' With some difficulty she slid her finger down the inside of her trousers, releasing the button that fastened over her left hip. 'And you're fat,' she said. 'Getting fatter. You're going to have to do something. Take yourself in hand. Spend weekends at the gym instead of gluggling Chablis and stuffing down takeaways.'

'It's the first sign of madness, you know.'

Megan bumped her nose on the seatbelt anchor as she whipped her head towards the window. Delva was leaning in, a face-splitting grin displaying her gleaming teeth.

'What are you doing, sitting here talking to yourself? Come and sit in the OB van. You can meet the rest of the team.'

Glad to be pulled from the mire of self-loathing, Megan followed her to the monstrous white vehicle with the BTV logo emblazoned on the sides. The Outside Broadcast van was parked a short distance from the gates of St Mary's, and the shadow of Balsall Gate's barbed-wire-topped walls fell across its roof. The back of the van was piled with cables and camera equipment, but, perched on a fold-down bench near the cab, were a couple who didn't look much older than Megan's students. They were both striking-looking. He had a strong, tanned face with long brown hair tied back in a pony tail and a silver stud in one earlobe. She was dark and pretty, her hair falling in corkscrew curls over her shoulders. Both were dressed in unisex, outdoor clothes.

'Tim, Natalie, this is Dr Megan Rhys.' Delva ushered her into the van, offering her an upturned box with a mud-coloured cushion on it. 'These two are from the research team,' Delva said, settling herself onto a similar makeshift seat. 'Natalie's the one that's been visiting Balsall Gate.'

'Oh, right.' Megan smiled to mask the stab of jealousy she felt. So this was the blonde girl she had seen laughing and chatting with Dom in the visitors' room. Obviously she had been wearing a wig: she would never have recognised her.

'And Tim's the ex-copper I was telling you about – looks far too young, doesn't he?' she chuckled, 'Makes me feel as old as Methuselah!'

'You've been looking through the court records, haven't you?' Megan addressed the question to Tim. 'You're quite sure there was no third man?'

Tim and Natalie exchanged glances before shaking their heads.

'You're talking about the third member of the gang who murdered Moses Smith?' Tim flicked the trailing ends of the pony tail off his shoulder as he spoke. 'There was no third person sentenced at that time. But it was a long time after the murder, wasn't it? More than a decade. I guess the third guy must have been off the scene by then.'

'It would help if we had a name, wouldn't it?' Delva said. 'I mean, if these prison murders are about Moses Smith's death, this third man's life could be in danger.'

Megan nodded. It felt like walking through treacle: this whole investigation was going in slow motion. There was so much that needed to be done: so much the police could be doing, but it felt as if she and Delva's team were the only ones doing any real detective work.

'Anyway,' Delva said, looking at the researchers, 'It's going to be a long evening and I could do with a caffeine fix. Would you two nip round the corner and see if you can find a Costas or a Starbucks or something?'

'There's a Starbucks about half a mile that way,' Megan said, jabbing her thumb towards the left side of the van. 'It's just across the road from the university.'

'I know it.' Natalie piped up. 'I did my degree at Heartland.'

'Oh?' Megan attempted another joyless smile. 'What did you study?'

'Biochemistry.'

'Really? And you've gone into television?' Megan was genuinely surprised. She had expected the girl to say English or Media Studies. It seemed an odd career path for a science graduate but, as she well knew, the vast majority of students ended up in jobs that bore no relation to the subjects they had studied.

'I wish I hadn't chosen it now,' Natalie replied, looking up at Megan through long dark lashes. 'I've been telling the

Balsall Gate inmates I'm a Sociology student but actually I wish I'd taken a degree in something like that. I find prisoners absolutely fascinating.'

I bet you do, Megan thought. It annoyed her to picture this girl lying to Dom; batting her eyelashes at him as she tried to win him over.

'Right. What shall we get you?' Tim rose to his feet, bending his head to avoid bumping it on the roof of the van. 'Cappuccino with an extra shot for you, Delva? And what about Dr Rhys?'

'A double espresso, please.' That was something else she was going to have to cut down on. This would be her third one today but she felt she needed it – it was either that or take up smoking again. As Tim and Natalie squeezed past the piles of cable she noticed his hand brush her waist. 'Are they an item?' she asked Delva when the van door slammed shut.

'That didn't take you long,' Delva chuckled. 'I think it's quite recent. They're at the stage where they find it hard to keep their hands off each other. I caught them having a snog in the newsroom kitchen the other day. Quite sweet, isn't it?'

Megan nodded. A wave of relief washed over her. Natalie no longer seemed quite such a threat. Some higher part of her brain told her how ridiculous this was; getting jealous over a twenty-something who may or may not have been flirting with the object of her misguided fantasies. She shuddered to think what her academic colleagues would make of it if they knew.

'They worked their socks off on the Birmingham Six theory,' Delva said, jerking her head in the direction Tim and Natalie had taken. 'Shame my hunch didn't stand up. It would have been an amazing story.'

Megan opened her mouth to agree but was caught short

by her mobile ringing again. She bit her lip as she plunged her hand into her bag. If it was Jonathan she wasn't going to answer. She couldn't face any more heavy stuff. But it was a number she didn't recognise.

'Dr Rhys? It's David Dunn. Sorry I didn't get back to you earlier but I wanted to speak to all the staff.'

'Oh, that's okay.' The sudden announcement of the exhumation and its aftermath had made her forget that he was meant to be calling her. 'What did they say?'

'Not a lot, I'm afraid. No one reported seeing anyone suspicious loitering about in the reception area. So I can only conclude that the culprit is one of our own students, which I find rather alarming.' Or one of your staff, she thought. She began to voice this but he spoke over her. 'I was wondering, are you involved in this exhumation I've heard about on the news? I gather there's a link with a drugs death in Balsall Gate jail?'

She wondered how he'd worked that out on the limited information she'd given him. 'I'm afraid I can't comment on that,' she said tersely. 'It's a police matter.'

'Oh, I was just interested, that's all.' He sounded slightly chastened. 'I do hope that you'll keep me informed of what's happening with your inquiries, though. I'm very concerned about the safety of my students and I need to know the full picture.'

'I understand your concern. Obviously if anything relevant arises I'll be in touch.'

'Okay, Dr Rhys. Good luck with it, and please, if you need any help at all, don't hesitate to contact me, will you?'

'Who was it?' Delva asked as Megan slid the phone back into her bag.

'The warden from Linden House – the one you thought was a bit of a smoothie.'

'Oh, him.' Delva pursed her lips. 'Sounded as if he was

getting a bit nosey.'

'That's what I thought. Seems he's got hold of more of the story than I gave him the other night. I wonder where from?'

Delva shrugged. 'Could be one of his staff. I mean, the university's so near to the prison: it wouldn't be much of a surprise if someone at Linden House was related to someone who works at Balsall Gate, would it?'

'I suppose not.' Megan's eyes narrowed. 'I wonder if that's the key to this? Some screw using contacts at the university as a cover? Anyway, it's reminded me of something: I must give that letter to DS Willis – the one Dom Wilde gave me. If it's got prints on it we can get everyone at Linden House checked out – see if there's a match.'

'That'll be a long job, won't it?' Delva said doubtfully.

'I know, but it's the only solid lead we've got at the moment.'

The rattle of a handle signalled the return of the researchers. When the coffees had been distributed, they all sat with faces glued to the windows, watching for anyone suspicious approaching the gates of the graveyard. There was far less interest than Megan had expected. Apart from an old man walking his dog and the girl with the pushchair she had seen earlier coming back the other way with a bag of shopping slung from the handle, there was no one.

By seven-thirty the light was beginning to fade. 'I think I'll make myself scarce,' Megan said, as a police car rolled into view. 'Willis has banned me from talking to you lot. He's prickly enough as it is, so I'd better not wind him up.'

By sneaking round the side of the OB van she managed to get back to her car without being seen by the five uniformed men who emerged from the patrol car. Watching in her rear view mirror she saw a large black vehicle pull up behind the police car. It had the shape of a hearse but without the large side windows. This must be the transport for the coffin, she thought.

She gave it a few minutes, then got out of the car and made her way to the cordon, where one of the five policemen had stationed himself. She flashed her ID and he let her through without a word. As she picked her way past the headstones there was a sudden flash. The arc-lights had come on. Glancing around the periphery of the churchyard she could now see knots of people wandering up to the cordon, drawn like moths to a flame. It was impossible to make out faces: she hoped Tim and Natalie would do the rounds once the cameras were rolling. It would be easy enough for them to blend in once people were distracted by the media circus.

There were only six people behind the screens. Willis was chatting to the driver of the mini-digger and the four other uniformed officers she'd spotted in the patrol car had put on yellow overalls and were erecting a metal structure that looked like some sort of pulley. There was no acknowledgement from the detective sergeant other than a curt nod in her direction during a momentary lull in his conversation with the digger man.

Darkness had fallen by the time the pulley was in place. The men stood back as Willis signed to the driver to start up the digger. Megan strained her eyes as turf and soil peeled away. The arc lights cast a cold white glare over the scene. Within minutes a wide trench had been carved out. There was a juddering sound as the scoop made contact with the coffin. Willis and the others moved forward, shouting instructions as the digger manouevred at snail's pace along the edge of the trench. Megan could see that the impact of the scoop had splintered the lid. No doubt the coffin was the cheapest type: after seventeen years in the ground it would have been no surprise to have found it had collapsed. She wondered if it would survive being hauled out. It vibrated alarmingly as the digger excavated the earth at each end. Harnesses were lowered and looped under it. Megan held her breath as it swayed into the air. If it burst now Moses Smith's remains would be scattered everywhere. Amazingly the coffin landed, intact, on the collapsible metal trolley laid beside the trench.

They went in procession to the gates. It was like a funeral in reverse, the coffin borne from its resting place by the policemen, with Willis walking sombrely in front of it. The mumbled conversations of the onlookers came to an abrupt halt. Shrouded in a black sheet, there was nothing visible as the bones made their way back to the land of the living. But there was no doubt Moses Smith was getting far more attention at this moment than he had ever received in life.

He was not the only one arriving at the mortuary that evening. As Megan drew up beside the black van she saw an ambulance parked outside the entrance. Paramedics were bringing in the body of a young man killed in a road accident. Megan had to pass by the corpse on her way to the post-mortem room. He looked barely old enough to drive. There wasn't a mark on him apart from a trickle of dried blood beneath his nose His blue eyes were open, their unblinking gaze demanding an explanation.

'Don't s'pose old Moses'll smell as sweet as that one.' It was one of the uniformed officers who spoke, chuckling as he jerked his head at the crash victim. Megan shuddered. She had seen death many times but she could never be blasé about it; could not bring herself to participate in the black humour the police and medical staff used to get them through. The link with life was so fragile; snatched away in an instant.

Alistair Hodge was waiting for them. Megan thought he

looked tired. He had probably been here all day and was anxious to get this over with and get home. There wouldn't be a lot for him to do. It was just a matter of removing the remains, bagging them up and selecting suitable material for a DNA test.

The smell became more pronounced when they entered the post-mortem room. It was a musty, earthy smell. It reminded Megan of an old trunk in the damp-ridden box room of her uncle's house. She'd climbed into it once during a game of hide and seek, almost gagging as she buried her face in a forgotten jumble of mildewed fabric.

'You got the crowbar?' DS Willis was addressing the officer who had made the quip about the dead boy. He was the only one of the four uniformed officers still present, which was just as well, Megan thought. The overhead fans were going like the clappers but the atmosphere was still stifling and it was about to get much worse.

'Don't think we're going to need it, Sarge,' he replied. 'It's loose already.' With a grunt he prised the lid right off. It fell to the floor with a splintering sound, particles of earth shooting in all directions. Now the smell was overpowering: like nothing Megan had never encountered. It was a stench she could only describe as old and rotten. The mummified remains of the baby had smelt of almost nothing; like dry paper kept in a cupboard for years and years. But this was an evil smell. Without looking inside she knew that the bones would be moist; greasy. There would probably be hair still attached to the skull and the tattered remains of whatever clothing Moses Smith was buried in. With her hand to her mouth, she moved towards the open coffin.

'He was a Villa fan, then.' This time it was Alastair Hodge who tried to lighten the atmosphere. He pointed a gloved finger at a rolled-up scarf lying near the feet of the skeleton in the familiar claret-and-blue of Aston Villa football club.

'Shall I bag it up, Sarge?'

Willis nodded and the officer stretched out his hand slowly, grasping the frayed woollen fabric between the tips of his finger and thumb, as if the latex that covered them was not enough to protect his skin from this contaminated object. Megan noticed a bead of sweat coursing down the side of his face as he leaned in. Suddenly he froze. 'Hold up,' he said. 'There's something…'

'What it is?' Willis glanced at the pathologist with nervous eyes.'

With a brisk movement Alastair Hodge took the scarf from the policeman's grasp. 'There's something wrapped up in it,' he said. 'Something hard.'

Chapter 22

'What is it?' Megan stared at the bundle in the pathologist's hands. Very gently he began to unravel the fabric. The stripes were the colour of the sky and of dried blood.

She held her breath. Could it be the knife used to murder Moses Smith? What better place to hide it than his coffin? If it *was* the knife, his killers must have been known to the family...

'Oh.' Alastair Hodge stopped unwinding the scarf, his finger and thumb fastening on something inside. 'It's a photograph.' He slid it out of its woollen cocoon. The plastic frame was undamaged and the glass intact, although there looked to be damp inside it. Despite the wave of mildew sweeping up the left hand side of the picture, Megan could clearly see the faces of a woman and a child. Without a word, Hodge passed it to Willis, who shrugged before handing it to Megan.

'Not really worth turning out for, was it?' he said in the monotonous voice she'd come to loathe. She took the photograph, avoiding his eyes. The woman was very young: barely out of her teens by the look of her. This must be Moses Smith's girlfriend: the newspaper report had said she was nineteen at the time of the murder.

She had a strange feeling of *déjà vu* as she stared at the snapshot. There was something strangely familiar about the woman. She had long, dark hair swept sideways by the wind and her eyes were heavily outlined with Goth-style makeup. Where had she seen that face before? The skin between

Megan's eyebrows puckered as she turned her attention to the child – a little girl – who looked like a miniature version of the woman, minus the make-up. Her wispy hair was caught up in ponytails tied with pink ribbons. She looked about two years old. This must be the child mentioned in the article, Megan thought. Not a newborn baby, as she had suspected. So if this little girl was the dead man's child, who was the baby boy found in the shoebox?

Something clicked in her brain. A memory of Dom Wilde, his hand outstretched, showing her something. It was the woman in the photograph: the snap Dom had shown her of the young mother cradling his baby daughter had the same face as the one she was staring at now. She felt a pulsing in the side of her head. Her gloved fingers tightened their grip on the picture frame as she moved it closer to her face. Were her eyes deceiving her?

'Don't think there's much point us hanging around.' Willis' voice cut across her thoughts. It sounded different; muffled. Megan glanced up from the photograph to see that he was holding a handkerchief to his mouth. 'How long until the DNA results come through?'

'Hard to say,' Hodge replied. 'Depends how long it takes to extract a good enough sample – we'll try the hair follicles, but we might have to take a piece of bone. We're talking the best part of a week anyhow.'

Willis nodded, taking a step backwards.

'I… er…' Megan straightened up, laying the photograph down as she looked around the room for her bag. Her mind was a jumble and she blinked, trying to recall the thing she had told herself not to forget to ask Willis. 'Before you go,' she mumbled, 'there's something I need to give you.' She spotted her bag on the hook on the door and went to fish out the Jodie Shepherd letter. 'I'd like you to get this fingerprinted, please. It might speed things up if there's anything on it.'

He stood in the doorway, the handkerchief still clasped to his mouth, while she gave a brief explanation. There was plenty more she could have told him, but given his behaviour, she didn't feel inclined to. Save it for the case conference on Thursday, she thought. It would be interesting to see his face when she told his bosses things he didn't have a clue about.

When he'd gone she turned her attention back to the photograph. 'Can I get a photocopy of this? There's someone I'd like to show it to.' She had to get it to Dom. Compare it with the snapshot he carried around with him. If there was any chance of her being right about the woman it would change everything.

So many questions were forming in her mind. Without being able to compare the images she couldn't be absolutely sure they were one and the same. It could easily be some relative of his ex-partner – a sister or a cousin. But what if *was* her? She felt herself shiver. What was her picture doing in the coffin of Moses Smith – a man Dom claimed he had never heard of?

Hodge adjusted his glasses, which had slipped down his nose, and gave her directions to the path lab's office. Once again she passed the body of the road crash victim. Apparently he was still awaiting identification before being tagged and moved into a fridge. A white sheet now covered his face. She winced at the thought of some poor relative being brought to this place; standing in terrified silence as the sheet was pulled back. As she hurried towards the office she realised that she had no idea what Moses Smith had looked like. There had been no photograph of him in the newspaper article. It was strange, seeing his skeleton but having no image of the man when he was alive.

The photocopying done, she returned the picture to the pathologist. It was nearly a quarter past nine. No chance of going to the prison at this time of the night. She was going to have wait until tomorrow to see Dominic.

As she made her way to the car park she thought about Delva, waiting at home with the jerk chicken dish she'd promised to cook. With a twinge of guilt Megan realised that she wasn't feeling the slightest bit hungry. Not surprising really, she thought, as she pressed the button on her key fob; the smell of the mortuary was the best appetite-suppressant she'd ever encountered.

She turned the key in the ignition and heard the reassuring purr of the engine. Moving the gear stick into reverse she edged out of the parking space. There was a sudden judder and she rammed her foot down on the brake. One of her back wheels had gone over something.

'Shit!' she hissed. Her hand trembled as she opened the door. Was it a speed bump she'd missed in the dark? She was trying to rationalise it; telling herself this wasn't what she feared it might be. They couldn't have followed her *here*… could they?

With a deep breath she walked towards the back of the car. 'Oh Christ!' She grabbed the boot to stop herself collapsing. In the red glow of her taillights she could see a baby's head. She had driven over a baby. 'God… please… no!' she stammered, on her knees now, her hands clawing the air. What should she do? Move the car? Call an ambulance? Run inside and get Alistair? All these options tumbled through her mind as she stared helplessly at the white frilly bonnet still attached to the tiny head. Something, some instinct, made her reach out to it. And the moment her fingers touched it, she knew. There was something about the feel of it the head, even through the thin white cotton. It was hard: there was no flesh on the skull. She retched as she pulled the bonnet away. What she was expecting to see was the head of the little boy; the mummified corpse that Jonathan was supposed to be collecting tomorrow. Some sick joker had stolen it and put it under the wheels of her car.

But she was wrong. Even in the dim red light she could see that it was too clean, too white. She was shaking so violently she could barely control her hands as she reached out again. It was smooth. Cold. Her fingers told her brain that this was plastic. That what she was touching was no baby, dead or alive, but a doll.

Megan wasn't sure how she made it to Delva's house. When she went over it all the next morning she couldn't remember anything about the journey. All she could recall was ringing the bell and stumbling through the front door. Delva had been standing there in a blue and white striped apron with a spatula in her hand. Megan had opened her mouth to explain but the words had come out in a jumble. Delva had tried to catch her when she passed out. The spatula had flown into the air, smearing the wallpaper with sauce from the jerk chicken.

Megan saw the mark in the morning when she left for Balsall Gate jail. Delva had begged her not to go; told her she ought to rest. But she was fine. It had been a shock, yes, but she had been overwrought. The exhumation had got to her; made her paranoid. She told Delva that she had been making something out of nothing. It was just a doll, lost or abandoned by some child. The fact that it had been behind her car was probably pure coincidence. There was no logical reason to suspect that it had been put there on purpose.

Delva told her that she looked washed out; that she had been spending too much time on the case and needed to forget it for a while. But she couldn't. She had to get to Dominic, show him that photograph. And then she would phone Willis. Nag him about fingerprinting the letter.

Despite what she'd said to Delva, though, she couldn't help walking around the car two or three times before she got into it. She needed to reassure herself that no one had tampered with it during the night. She found nothing, but the uneasy feeling stayed with her. As she drove past St Mary's graveyard she noticed that the screens and the digger had gone. She couldn't see it from the road, but her mind's eye recalled the deep, dark, vacant hole that awaited the return of Moses Smith's remains. She thought about the woman and child in the photograph. Whoever had put it inside the coffin must have loved him. So why hadn't they come forward? Tried to stop the disinterrment going ahead? Either they didn't know or they were scared of retribution.

She was still mulling these possibilities over as she made her way to the room where Dominic was waiting. Her first impression was that he looked better than he had yesterday. His face had some colour and his eyes looked brighter.

'I had the first decent night's sleep I've had in ages,' he said. 'It sounds awful, I know, but I've got Moses Smith to thank for that. It was a big event in here, the exhumation. The lads on the cemetery side of the jail were giving a running commentary. It turned into a bit of a party – from what I heard there was a fair bit of hooch doing the rounds. Anyway, it must have tired them all out. I didn't hear a peep out of anyone till breakfast.' He smiled at her, but then his face changed. 'You look tired. Are you okay? It can't have been a barrel of laughs, seeing something like that.'

'I'm fine,' she lied. 'It was a bit of a late night, that's all, by the time I got back from the mortuary. Anyway,' she looked away as she reached into her jacket in case he saw through her fake smile. 'I've brought something to show you: something we found with the body.' She took out the photocopy of the picture from the coffin and passed it to him. 'It was in a frame, wrapped up in an Aston Villa scarf,' she said. 'I'm assuming that's the girlfriend and the child they mentioned in the newspaper report of his death.' She passed it to him, watching his face. For a moment all she could hear was his breathing. Then his features went completely rigid. He looked as if he'd seen a ghost.

'It's her,' he whispered. 'It's Sonia.' He looked at her, bewilderment in his eyes, his hand shaking as he felt in his pocket for the dog-eared hospital snapshot. He thrust it into her hand. Side by side, there was no mistaking the likeness. 'What the hell's her picture doing in that guy's coffin?' He stared at it, raking his hair. 'And who's this?' He brought a trembling finger level with the child in the photocopied image. 'Could it... could she be...' he tailed off, turning his troubled face to Megan

'You think it's your daughter?' she whispered. 'You think it's Elysha?'

Chapter 23

Megan eyes narrowed as she turned her attention back to the pictures in her hand. The photocopy was black and white and it lacked the sharpness of the original, colour version. 'Are you *sure* that this woman is your Sonia?'

'As sure as I can be,' Dom replied.

Megan glanced from one image to the other. 'The make-up makes her look a bit older, but it certainly looks like the same person.' She looked at him, perplexed. 'But I thought you said you didn't know Moses Smith?'

'I didn't.' He screwed his eyes tight shut, as if to banish the woman's face and the memories it brought back. 'Like I told you, I lost track of Sonia after she hooked up with Leroy Spinks. Christ, I wasn't even sure she was still alive...'

'Well, I guess that's understandable, if she was moving in that kind of world. But she must have got away from her pimp, though, mustn't she?' Megan laid the photos down on the coffee table, thinking it through. 'Perhaps she was taken in by Moses. If he was a heroin addict, he wasn't exactly a great catch; but if she was desperate, if she had no money and nowhere to hide...'

'Yes, that makes sense, doesn't it?'

'But why would she have put that photo in the grave with him? If it wasn't his child, I mean?'

'She probably told the kid he was her father. She hated my guts, so I guess she wanted to write me out of her life.'

Megan considered this. 'But what about the baby in the shoebox? How does he fit in to all this?'

'That might have been their baby,' Dom picked up the picture from the coffin, his face set. 'She looks pregnant to me.'

'Does she?' Megan took it from him, bringing the picture closer to her face. 'How can you tell?'

'That top she's wearing,' he said. 'She was always dead skinny and she liked to show her figure off. She would never have worn something that baggy unless she had to.'

'What if she was pregnant when he was murdered?' Megan said, voicing the thought that had occurred to her immediately after Carl Kelly's death; the idea that had surfaced when she was pondering the cause of Carl's obsessive belief that Moses Smith was coming back to haunt him. 'The newspaper report said there was one child, not two: could the men who killed Moses have done something to her? Something that made her lose her baby?' She glanced at Dom, who was staring at the window. 'Perhaps she was in shock: that would explain why she didn't tell anyone about it; why she hid the baby's body.'

She heard Dom suck in his breath. In a sudden movement he reached for her, grasping her fingers with his. 'Elysha would have been there, wouldn't she?' His forehead was beaded with perspiration and his eyes were searching hers, wide with fear.

Oh God, she thought, a two-year-old caught up in something like that. It didn't bear thinking about. 'I don't know, Dom,' she said gently. 'She might not have been: perhaps she was with a neighbour or a relative or…'

'No,' he cut in, 'She would have been there, I'm certain. Sonia and Moses were both at home when Carl and the others came for him. The newspaper said so. What if she saw it, Meg? What if they hurt her?'

She stroked his thumb with her fingers. 'They can't have hurt her, can they? You know she's alive; she's on the electoral roll and you've got her address.'

'Yes,' he nodded hard. 'Yes, I have. I've got to find her, Meg, make sure she's all right.'

'I'll find her for you, Dom.'

His eyes filled up and he blinked furiously to stop them brimming over. Without thinking she reached out and pulled him to her, kissing his forehead. She could feel his tears on her chin. 'That letter you were going to write,' she whispered, 'Did you finish it?'

She felt his head shake against her neck then he pulled away, groping in the pocket of his trousers for a handkerchief. 'I've been trying to work out what to say. It's so hard, after all this time, trying to explain.' He was looking at the floor, as if he couldn't bring himself to acknowledge what had passed between them.

'I'll explain it to her, if you like: it might be easier for her, hearing it from someone else. If you give me her address, I'll go there now. Can you get it for me?'

'I don't need to,' he replied. 'Have you got a pen?'

She wasn't surprised that he had memorised it: this was the most important thing in his life and he must have spent hours in his cell imagining the place where his daughter was living. 'Oh,' she said, taking the piece of paper from him, 'It's in Balsall Gate.'

'Yes.' With a heavy sigh he closed his eyes. 'I reckon you could see the house from Alpha wing. Weird, isn't it? All these years she's been so close and I never knew.'

'I'll have to play it carefully, Dom. I can't just come out with it. In fact I probably won't mention you at all to begin with. I'll have to pretend I'm looking for her mother, which I am anyway, of course, because she's the one who's most likely to be able to shed some light on all of this.'

He looked at her doubtfully. 'You'll have to come up with something pretty good. For all I know she might still

be living with her mother. Given that Sonia hasn't come
forward up to now she's going to run a mile if she finds out
who you are.'

'I know. But don't worry, I'll think of something between
here and your daughter's house.' She rose from the chair
and the draught from the window caught the moisture on her
chin. In a swift, involuntary movement she brushed her face
with the tips of her fingers. His tears. She turned away, not
sure how to say goodbye this time.

'If you see her, will you give her this?'

She turned to see him holding out the hospital
photograph.

'I was going to put it in the letter.'

Megan nodded as she tucked the photograph into her
pocket. 'I'll make sure she sees it,' she said, unable to look
at him. 'Call me this evening if you can,' she said over her
shoulder as she reached the door. 'I'll let you know how I
got on.'

Fergus was waiting outside for her. As he stood aside to
let her pass she heard Dom call out to her: 'Goodbye, Dr
Rhys. Thank you.' Strange, he hadn't called her that since
their first meeting. Why was he suddenly being so formal?
Was it because of Fergus? A sudden, cold sensation gripped
her, like icy fingers squeezing her heart. Something about
those words sounded so…she struggled for the right word…
so *final*.

She tried to push it from her mind as she made her way
through security to the car park. He was upset; worried. She
had seen for herself how much the shock of it had affected
him. He would be fine once she had some good news for
him. With an air of determination she climbed into the car
and slammed the door.

* * *

The address he had given her was within half a mile of the prison. In less than ten minutes she was parked at the top end of a row of scruffy maisonettes. They had been built in the early eighties to replace one of the many bulldozed tower blocks and they were showing obvious signs of wear and tear. The window frames looked rotten, with paint peeling away from the sills, and most of the tiny front gardens were strewn with rubbish. As she walked along the pavement looking for number twenty-three she saw a couple of syringes and a used condom lying against one of the broken picket fences. Was this where Dom's little girl had grown up, she wondered? Not the best place for a child.

She thought about what sort of person Elysha might have become; what kind of mother Sonia was likely to have turned into after seeing her partner murdered and possibly miscarrying a baby at the same time. Drugs had apparently been part of their lives before the murder. It wouldn't be much of a surprise if Sonia had become heavily dependent on them after an experience like that – especially if she'd become a prostitute.

She wondered if either of them could have any direct involvement in the murders of Carl Kelly and Patrick Ryan. It would certainly explain why neither had come forward in response to the appeals on the news. Elysha was just about old enough to pass for early twenties. Could she be the one who had hoodwinked her way into the jails? Or was it her mother? Dom had said she was always skinny. She would be in her mid-thirties now, but perhaps she could pass for someone much younger. Why wait until now, though – seventeen years after the event – to take revenge? These men had been on the loose for years after Moses Smith's death. Killing them on the outside would surely have been a far easier option than getting into a prison to do it. And then there was the question of the baby. If it was Sonia's, why would she draw attention to herself by burying it in her partner's grave within days of killing his murderer?

The other problematic piece of the jigsaw was the hall of residence. To steal the identity of two students would require a detailed knowledge of Linden House and the students who lived there. Could Elysha be a student? Did one of them work there? However unlikely their involvement seemed, she would have to call David Dunn and ask him. And it would be better to know that in advance of going to the house.

Walking back up the street she pulled out her phone then searched her bag for the card Dunn had given her. She tried his mobile first, but it went straight to voicemail. She left a message for him to call her back then tried the hall of residence. One of the porters answered. He told her rather brusquely that the warden was away at a conference and wouldn't be back until the evening. She explained who she was and asked if there was anyone by the name of Sonia or Elysha Smith working at Linden House. He replied in a stiff, jobs-worth manner that he wasn't allowed to give out such information and she would have to wait until the warden came back.

Swearing under her breath she ended the call. She was either going to have to put this off until the evening or go in blind. The thought of leaving it was frustrating: what if she came back tonight and there was no one in? She wanted to see Elysha and she was confident she could blag her way in without arousing suspicion.

Number twenty-three was the second-to-last house in the row. It looked no more or less down-at-heel than the neighbouring maisonettes. There were a couple of black bin liners in the garden, one ripped slightly to expose the corner of a packet of cigarettes and what looked like dried up potato peelings. There were net curtains at all the windows, so it was impossible to see inside the house from the road. There was no doorbell so she rapped loudly on the reinforced frosted glass that formed the top part of the front door. She stepped back, listening for signs of life. But there were none. She knocked again. Still no response.

'They'm not there, love.'

Megan turned to see a neighbour standing on the step on the other side of the low fence. She looked about fifty, her dyed blonde hair showing a tangle of dark roots. She was wearing a short, pink nightdress and a pair of huge, padded lion's paw slippers. A curl of cigarette smoke rose from her right hand.

'Oh?' Megan said, 'Do you know when they'll be back?'

The woman eyed her suspiciously. 'Where yer from? The Social?'

'No. I'm a friend. Of Elysha's.'

'Yer from the Starbucks up the road?'

Something clicked in Megan's brain: A café: Dom had said Carl's girfriend worked in a café. Could it be Starbucks? Was this the connection? 'Yes,' she replied, sticking her chin out as if she believed it.

'She been skiving off, has she?' The neighbour took a drag of her cigarette, blowing it towards the sky as if this was not unexpected news. 'I reckon they've done a runner. I ai' seen none of 'em since last week.'

'Really?' Megan folded her arms and took a step closer to the fence, wondering how many people lived in the house and who the others were. 'I don't suppose you know where they might have gone, do you?'

The woman shrugged. 'The boyfriend's, mebbe.'

'Boyfriend?' Did she mean Elysha's boyfriend? Or someone else's? Could Sonia be living there with a new man? Not wanting to reveal her ignorance, she said: 'Does he live near here?'

The woman stubbed her cigarette out on the fence and

tossed it across the garden onto the pavement. 'I ai' gorra clue where he lives. 'Is name's Paul summat. It's on the van but I cor remember it.'

'His van?'

'Yeah.' The woman stubbed her cigarette out on the fence and tossed it across the garden onto the pavement. 'PD Pest Control. I cor tell yer no more'n that.' With a toss of her head she disappeared through her front door, slamming it behind her.

Megan stared at a flake of blue paint as it floated onto the step, dislodged by the impact. The woman's words were ringing in her ears. *PD Pest Control.* She gave an involuntary shiver. There was no denying a connection now. She grabbed her mobile and punched out the number of one of the directory enquiry services. In less than sixty seconds the number of PD Pest Control was texted to her phone. A mobile number. She saved it in her contacts and got back into the car. She would call the number and pretend to be a client. Ask for a face-to-face meeting to discuss some complicated infestation problem.

Further up the road she had spotted a phone box. She would make the call from there. She pulled up alongside it, hoping it hadn't been vandalised. It looked okay. She delved into her purse for coins and punched out the number. Her shoulders tensed as she heard it ring out. But after two rings it went to voicemail. A tinny male voice with a strong Birmingham accent announced the name of the company and asked the caller to leave their number. *Damn*, she thought. There was no way she was going to give him that. She was going to have to try again later, or google him back at the office, find out the address and just pitch up there.

But first she would try Starbucks. *The Starbucks up the road*, the woman had said. That had to be the one on the Heartland campus: the one opposite her office. The one she called at nearly every day of the week. She had almost certainly been served coffee by Dom's daughter. And there was a good chance she would be there now.

It took a matter of minutes to drive back to the office, park the car and step across the road to the café. She approached the counter a little warily. There was no sign of a female member of staff – just two young men serving. She'd seen them both before. One was a student from Greece and the other a migrant worker from Slovenia.

'Excuse me,' she said to the Slovenian, 'I'm looking for Elysha…' she hesitated. She had almost said 'Wilde' but stopped herself just in time. 'Elysha Smith,' she said.

'Ellie?' he smiled at her.

'Yes. Is she working today?'

He frowned and turned to the Greek boy. 'Andris, is Ellie on today?'

'No, she's off,' he replied, shaking coffee grounds out of a shiny silver funnel. 'She's in tomorrow, I think.'

'Okay, thanks.' She ordered a coffee, wondering if there was anything else she could ask without arousing suspicion. There was no way they would give out her mobile number. She couldn't afford to say anything that might alert Elysha to the fact that someone was on her trail. With a nod she took the cardboard cup and headed for the door. She would try the pest control man again and if that failed she would have to come back here in the morning.

She walked towards the office, pausing at the edge of the pavement to take a big slug of expresso. There was a cluster of four phone booths across the road. The first one she went into had a slew of vomit down the perspex partition. With a shudder she stepped into the next one. All she had left in the way of usable coins was a fifty pence piece. She dialled the number without much hope but to her surprise it was answered after the first ring.

'PD Pest Control.' It was a live version of the voice she'd heard earlier.

'Oh, er, good morning. Afternoon, I mean.' She scrambled back into gear. 'I was wondering if you could help me?'

'What's the problem?'

'Well, it's vermin.'

'What kind of vermin? Rats? Mice? Pigeons?'

'I'm not sure, actually – it's a bit complicated. I was wondering if I could talk it over with you. Where are you based?'

'I'm in Highgate. Near the mosque. Coburg Road'

'Oh, yes, I know. It's not far from me. Could I come round?' She pulled her lips in tight against her teeth.

'Well I'm there now, actually. Just popped back for a bit of lunch. I'll be here for the next half hour or so if that suits. Otherwise it'll have to be tonight.'

'Okay, give me twenty minutes and I'll be there.' She scribbled down the number of the house and replaced the receiver. There was no time to go back to the office. She would have to plan out what to say in the car on the way over.

Number four Coburg Road wasn't difficult to find. A white transit van with PD Pest Control in large no-nonsense lettering was parked right outside it. The house was in a street dating from the same era as her own. But unlike the terrace she lived in these were very narrow, low-roofed buildings. From the outside number four looked no bigger than the maisonette she had been to this morning.

She parked in the next street. No sense in giving away any more of herself than she needed to. There was a weather beaten gate, half off its hinges, leading to a tiny front yard with tall dandelions sprouting from the cracks in the Victorian paving slabs. Tobacco-coloured blinds were drawn down over the single bay window. Megan stepped up to the front door. Dead leaves from last autumn had settled in the corners of the porch, adding to the neglected look. Gingerly she stretched out her hand to lift the tarnished brass knocker.

For a moment she could hear nothing but the distant hum of traffic. Then she caught the shuffle of footsteps. The door opened no more than two inches. But it was enough. Enough to recognise the face behind it.

Chapter 24

It was the woman in the photographs. Sonia Smith. As the door opened wider Megan could see that her hair was still long and black. It had the flat, brittle, Sindy doll quality created by decades of dying and straightening. But she certainly didn't look thirty-six. Her skin was taut and smooth under its layer of makeup. The eyes were no longer ringed with heavy black eyeliner but without it she seemed more attractive than she had looked seventeen years ago. She was staring at Megan in an uncertain, rather wary way.

'I'm sorry to trouble you,' Megan began. Her mind was racing ahead. Imagining this woman walking into Strangeways in a blonde wig. Standing in line as the sniffer dogs went up and down the row of visitors. How would she have done it? Wrapped it in clingfilm and put it in her mouth? That was the usual method of throwing the dogs off the scent. Perhaps she would have gone into the visiting room with the fiver they were allowed to carry for refreshments; bought a packet of crisps from the little old ladies serving the tea, then spat the gear into it at an opportune moment. 'I... er...' She forced her mind back to the present. 'I'm here to see Paul. I spoke to him earlier about him doing some work for me.'

'Oh, yeah.' Her face relaxed. 'He's having a sandwich in the back. Do you want to come through?'

Megan followed the woman through the narrow hallway. Sonia's low-cut jeans clung tightly to her small buttocks. A gold belt snaked round a waist unmarred by any rolls of fat. From behind, she could be mistaken for a teenager. Was this the killer? Had she delivered those fatal packages to Carl Kelly and Patrick Ryan?

'He's in here.' Sonia pushed open the door to the kitchen and stood aside to let Megan through. 'Paul! Visitor for you.' As she squeezed past Megan caught a scent of something; a hint of some perfume she recognised but couldn't place. The scent faded and behind her she heard the woman's slippered feet padding up the stairs. She peered into the kitchen. An orange blind obscured the only window, giving the room a sunset glow. In the far corner she caught sight of the top of a man's head. The rest of his upper body was obscured by the newspaper held up to his face. He lowered it as she approached and she saw roundish, friendly features and mousey hair tinged with grey. A slightly bulging stomach nudged the table as he turned towards her. Crumbs clung to the bobbly fabric of his jumper.

''Ow do? Good timing – just finished me sandwich.' He waved at the bench seat across the table. 'This is what passes as the office. Sorry about the mess.' He pushed the remains of his lunch out of the way. Two crusts of bread with bits of what looked like Branston pickle oozing out of them. And a half-drunk mug of tea with the claret and blue Aston Villa logo emblazoned on it. 'What's the problem, then, cock?'

She'd never quite got used to this uniquely regional form of address, used without reference to gender. 'Well,' she said, perching herself on the corner of the bench, 'something's making a mess of the garden, but I'm not quite sure what it is.'

He leaned towards her and she was aware of an odour unrelated to the pickle or the unfinished tea. It was a smell of neglect, of excess, like sweaty feet or rancid vomit. But it was neither of those things. She couldn't put her finger on it. She wondered how someone like Sonia had been drawn into a relationship with a man like this. Was he her partner in crime? Had she traded herself for a means of murdering her enemies?

'What sort of mess?' he said. 'Are we talking damaged plants or holes in the ground or what?'

'Holes in the ground,' she replied, nodding to lend conviction to the story. 'Loads of them all over the lawn.'

'Sounds like a mole problem then.'

'Do you think so? I didn't think you got moles in the centre of Birmingham.'

'Oh, the little buggers'll get anywhere,' he said. 'But don't you worry, I've got just the thing.'

'What?' She looked at him, the pulse in her neck beating hard enough for her to feel it.

'Traps,' he said.

'Oh.' Her heart sank. Was this another blind alley? Had she allowed her imagination to run away with her? 'What sort of traps,' she asked, playing for time while she tried to think up another angle.

'Steel ones. They're the latest thing.'

'I hope they're not cruel. I couldn't bear to think of hurting the poor little things.'

'They're very quick, actually. They don't suffer at all. I'll show you one if you like.' He pushed the table towards her and got to his feet. 'Come and have a look in the van.'

She hesitated for a moment before following him. What if he'd rumbled her? What if he was taking her outside to bundle her into the van and get rid of her? She looked at his beaming face. It was hard to imagine this man as a cold, calculating killer. But, she reminded herself, killing was what he did for a living: he despatched animals without a second thought, so why not people? With a deep breath she rose from the bench. There might be something else in the van, some clue as to whether or not he was involved in the murders. This was no time for bottling out.

There was no sign of Sonia as they walked back along the hall to the front door. As they stepped out onto the pavement Megan glanced at the upstairs windows, wondering if she was watching. But if she was there she was well hidden: both bedrooms had their curtains drawn. Why was she holing herself up like this? Who was she afraid of?

The van's doors opened with a rumble of metal on metal. The stench hit Megan as she stepped off the pavement. It was an overpowering version of the odour that clung to the man. And now she could see where it came from. A large plastic dustbin sat in the middle of the van's floor, flies buzzing round the dead animals spilling out of it. She caught sight of a fox's brush draped over the body of the largest rat she had ever seen. The limp heads of two magpies hung over the front of the bin, their eyes dull in death. And in amongst the heap of grey and brown fur in the middle was what looked like the snout of a mole.

'Sorry about the whiff. I haven't had chance to get this lot incinerated. Problem with the van.' He turned and grinned at her. 'This is what I'm after.' He leaned in and pulled something from under a moth-eaten tartan blanket. The bars of the trap glinted as the sunlight caught them. He chuckled as he handed it to her. 'Don't worry – it's not going to take your fingers off!'

Gingerly she took it. Pretended to examine it. She was thinking about the mole in the dustbin. There were probably dozens more in there. Was this where it had come from, the one the AA man had found in her car?

'Of course, we used to use poison.' He winked at her. 'Not s'posed to do that anymore – bloody EC interfering as usual – but if the traps don't do the trick…' He broke off, tapping the side of his nose.

She nodded slowly. 'What kind of poison did you used to use?'

'Strychnine.' He gave a mock shudder. 'Really nasty stuff. You wouldn't want that. Not if you're an animal lover.'

She handed the trap back to him, her eyes searching the van's dim interior. There were boxes and containers of all shapes and sizes. Any one of them could have strychnine inside and he'd as good as told her it was still an option. 'How many of these traps have you got?' she asked. 'You see, it's a very big garden: in fact, it's grounds rather than an actual garden: it's one of the halls of residence at the university.'

'Oh? Which one?'

'Linden House.' She watched his face intently. The eyes creased at the corners.

'I know it,' he said. 'My girlfriend's daughter was living there up until a week or so ago. They're nice, those grounds. Didn't know they had a mole problem.'

'Oh really?' Megan smiled back. She mustn't sound too eager. 'What's her name?'

'Elysha. Elysha Smith. She's doing International Politics. Very bright girl.'

'But you say she's left us? Is she okay? I hope living in hall hasn't put her off.'

'Oh, no. It's nothing like that. I think she had a row with her boyfriend or something.' He shrugged. 'You know what they're like at that age. She's moved in with one of her friends now, I think.'

Megan's mind was racing ahead as he spoke. Now both mother and daughter had a strong connection to the murders. Had one of them done it? Both of them? And was this man an accessory? Would he really have been so open with her if he was?

'Anyway,' he went on, pushing the trap back under the blanket, 'I've got plenty of these little beauties and I can always get my hands on a few more.'

'Okay,' she said, stepping back from the van and its macabre cargo, 'Can you give me a ballpark figure for the job? Obviously I'll have to discuss it with my boss but I just need to give him a rough idea.'

'Shouldn't be much over a couple of hundred,' he replied. 'I'd have to come and have a proper look first.'

'Have you got a card?'

He fished in the pocket of his overalls and brought one out. There was a smear of what looked like dried blood in the top right hand corner. It had his name in full below the business logo: Paul Deboney. It was almost certainly one of those cards that were printed pronto at motorway service stations: fifty for three quid, write anything you want.

'Thanks.' She tucked it into the front pocket of her handbag. 'I'll get back to you as soon as I can.' As she turned to walk down the street she glanced up at the bedroom windows again. Was that a flicker of movement in one of the sets of curtains? She couldn't be sure. As she made her way along the pavement she felt eyes boring into her back. His or hers? She needed time to think this out. To assemble all the pieces of the jigsaw.

On the drive back to the university her stomach was doing strange things. It was gurgling as it would when she was ferociously hungry but she felt nauseous at the same time. The smell of Paul Deboney's van was clinging to her clothes, making the thought of food quite repulsive. The route to the office took her past a juice bar called Gingers. Perhaps that would be okay: a fruit smoothie or some vegetable-based concoction: anything that didn't involve meat, anyway.

As she sucked blueberry seeds through a fat straw she thought about Sonia Smith. Tried to imagine her as she was seventeen years ago, trapped in a flat with three knife-wielding men, possibly made to watch her partner being stabbed to death. Perhaps Elysha had been in the room as well, too young to understand what was going on. Or maybe she had been asleep upstairs. Either way Sonia would have been terrified for her and for her unborn child, if what Dom had guessed at was true. Why hadn't Kelly and his gang killed them all? Had some kind of morality kicked in when they realised she was pregnant? Weren't they afraid that if she lived she might identify them? Or had they made some threat to ensure her silence? Said the child would die if she grassed them up?

She drained her glass with an embarrassingly loud slurp of the straw but no one turned to look at her. Not even the girl behind the counter. She thought of Elysha, tried to bring her face to mind, framed by the giant coffee machines at Starbucks. There were three or four girls who had served her on a regular basis over the past six months or so. There was the black student with the Yorkshire accent; a small dark-eyed girl whose English sounded East European. And there were a couple of white girls whose voices blended in with the locals. One quite plump and pretty with a piercing through her eyebrow and the other tall and slim with elfin features and a reluctance to engage in the small talk Megan always tried to make when she went in there. Elysha must be one of these two. But which one?

When she arrived back at the office she searched for Elysha on the university's intranet system. Her name and email address were there all right. Next she called up the course registers for the Department of International Politics. What Paul Deboney had said was absolutely accurate; she was a first year student and David Dunn was her tutor. But her address was down as Linden House: had Deboney lied about that? Probably not, she thought: it was much more likely to be a case of the system lagging behind the action.

Her train of thought was interrupted by her mobile ringing out. Perhaps that was David Dunn now, picking up the message she'd left this morning. He would be able to tell her a lot more about Dom Wilde's long-lost daughter. She snatched up the phone. But it was Delva's voice she heard.

'Meg, are you okay?' There was no pause for a reply. 'I've got some news: Tim's come up with something. He's found a third man.'

'What?' Megan almost dropped the phone.

'Someone else was convicted with Kelly and Ryan.'

A surge of adrenaline whizzed up the smoothie in her stomach. 'How the hell did he miss that when he went through the records the first time?'

'He didn't miss it. The other guy, Lee Deacon, was dealt with by the Magistrates' Court because he pleaded guilty. He was only sent to Crown Court for sentencing and he appeared on a different day from the other two. He's the right age, Meg, forty-one, which makes him easily old enough to have been in on the attack on Moses Smith. Tim's checked with the Ministry of Justice: he's in an open prison near Redditch.'

'Hewell Grange?'

'Yes, do you know it?'

'I do.' Megan pulled open a drawer with her free hand, fishing out a fat black contacts book. 'I'll get on to the governor. I just hope to God we're not too late.'

Chapter 25

A plan formed in Megan's mind as she dialled the number of the prison. Hewell Grange was only about forty minutes' drive from Birmingham: she would go and talk to Lee Deacon herself; warn him of the danger and find out exactly what these killings were all about.

It took a while to get through to the governor and as she waited she felt her stress levels rising. What if today was a visiting day? She looked at her watch. Sonia Smith could easily have driven to Redditch in the time that had elapsed since she'd left the house. Deacon could be literally minutes from death. What the hell were the admin people playing at?

'Good afternoon. Can I help you?' A female voice cut across the tinny music.

'I'm trying to get through to the governor.' Impatience got the better of her, making her voice louder than usual and her tone sharper.

'Yes, this is the governor.'

'Oh.' This took her by surprise. The last time she had visited the jail there had been a man in charge and she wasn't aware that he had been replaced.

'Hazel Gorman,' the voice said. Megan thought she detected a hint of annoyance. Not surprising if the woman realised she'd been taken for one of the switchboard operators.

'I'm sorry,' she replied. 'It's Dr Megan Rhys – Heartland University. I met your predecessor a year or so ago – I didn't

realise he'd moved on.' There was silence at the other end of
the line. Megan wondered what had happened but now was
not the time to ask. She explained the situation as succinctly
as she could. 'So Lee Deacon needs protection,' she said,
pausing for a second to draw breath. 'His life could be in
danger.'

'But Lee Deacon's not here.'

'What? He's been transferred to another prison?'

'No. He's out of the prison today, on an acclimatisation
visit to Redditch town centre.'

'Is he?' Megan gave a small sigh of relief. These visits
were designed to get prisoners ready for life in the outside
world. A prison officer always accompanied the inmate and
was not allowed to let him out of sight. So Deacon was safe
– for the time being. 'I need to know who's been coming to
see him,' Megan said. 'When's the next visiting day?'

'Tomorrow.'

'Can you get me a list of who's been visiting over the past
few weeks? Especially if there's anyone young and female
with a Birmingham address.'

'Hang on a second.' Megan heard the tap of a computer
keyboard. 'The last one was a Louise Deacon, of 298 Curzon
Street, Bordesley Green. She came a week ago.'

'Would that be his wife?' It hadn't occurred to her that
there might be a wife on the scene. That would surely scupper
the killer's lonely-hearts strategy.

'Er…' She heard a couple more clicks. 'No, it's his
mother.'

'Okay,' Megan said, 'What about tomorrow? Is there a
visiting order for anyone else?'

'I'm just checking,' the governor replied. 'Yes, there is.
It's for a Ruby Owens, Flat 4, Grendon Gardens, Balsall Gate.
It's her third visit and she started coming in February.'

'Balsall Gate?' Megan's fingers tightened their grip on

the receiver. 'Does it give a date of birth? Phone number? Any other details?'

'Date of birth is 26.11.86. No phone number. Just "friend" in the description box.'

'That fits the age of the suspect visitors at the other two prisons. I need to talk to Lee Deacon. What time's he due back?'

'Not till about six o'clock tonight.'

'Can I come then?' In a few more minutes it was all arranged. The woman's initial frostiness had given way to concerned interest. Megan got the impression she wasn't convinced by the threat to Deacon but didn't want to be seen to be taking any chances. Governors of open prisons were always coming in for stick from the media. Hazel Gorman was apparently making sure she wasn't going to be their next scapegoat. 'We can discuss what to do about Ruby Owens when I've spoken to Lee Deacon,' Megan went on. 'I don't want anyone alerting her in any way, so he mustn't know we suspect her. If she turns up tomorrow we'll have to come up with some way of holding on to her without letting her get anywhere near Deacon. She'll probably have to be strip-searched as soon as she arrives.'

'We don't generally do strip searches.'

'Well, I'm afraid you're going to have to make an exception in this case, unless you want a death on your hands.'

There was a momentary pause. 'I presume there'll be a police presence?'

'Of course.' Megan said it with an air of conviction. Willis was going have to play ball on this one. But she wasn't going to call him until she'd sussed Deacon out. She didn't want him screwing things up at this critical stage.

Replacing the receiver she checked her watch again. Another three hours before she could go to Hewell Grange. She decided to phone Balsall Gate prison and leave a message for Dominic. It was annoying, not being able to phone him direct. She couldn't bear to think of him sitting in his cell, waiting until this evening to phone her, not knowing what was going on. Of course, she couldn't tell him everything. Until she had a clearer idea of what was going on there was no way she was going to burden him with the suspicion that his daughter could be mixed up in the murders. But she could let him know that she was doing a degree at Heartland; that although she was no longer living at the address he had she was traceable through her job at Starbucks. None of this could be conveyed via the admin people at the prison: all she could do was ask them to ask him to phone her. She dug her nails into her palms as she ended the call. She was willing it to be Sonia; praying for her to be the one who had murdered Kelly and Ryan. But she couldn't deny the evidence: Elysha had been living at Linden House. It was looking much more likely that both mother and daughter were involved. How the hell was Dom going to cope with news like that?

She scanned the notes she had scribbled while talking to the governor of Hewell Grange. The address of the suspect visitor was puzzling: 14 Grendon Gardens, Balsall Gate. Why a different address this time? Why not Linden House? Had someone – possibly Elysha – seen her going to the hall of residence and decided it was no longer safe to use as an address? Paul Deboney had said she moved out a week or so ago but perhaps it was more recent than that? She thought about it for a moment. Visiting orders couldn't be obtained as quickly as that: it was only three days since she had been to Linden House and her visit had been on a Saturday night. No, she thought, it wouldn't be possible to turn things round in that time. So could her hunch about this girl be wrong?

Grabbing her bag and jacket, she made for the door. She had to go there. Watch the place and see who went in and out. Find out if this Ruby Owens was yet another alias for

Elysha or for Sonia and whether anyone else was involved.

As she headed for the car park she called up Delva's number. She would want to know what the governor had said about Lee Deacon. She decided not to tell her about Dom's daughter, though. It would just complicate things. Better to wait until she'd seen the girl for herself and weighed her up. So she stuck to the facts, telling Delva about the visitor Deacon was due to see tomorrow and her plan to check her out.

'You're going to this person's house? Are you mad?'

'Don't worry, I'm just going to hang around outside and see who comes and goes.'

'Can't you wait until later? I could come with you; I finish at six-thirty.'

'I'm sorry, I can't. I've got to be at Hewell Grange for six to catch Lee Deacon when he gets back from Redditch.'

'What about the police? Does Willis know about this?'

'Not yet, no. I don't want him wading in before I get the chance to talk to Deacon.'

Delva went silent. 'You'll keep your phone on, won't you?' she said, as if it was an errant child she was talking to.

'Of course I will. I'll be fine, honest.' Megan knew exactly what Delva was thinking: that she'd been anything but fine last night after finding that doll under the wheel of her car. It had shaken her up, it was true. But this was something different. It was a bit of straightforward detective work; that was all. Nothing to get worked up about.

She parked well away from Grendon Gardens in a multi-storey built for Balsall's Gate's once-thriving market square. The market was long gone and these days the car park was used by commuters who refused to pay the sky-high rates charged in the city centre. Megan was confident that no one would spot her car there. Now she could find a suitable spot to watch the flat without alerting anyone to her presence.

Grendon Gardens was a cluster of 1970s council flats built around a children's play area. The slide was a twisted wreck of rusting metal and there was nothing left of the swings apart from the frame and a few lengths of broken chain. The only item of play equipment still intact was a graffiti-covered concrete tunnel. The area was roped off but as she walked past Megan could see that people had been getting in. The usual detritus was clearly visible: empty cans, crisp packets and sweet wrappers lay alongside cannabis roaches and the shrivelled remains of condoms.

She paused as she reached the steps that led up to the first set of flats. They were low-rise; only three storeys high and from the numbering system there appeared to be twelve flats per block. She began to walk slowly along the weed-strewn gravel path that encircled Grendon Gardens It looked as though many of the flats were empty. They had that hollow, uncurtained look and despite the warm weather, none of the windows were open. Number fourteen was on the ground floor of the second block. There were yellowing net curtains at the windows, one set of which were billowing out like sails. As Megan got closer she could see that a pane of glass was missing. It didn't look as if it had been smashed in an act of vandalism: there were no shards sticking out round the edges. It looked as if the pane had been deliberately removed. She wondered why. Perhaps it *had* been smashed and the glass had been cleared away prior to a new pane being installed. But if that was the case, surely it would have been temporarily boarded up? Left like that, it was an open invitation for a break-in. Was number fourteen just another empty flat, then? A convenient address used for the purposes of getting a visiting order to Hewell Grange?

There was only one way to find out. Squatting down, Megan positioned herself so that her eyes were level with the window sill. As the net curtains billowed out with the breeze she got a glimpse of the room inside. It was a mess. She could see envelopes scattered across the floor, cigarette butts on the mantle piece and balls of scorched paper on the tiled hearth beneath the gas heater, as if someone had tried to make a fire and given up. Megan wondered whether to climb through the window. Even if the flat was empty, it might offer some clues to the identity of the woman who was due to visit Lee Deacon tomorrow. She straightened up and glanced around. There was no one about. Better to ring the bell first, though, she thought, just in case she was wrong about it being empty. If she heard someone coming to answer it she could dodge out of sight down the alley that ran between the neighbouring blocks.

The bell didn't look as if it had worked in a long time. There was a wire protruding from it which had rusted at the end. She lifted her hand to knock instead, but as her knuckles made contact with the wood the door moved. It wasn't locked. Not surprising, really, she thought as she stepped gingerly over the threshold. Whoever had been using it as a squat had probably ripped off the latch to save them the trouble of coming and going by the window each time.

The hall was strewn with an assortment of the same items she had seen in the playground. There was a scorched ironing board propped against the wall and she dragged it over to the door, wedging it under the handle to deter anyone who might wander in while she was carrying out her search. There wasn't a lot she could if they were determined enough to get through the window, though: she would just have to be as quick as she could.

The hall carpet had the sort of floral design beloved by elderly ladies, its pinks and greens spattered with various shades of brown. There was a smell of foetid rubbish about the place and as she picked her way through the debris she spotted a black bin bag through the open door of the kitchen. It was leaning against the wall, its contents bulging, and on the top was an aluminium takeaway container with what looked like the remains of a chicken korma inside it. So someone had been here fairly recently. She tiptoed further along the hall, almost tripping over something that was propped against a coat stand. It was a child's buggy, folded up, with a clear plastic rain cover over it. The green metallic paint on its handles was flaking and the cover was ripped on one side. It looked old and battered. Megan wondered if someone had dumped it here. She hoped so: this was no place for a baby to be living.

Further along the hall was a tiny bathroom. Its pink suite appeared to be stained with every kind of substance that could possibly emanate from a human being. She struggled not to retch as she backed away from it.

There was a bedroom at the end of the hallway. She could see an old-fashioned kidney-shaped dressing table with each of its three mirrors shattered. Bottles of talc and scent lay on their sides across the surface, their contents mingling in a sticky white mulch. A dark wood wardrobe stood in the corner, its door wide open to reveal nothing but half a dozen wire hangers. And in the centre of the room was a single bed with a faded pink dralon headboard and a bare, desecrated mattress.

Turning back along the hallway, Megan found herself in the lounge. From the viewpoint of the door she spotted something she hadn't been able to see through the window. There was a sleeping bag on the sofa. It was navy blue and new-looking. Someone was living here, then. That would explain the half-eaten curry in the kitchen. This room was the least offensive in the flat in terms of the amount of litter and the smell; perhaps that was why whoever it was had chosen to sleep in here instead of the bedroom. And the fact that they had apparently left their own rubbish in the kitchen instead of chucking it on the lounge carpet suggested that this squatter was not some spaced-out druggie or alcoholic tramp.

Something lying on the floor caught her eye. It was a card with a bouquet of yellow roses on it. It wasn't the picture that had drawn her attention but the number embossed in gold foil in the top right hand corner. It was the number eighty. She bent down and flipped it open. In spidery copperplate script she read the words: "To Ruby, wishing you many happy returns, love from Flo."

Beside the card an envelope lay face down. She turned it over. There was the name in full: Ruby Owens, Flat 14, Grendon Gardens, Balsall Gate. She nodded slowly. Another identity theft: not of a student this time but of an old woman who was either dead or in a nursing home, with no relatives to care what happened to her few possessions. Evidently the checks done on potential visitors to Hewell Grange were not particularly rigorous: the date of birth would have given the imposter away if only it had been checked out. But with the prison service as overloaded as it was, such oversights were hardly surprising. Whoever was doing this, they were exploiting the flaws in the system to full advantage.

As Megan stood up she noticed a black cardboard box on the coffee table. On closer inspection it turned out to be a shoebox. A Nike shoebox. The mummified baby leapt into her mind's eye and icy fingers clawed her belly. With shaking hands she lifted the lid. It was pure relief to see nothing but a jumble of paper. Then she noticed the scrawled note at the top of the pile. In pencil, on a scrap of lined, hole-punched paper, was her car registration number.

Chapter 26

A sudden gust of air from the window made the sweat on her neck feel clammy. Her first instinct was to run out of the door, to get as far away from this place as possible. But this was it: this was what she had been looking for. This box must belong to the person who had been trying to scare her off. And that person was either the killer or someone closely connected. Was it Sonia? Or someone else? Somewhere in this pile of papers there had to be a clue to their identity.

She thought of taking the box away with her. But that was no good. If they came back and found it missing they would know someone was on their trail and would simply disappear. She had to search the box here and do it quickly. She ran across to the window and peered through the nets. No sign of anyone coming. Taking the box off the table she hunched herself up on the carpet so that she was hidden from view by the sofa. Then she began to take each sheet out, careful to lay them in order, face down, as she did so. She must put everything back exactly as she had found it.

The first few pieces were printouts from the internet. They looked like the sort of thing a student might use for researching an essay. A cold hand squeezed her heart as she scanned them. There was information about the apartheid regime in South Africa; a review of a biography of Nelson Mandela – the sort of thing an undergraduate in International Politics was highly likely to be studying. Her mind was reeling. Could she be mistaken? Could it be some other student? *Please, no, not her: not Elysha.*

What she saw on the next printed sheet made her mouth go dry. The heading was: "The Effects of Strychnine on the Human Nervous System." There were three sides of A4 all about the way the drug killed and the history of its use. Without pausing to read them in detail she whipped out the next sheet on the pile. She froze when she saw what it was: not a computer printout, but notepaper bearing the familiar logo of Heartland University. Underneath the logo was printed: Dr David Dunn, BA (Cantab), PhD. Warden, Linden House. *Elysha's tutor.* Yesterday's date was handwritten in blue ink along with a message: "Darling, sorry to hear that your mum is not well. Hope she is better soon. I'll miss you heaps. Will take you for a romantic meal when you get back. Love you, x."

She leaned back against the base of the sofa, her mouth so parched she could barely swallow. So David Dunn was involved in all this. And she had played right into his hands by going to Linden House and telling him what she knew. The note left little room for doubt: he was having a relationship with Elysha. So did he know about the murders? Was he party to the theft of the identities of Jodie Shepherd and Rebecca Jordan? It seemed barely credible: Dunn was a respected academic. Why would he want to get mixed up in something like this? She looked at the note again. *Sorry to hear that your mum is not well...* But Elysha's mother had looked perfectly well a couple of hours ago. Had she lied to him? Needed an excuse to get out of the hall of residence and made up some story about Sonia being ill?

Megan glanced around the room. These must be Elysha's things in the flat: her sleeping bag on the sofa; her half-finished meal in the kitchen. She closed her eyes then opened them again, not wanting to believe it. But the evidence was overwhelming. Thank God she had spent last night at Delva's place: Elysha knew her car; probably knew which house she lived in as well by now. She could have broken in; put strychnine in the coffee jar or the sugar bowl.

In her head she began rehearsing how she would break it to Dom. She could picture his face; the confusion in his eyes as he took it in. And she couldn't bear it: couldn't stomach the thought of taking him this news.

She went to moisten her lips but her tongue felt as stiff as a sponge left out in the sun. Another possibility had occurred to her, one that she wouldn't allow to take shape: that Dom was somehow in on it: that he was behind it all. *No*, she thought. *It can't be true. Why would he have told me about her if it was?* She felt stunned, paralysed. What the hell was she going to do?

The sudden ring of her mobile made her jump. Her bag was several feet away, hanging from the arm of one of the two wooden chairs that stood either side of a tiny dining table. Scrabbling inside it she managed to grab the phone just before the voicemail message cut in. It was a number she didn't recognise.

'Hello?' Her voice echoed round the sparsely furnished room.

'Dr Rhys? Hazel Gorman, Hewell Grange.'

'Oh…' Megan tried to get her brain back into gear. 'What is it? Has something happened?'

'It's Lee Deacon. He's given his prison officer the slip.'

'What? He's escaped?'

'Yes. Apparently he asked to go to the toilet while they were in a café. He must have got out of the window. Anyway, the police are on their way to his mother's house in Bordesley Green – I think that's the place he's most likely to make for. But I thought I'd better let you know that there's no point you coming to Hewell Grange this evening. I'll give you a call if and when we find him.'

As Megan put the phone back she thought she heard

something. She stopped dead, her hand still on the zipper of her bag. Was that the door? The net curtains swirled in a gust of air. They brushed against her face, pulling a strand of hair across her eyes. Still she didn't move. She could hear nothing but the swish of the fabric against the window frame. There was no one there: she would be able to see anyone peering in through the nets. Perhaps the breeze had made the door rattle against the ironing board she had wedged against it: like everything else in this place it had obviously seen better days and was probably hanging on by a couple of screws. Whatever had made the noise, it was quiet now and she turned her attention back to the box. She must get the contents back in order, must leave everything exactly as she had found it.

She paused as she knelt beside the pile of papers. Would Lee Deacon's escape be on the news? She hoped not. She must ring Hazel Gorman back and tell her to suppress it. Elysha mustn't know that he'd done a runner. She had to be there tomorrow at visiting time: the only way to get hard evidence of her part in the murders was catching her with the strychnine on her.

As she got to her feet there was a sudden thud behind her, as if something heavy had fallen onto the carpet. She wheeled round to see a hooded figure wielding a baseball bat lurching towards her. The last thing she remembered was the taste of the carpet; its musty, sticky surface grazing her tongue as she slumped onto the floor.

Chapter 27

As Megan started to come round the first thing she was aware of was her mouth. Her tongue felt too big; like it belonged to someone else. In her semi-conscious state she felt as if she was chewing on cream crackers, unable to swallow because there were too many in her mouth and nothing on them to help them down. It wasn't until she opened her eyes that she realised what she could taste was some sort of paper. And her lips were clamped shut with what felt like parcel tape.

Panic kicked in as she tried to raise a hand to free them and found she couldn't move. Her arms and legs were tied with twine to the wooden dining chair her bag had been hanging from. Writhing against her bonds, she tried to shout. It came out as a muffled whimper. In a reflex action she started to swallow and gagged as the stuff in her mouth caught her epiglottis.

Then she saw a head rise from the sofa. A head whose hair and face were concealed by a black hoodie. The head gave way to a tall, slim body whose bottom half was clad in denim. The top was so baggy it was impossible to tell if her attacker was male or female. As the figure moved round the sofa Megan flinched. The right hand was wielding a six-inch-long kitchen knife.

'Shout out and you're dead.' The voice was female. Young female. Megan froze as the blade made contact with her neck. In a swift movement the girl raised the knife, slitting the parcel tape near Megan's left ear and ripping it off. The pain as it skinned her lips was intense but she didn't move. Grabbing her hair, the girl jerked Megan's head back, pulling out whatever had been stuffed into her mouth. Four crumpled Starbucks serviettes fell onto the carpet

'Who knows? Who have you told?' The girl's mouth was no more than an inch from her ear, her voice a rasping whisper. Her left hand still had a tight grip on Megan's hair while the other pressed the flat of the blade against her throat. Afraid even to cough, Megan made a choking, retching sound as saliva returned to her mouth. Was this Elysha? It had to be. Should she pretend she didn't know in the hope that the girl would let her go? Or use it to try to unnerve her: to play for time?

'Talk!' The point of the knife dug into the soft flesh between Megan's chin and her windpipe.

'Elysha.' She gasped it out, her throat so dry and sore she could hardly speak.

'How the fuck do you know my name?' There was a change in the voice: a note of uncertainty; a chink in the armour. Megan reminded herself that this was a teenage girl who had probably never seen anyone die. Even if Elysha had planned it all herself and delivered the means of death, Carl Kelly and Patrick Ryan had despatched themselves. She had been involved in a clever game, a murderous fantasy. But now it was real. And Megan sensed that beneath the bravado she was terrified. She must use this fear; exploit it.

With some difficulty she swallowed, forcing down saliva to lubricate her throat. 'I know a lot more about you than you realise.' She paused, the effort of speech making her cough. 'But if you think I'm going to shop you, you're wrong. No one could blame you for killing those men: they didn't deserve to live.' Her voice died as she felt something shoot up her larynx. As she coughed again a fragment of serviette flew out of her mouth.

'You think you can soften me up with that bollocks,' the

girl sneered. 'You don't know the half of it. Those bastards stabbed my dad to death and threw my mum down the stairs when she was nine months pregnant.'

Megan could feel her breath on the side of her face. Dom had been right, then. Sonya had been expecting a baby. Was this the little boy in the shoebox? She winced as she opened her mouth again, congealing blood sticking her lips together. 'So they killed him, too,' she whispered, 'Your baby brother?'

Her hair was yanked back hard. 'You should fucking know! You took him!' Now the knife was on the side of her neck, pressing so hard she could feel the blood pulsing against it. *Say something. Anything.* Her head was buzzing like a greenhouse full of flies. *Nobody's coming to the rescue. You're on your own.* 'I didn't take him,' she whispered. 'I ...'

'Yes you did!' The girl spat the words out. 'I heard you on the phone, talking about it when you came in for your fucking coffee! But that wasn't enough for you, was it? You had to make them take my Dad as well...' She tailed off, the knife shaking so much Megan could feel it grazing her skin. 'I wanted to run up to those bastards and shout: No! You can't do that – he's my father, leave him alone! But I couldn't. I just had to stand there with that fucking buggy and watch while all the sickos came out of the woodwork to feast their greedy eyes.'

So that was her. The girl with the buggy walking past the graveyard. Probably the same buggy she had seen lying in the hall when she came in. But the baby? Where was that baby? In an instant it came to her: The rain cover would have hidden the fact that it was not a baby being pushed along but a doll: Elysha must have followed the convoy of cars to the mortuary; waited outside for her to come out.

'Why, Elysha?' It sounded lame, pathetic. But she had to

know if her guess was right. 'Why did you leave that doll under my car?'

There was a long silence. When the girl spoke, it was through gritted teeth. 'I wanted you to feel the kind of pain I felt when I found my brother.'

'*You* found him?' Now it was all starting to make sense. 'How? When?'

'You really want to know?' she snarled. 'You really care? Oh, yeah, right!'

'It might not seem that way, but yes, I do care.' Megan licked her ragged lips, caught her breath as the saliva stung. 'When I found him in that shoebox I couldn't bear to think that no one knew who he was; who his mother was. I had to find out; had to try to give him a name…'

'He has a name!' Elysha's voice was so loud the words pierced her eardrum.

Megan said nothing. Waiting. Hoping that if she didn't ask the girl would offer it up and, in doing so, widen that chink in her armour.

'His name is Ben.' Silence for a few seconds, then it all came tumbling out, one sentence merging with the next: 'I found him in the wardrobe when she was out and I was looking for the shoes, the ones she borrowed without asking and there he was, bundled up like fish chips and I couldn't touch him, didn't know what to do so I left him on the bed in the newspaper and when she saw him she was screaming, crying, till I made her tell me.' Megan heard the click of the girl's tongue against the insides of her mouth as she swallowed. When she spoke again her voice was low and full of menace: 'I put him where I thought he'd be at peace: with his Dad: with *my* Dad. But you couldn't let them be, could you?'

'But they *will* be at peace, Elysha,' Megan said, fighting to keep her voice steady. 'They'll be buried together now – in the same coffin.' She paused. There was no response. But the pressure of the knife eased slightly. Now was the moment to play her trump card. If it failed, the words she was about to say would probably be the last she would ever utter. 'There's something I have to tell you,' she began, 'Something you don't know: Moses wasn't your real dad, Elysha. I know your father. He's a lovely man and he's desperate to meet you.'

For a long moment all Megan could hear was the swishing of the nets. Suddenly her head fell forward as Elysha loosened her grip on her hair. But this respite lasted only a second or two. Megan yelped as her head was yanked back again. This time the point of the knife was jabbing the skin above her jugular vein.

'You lying bitch,' the girl hissed. 'You'd say anything to stay alive, wouldn't you? What's the plan? Play for time till the cops come? Have you told them? Have you?' The last two words shot drops of spittle into Megan's ear.

'No,' she gasped, 'I haven't told them.' She was gambling everything on gaining the girl's confidence. She had to persuade her that it was true. 'If you think I'm lying about your father, just take a look in my bag. There's a photograph in my purse: a photo of him with you.'

She felt Elysha's weight shift. The chair wobbled as the girl squeezed round the back of it. Her left hand was still grasping Megan's hair but the knife was gone. Megan heard the zipper on her handbag being pulled open. She heard the click of the popper that fastened her purse. She had put the photo in the clear plastic pocket opposite her credit cards. Elysha would see it as soon as she opened it up.

'Who is he?' The voice sounded higher, like a boy's about to break. It made her sound even younger.

'His name is Dominic Wilde.' Megan hesitated, trying to judge how much to say. What she came out with was a sanitised version of the truth: 'He has a degree in English and he works as a counsellor.'

'This could be anybody.' The sneering tone had returned. 'He could be some bloke who came to visit my mum in hospital and had his picture taken for a laugh.'

'Look at the way they're sitting, Elysha. He's got one hand on your mum's shoulder and the other on you. Do you think just anyone would do that?'

Silence again. Megan hardly dared breathe. She had to convince her; had to make her believe that there was a reason to keep her alive. The sudden trill of Megan's phone made them both jump. *Christ, if only I could get to it!* Megan clenched her fists, the twine cutting into the skin where it pinioned her at the elbows. Suddenly it occurred to her: the one thing she could say to make Elysha pick it up: 'That's probably him,' she urged. 'I told him I was going to look for you. You should answer it. He doesn't know anything about…' She stopped as the ringing stopped. Too late. The voicemail must have cut in. Bitter tears stung her eyes. Who had it been? Delva? David Dunn? Or Jonathan, even? He would be here now, in Birmingham, collecting Elysha's stillborn baby brother for a test that was now completely unnecessary. If she hadn't decided to break things off he might have been with her now…

'She's driving at the moment – who is it?'

Megan caught her breath. She had answered it. Elysha had answered the phone.

'Did you say Dominic? Dominic Wilde?'

Adrenaline surged through Megan's body. She closed her eyes tight, making a fervent, silent prayer: *Please, please don't hang up; tell him who you are; listen to what he has to say.*

'Yes, this is Elysha, —Yes, she told me, but why should I believe her? Why should I believe either of you? —Well, you say that, but you can't be my real dad. If you were, you'd never have left me to deal with all this *shit* on my own. —No, I don't want to talk about it and I don't want to see you. —Just fuck off out of it and leave me alone!'

Megan felt as if she'd taken a second blow from the baseball bat. If Elysha had been her own child the pain could not be more acute, imaging Dominic's anguish as his hopes and dreams were shattered.

There was a flash of silver as her phone flew across the room and smashed against the mantle piece. So that was it: her one chance gone. There was now no reason for Elysha to keep her alive.

'Where does he live?' The girl's voice was gruff, as if she was fighting back tears. Megan sensed then that something had changed; that despite the angry words he had somehow got through to her.

'He lives near here. In Balsall Gate.' Megan had a fleeting fantasy of the two of them going to the prison to visit him; of seeing Dom reunited with his daughter. If she kept quiet about it no one need ever know that Elysha was the killer. What good would it do to turn her in? She had killed for a reason. For a very good reason. Could Megan be so sure she wouldn't have done the same thing in those circumstances? *You can't do that.* It was a fantasy. But she could use it.

'Will you take me there?'

Megan bit her lip, wincing as her teeth grazed raw skin. She must say yes, must say whatever she had to. The only thing that mattered was getting out of this place alive. As her mouth formed the word there was a sudden yell from outside.

'Ruby! You in there?' It was a man's voice: a voice that Megan didn't recognise.

'Who the fuck's that?' The girl had the knife at her throat again.

'I don't know,' Megan mumbled. 'I haven't told anyone, I swear to you.' She felt the blade move away again. Elysha was in front of her now, crouching, looking at the window. Keeping her head down, she crept across the room to peer through the net curtains.

'Jesus! What's he doing here?' The girl turned to Megan. 'Keep your mouth shut, or you're dead,' she hissed. She darted into the hall, closing the lounge door behind her. Megan heard the man's voice again, saying something she couldn't quite make out. Elysha was saying something back: arguing with him, by the sound of it. Megan realised this was her chance. While they were talking she shuffled herself sideways so the chair she was tied to was facing the table. She was hoping against hope that Elysha had left the knife behind when she went to the door. But she hadn't. Straining at the twine that held her arms, Megan cast about the room for something sharp, her eyes ranging over the mantelpiece, the sofa and the carpet. There was nothing. Then she remembered the nail scissors in her handbag. Shuffling a couple of inches closer to the table she managed to grasp the leather strap with her teeth. Pulling it towards her, she saw that it was still unzipped. She manoeuvred it with her mouth, tipping it over, spilling the contents onto the table. With her nose and chin she sifted through the junk until she located the scissors. *Thank God for those bloody prunes*, she thought.

All the time she could hear the voices in the hall getting louder. The man shouted an obscenity. Elysha shouted back: 'Fuck off yourself, Lee!'

Megan gasped. It couldn't be, could it? Lee Deacon? But of course: he had her address. It was on the visiting order. He must be so besotted with Elysha that he had given his jailer the slip to come and lay claim to her. *Christ*, she thought, *she's got the knife – she's going to kill him!* With a nudge of her nose she knocked the scissors into her lap. She had just enough mobility in the lower part of her right arm to reach them. In a matter of seconds she had snipped through enough of the twine to release herself. As she ripped the remaining bonds from her legs she heard a roar from outside.

'You fucking prick-tease!' the man bellowed. There was a crash and something thumped against the wall dividing the lounge from the hallway. Megan lurched towards the door, her limbs stiff and clumsy. The voice in her head was hissing, *Run! Get out of the window while you've got the chance!* But she couldn't. She couldn't leave Elysha. By the sound of it, the bastard was about to rape her.

She burst into the hallway to see a shaven-headed hulk of a man pinioning Elysha to the wall. One of his hands was holding both her wrists above her head and the other was tugging at her jeans. Her hood had come off in the struggle and Megan had a fleeting glimpse of a pale, delicate face framed with short, black, wispy hair. It was a face she had seen many times, bobbing about behind the counter at Starbucks.

'Get off her!' Megan launched herself towards him.

Lee Deacon turned a pair of large, surprised blue eyes on her. 'Who the fuck...' He never finished the sentence. Seizing her chance, Elysha broke free. Megan saw her whip the knife out of the pouch of her hoodie.

'No, Elysha!'

She was too late. The girl was jabbing the knife into his groin. He let out a howl of pain, staggering back against the opposite wall. Megan watched, paralysed with horror, as he slid to the floor. A huge stain was spreading down the left leg of his jeans. Both hands were clutching his groin and his face was screwed up in agony.

'Bitch!'' he groaned. 'You fucking bitch! I'm fucking bleeding to death!'

'Elysha – call an ambulance, quick!' Megan ran to Deacon, kneeling on the carpet beside him. Pulling off her scarf, she held it to the wound in a bid to stop the bleeding.

'Get away from him!'

Megan glanced up to see Elysha pointing the knife at her.

'You think I'm going to let him live? Let him grass me up?'

Oh God, Megan thought, *If I try to save him she's going to kill me.* 'Elysha,' she pleaded, 'This isn't you: you're no cold-blooded killer. You don't…'

'Shut up!' the girl screamed. 'Just shut the fuck up!'

'No, listen to me!' Megan could see that the hand holding the knife was shaking. 'Everything you've done up to now is the sort of thing a court would understand: a good lawyer would say the balance of your mind was disturbed by the terrible things you'd found out; that what you did to Kelly and Ryan wasn't technically murder. But if you leave this man to die you're looking at a life sentence.'

'Only if they catch me!' She waved the knife at the walls of the flat 'Who's going to know? Ruby Owens no longer exists!'

'No, she doesn't – but you do' Megan rose to her feet and took a step towards Elysha. The girl's eyes flashed and Megan blinked. It was like looking at Dominic. He'd once been like this: worse than this, by his own admission. And yet he was now, without question, a good man; better than most on the outside. Surely some grain of this would exist in his daughter? There was something in those eyes that made her believe it. 'You leave him to die and stick that thing into me and that's all you're going to do for the rest of your life: just exist. Your real father knows exactly what that feels like: he's spent most of his adult life in jail because of it. But now he's made something of himself and do you know why? It's because of you. The thought of meeting you, of getting to know you, is all he lives for.'

Elysha's nostrils flared as she grunted. 'Do you think I care?'

'You might not now. But how do you think you'll feel twenty years down the line? You've spent the last seventeen years without a dad – now you've got the chance to find out what it's like to have one. Do you really want to throw that away?'

The eyes narrowed. The hand holding the knife jerked forward. Then stopped. The pale, delicate face crumpled like a paper flower in the rain. 'Help me,' she whispered.

As Megan reached forward to take the knife a burst of sound ricocheted around the walls. It was the howling feedback of a megaphone. A voice crackled: 'Lee Deacon: this is the police. The building is surrounded. Give yourself up!'

Chapter 28

Delva Lobelo was with BTV's news editor, going through last-minute changes to the evening bulletin, when the phone rang.

'This is DS Willis, West Midlands police. I thought you'd like to know there's been a development in the Balsall Gate case.'

'There has? Can you hang on a second?' Delva put one hand over the receiver and repeated the sergeant's words to the news editor while grabbing her pen and notebook. 'Fire away,' she said into the phone.

'We've arrested a nineteen-year-old female on suspicion of the murder of Carl Kelly. We're also questioning the suspect about a second suspicious death at Strangeways prison in Manchester.'

'You did say female?' Delva was scribbling it down in shorthand and the news editor came round the desk, reading over her shoulder. 'Is it the lonely hearts girl? The one who was visiting them in prison?'

'I'm afraid I can't comment on that,' Willis said, his voice as expressionless as ever. 'All I can confirm is her name and date of birth: it's Elysha Smith. – that's E-l-y-s-h-a – and the DOB is the twenty-second of the sixth, nineteen-eighty-eight.'

'What about her address? Is she local?'

'She is, yes, but I'm unable to give you details at this stage.'

Delva clapped her hand over the receiver again as the

news editor bent to hiss in her ear. She rephrased his question to Willis. 'I didn't know the case had got this far. Was Megan Rhys involved?'

She heard him clear his throat before he answered. 'Let's just say that she was with the suspect at the time of her arrest. We believed that we were dealing with a hostage situation at an address in the Balsall Gate area.'

'A hostage situation?' Delva stopped writing in mid-sentence. 'Is Megan okay?'

'She was unharmed and is assisting us with our enquiries.'

Delva let out a sigh of relief. God, she thought, he sounds more like a robot than a human being. 'Was Megan Rhys the hostage?' she persisted. 'Was it the girl you arrested threatening her?'

'I can't comment on that,' he replied. 'All I can say is that an escaped prisoner – Lee Deacon – was escorted from the scene with stab wounds and taken to Heartland Hospital, where his condition is serious but stable.'

Megan was at number four Coburg Road when the news bulletin went out. She and Detective Superintendent Martin Leverton were sitting with Sonia Smith in the kitchen. Leverton was an old acquaintance of hers – not exactly a friend – but they had worked together a year or so ago on the prostitute murders, as a result of which she had won his grudging respect. To her relief he had been put in charge since Elysha's arrest and Willis had been demoted to media liaison. She had offered up what she knew about Sonia and her boyfriend on the understanding that she would be allowed to play a part in what followed.

Paul Deboney had already been taken away for questioning but from the look on his face when they arrived, he had no idea that the batch of strychnine in his van had been taken. He had appeared equally baffled when the names of Carl Kelly and Patrick Ryan were read out. Apparently Sonia had told him that Elysha's father had died in a car accident.

'That's what I told Elysha, too.' Sonia was staring at the orange blind drawn over the window as if it was a cinema screen. 'I couldn't tell her what really happened. When she found the baby I...' she faltered, her eyes brimming with tears.

'She told me they pushed you down the stairs,' Megan said gently. Sonia had been in a state of shock after they broke the news that Elysha had been arrested. Megan's instinct was that, like Paul Deboney, she had played no part in the murders. But she must have known about the baby being found in Moses' grave. It had been all over the news. She would also have heard about Carl Kelly's death. There were still so many unanswered questions: How had Elysha known who the men were? Where to find them? Was Sonia really as innocent as she appeared to be? Megan tried again: 'You must have been terrified when those men burst in like that.'

Sonia's hair fell forward, hiding her eyes as she nodded. 'I didn't tell Elysha everything. I couldn't.' Megan saw her lips go white as she pressed them together. 'They didn't throw me down the stairs. They raped me.' It came out in a whisper. Megan heard Leverton clear his throat and swallow. She felt a wave of nausea. It was a horrible thing to contemplate: a woman nine months' pregnant being gang raped and miscarrying her baby. No wonder Carl Kelly had had nightmares. He must have known what he was doing that night. Or had he been so drugged up he hadn't realised the consequences of what he and the others were inflicting? Had it happened while they were still there? Was it the dead child who had appeared in Kelly's dreams, rather than the father he had stabbed to death?

'I couldn't let Ben go.' Sonia's eyes were still obscured by her hair but Megan saw a tear run down her chin and fall to the carpet. 'He was the only thing I had to remind me of Mo.' She shook her head. 'People thought Mo was bad, but he wasn't. The only thing he ever took was skunk – nothing else. And he was the only man I'd ever met who didn't…' The words trailed away to nothing. Megan caught her breath. *So the poor bastard was murdered for the price of a few grams of cannabis.* She wondered what Sonia had intended to say next and she thought of Dom, remembering what he'd said about his serial infidelities while he was with Sonia. Then there had been the pimp, Leroy Spinks. Living with a bloke with nothing worse than a dope habit must have been paradise compared to what she'd endured before.

'Sonia, there's something I have to ask you. It might help Elysha when this comes to court. When Moses was killed it said in the paper that you didn't know who they were; that they were wearing masks…'

'No.' Sonia said the word firmly, brushing the hair away from her eyes. 'I knew them. But they said they'd come back and kill me too if I grassed them up. I was so bloody scared I took Elysha and ran. All we had was the clothes we stood up in and Ben.' She dropped her head again. 'He was wrapped up in newspaper in a carrier bag. We hid in a doss house for six months with the bed against the door every night to keep the drunks out.'

Megan could see more tears plopping onto the carpet. She fumbled in her bag for a tissue but Leverton beat her to it, offering a large, neatly pressed white handkerchief. 'What I need to ask you,' she said softly, 'is how Elysha knew who to look for. How she knew where to find them.'

'I told her when I came home and found Ben on my bed.' Sonia sniffed loudly and blew her nose. 'It was the day after

my birthday. I'd borrowed a pair of her shoes because Paul
was taking me out. That's how she found him. She was
looking for those bloody shoes. It nearly killed her, finding
him like that.'

Megan could hear Elysha's voice in her head. *I wanted
you to feel the kind of pain I felt when I found my baby
brother*... No wonder she had plotted the most horrible death
imaginable for the men who were responsible for his death.
'So you had to tell her, then?' she asked. 'And she wanted to
know their names?'

'Yes. I told her they were all in prison. I thought she'd
be satisfied with that. It never occurred to me that she'd go
looking for them.'

Megan looked at her for a long moment. No, she thought,
I don't suppose it did. She glanced at Leverton, whose eyes
gave a barely perceptible look of assent. He believed Sonia
too.

An hour later Megan was at West Midlands Police
headquarters. She was in a windowless room, watching
through a one-way viewing panel as Elysha Smith was
interviewed by Leverton and another senior officer from the
Greater Manchester force. The girl was just providing the
last piece of the jigsaw, giving an account of how she had
tracked down Moses Smith's killers. Megan was struck by
the ingenuity she had shown but was equally shocked by the
distant, emotionless way she described it.

Elysha was telling the two policemen that she had
handwritten three letters, one to each of her intended victims,
signing each one with a different name. She had colour-
photocopied the letters so that they looked like originals,
sending one copy of each to every prison within a hundred-
mile radius of Birmingham. It was that simple: in less than a

fortnight she had located all three men and made plans to visit them. The honey trap was laid and the drugs were offered on the second visit. They were delivered on the third.

When Elysha stopped speaking she sat rigid in the chair, staring into space, like a machine that had been turned off. It was as if something inside her had shut down. To Megan, it was plain that she needed help: somebody to support her. Sonia had come and gone, hysterical at the sight of her daughter in a police cell and unable to communicate. David Dunn had been contacted and was on his way back from the conference he was attending. He had agreed to be interviewed but expressed no desire to offer support to Elysha. The obvious person to counsel the girl was Dom. Not because he was her father, but because of his compassion. He was a rescuer of souls and that was exactly what Elysha needed at this moment.

Megan's thoughts were interrupted by the clunk of the door opening. A young WPC had brought her a cup of coffee and a plate of biscuits. 'You were mentioned in dispatches, Dr Rhys,' the woman said, as she laid the tray down in front of her.

'Dispatches?' Megan looked at her, puzzled, as she reached for the chocolate biscuit in the middle of the plate.

'They mentioned your name on the news.'

The biscuit stopped midway between the plate and Megan's mouth. 'You mean it's been released to the media already? What did they say?'

'Not much. Just her name,' the WPC said, nodding at the viewing panel. 'And the fact that Lee Deacon's in hospital.'

Megan bit her knuckles as the woman disappeared behind the door. What if Dom had heard it? He'd be going frantic with worry. She must phone the prison: try to persuade them to let him out for a few hours to meet his daughter and talk to her, however briefly.

Instinctively she reached for her mobile, then remembered it was lying in bits on the floor of the derelict flat in Balsall Gate. She had to go to the front desk of the police station to make the call, only to be told that the governor of the prison was unavailable. Only he had the authority to issue a temporary leave permit – even for a model inmate like Dominic.

'Can I at least come and see him, then?' Megan said urgently.

'Well, it's not usual to allow anyone other than staff in at this time of the evening…' the duty officer tailed off. Megan could hear shouts in the background: the familiar evening chorus of men on lock-up, trying to communicate with each other through barred windows. They were probably passing round the news that some girl had been done for killing one of their mates. Poor Dom, she thought, having to listen to that.

'It's very important that I talk to him,' she persisted. 'His daughter is in a lot of trouble and I need to explain the circumstances to him.'

There was a brief silence at the other end of the phone, followed by a small sigh. 'I'll see if we can make an exception for you, Dr Rhys, as it's Dom Wilde we're talking about. Can I call you back in a couple of minutes?'

Megan paced up and down the corridor until the news came back that her request had been granted. Grabbing her bag, she ran down the corridor to the exit that gave onto the car park. It was twilight outside and by the time she had driven across the city to the prison, darkness had fallen. She had never been there at night. Harsh white light bounced off the stone walls and a stiff breeze made the barbed wire hum like a swarm of angry bees. She wondered how Elysha would fare in whatever institution she was sent to: it was highly unlikely she would avoid a custodial sentence but maybe the judge would be lenient.

'Dr Rhys?' The man on the gate was the smiley one; the one who always greeted her like an old friend. But he wasn't smiling now. 'We've been trying to get hold of you.'

'Oh...' her stomach lurched. She could tell from his face that something was very wrong. 'I... er...' she mumbled. 'My mobile... I haven't got it...' Panic rose like bile in her stomach. 'It's Dominic Wilde, isn't it? What's happened?' Her mind crowded with a host of possibilities. Had the news made him flip? Had he attacked a guard? Another inmate? Or even tried to escape?

'Yes, I'm afraid it is him, ma'am.' The guard dropped his head. 'It was a hell of a thing. A couple of the lads found him hanging in his cell. They tried to revive him but he was already gone.'

The walls and the floor began to melt. She clutched at the counter to stop herself collapsing.

'Are you all right, ma'am? It's a shock, isn't it? That's how we all feel. Of all the people...' The sentence trailed away to nothing as he bent to reach for something under the counter. 'He left this for you. It's evidence, of course, so I'm afraid I can't allow you to take it away but I thought you should read it before anyone else did.'

Megan couldn't open the envelope until she sat down. It was warm in the warder's lodge but she was shivering violently. There were two letters inside, one for her and one sealed up in a second envelope addressed to Elysha. As she began to read the tears she had been fighting back spilled down her face and stung her lips.

Dear Meg,
    I wish I'd met you twenty years ago. If I had, I wouldn't have messed my life up so completely. Elysha would never have been born and she

*wouldn't have gone on to become a monster
like me. They say that the sins of the fathers are
visited on the children – when I saw the news
tonight I realised what a terrible legacy I'd left.*

*For a while I truly believed my life had
changed and your presence in it – however
brief – gave me a feeling of joy that I've never
experienced before – and will never feel again.
I've known guilt in the past, but nothing on this
scale. All that Elysha has become is because of
me.*

*A few days ago you asked me if I had ever
considered suicide. I told you then that what
stopped me killing myself was knowing I had
the choice. I still have that choice but now the
circumstances are different. I don't deserve to
live and I no longer want to. That's my decision
– no turning back, no cry for help.*

*You promised to find my daughter and you
kept that promise. You mustn't feel in any way to
blame for what I'm about to do. Can I ask you
to do something else for me? Will you make sure
she gets the letter I've enclosed? I know I've
ruined her life, but if our friendship has meant
anything to you, will you be a friend to her?*

*If there's one positive thing I can achieve by
my death, it's to right some of the wrongs in this
place. There were things I kept from you – things
I couldn't reveal while I was still inside. But I
can tell you now. There are two men controlling
this jail. You'll have met both of them. Their
names are Al Budgen and Gerry Kirk – as
sadistic a pair of perverts as you are ever likely
to find wearing a prison officer's uniform. Until*

last year there was a third – Charlie Hutchins
– the screw who was attacked in the laundry. I
couldn't tell you before who it was that beat him
up. That's because it was me. I did it because
Hutchins had raped a young lad I'd counselled
the previous day – a lad who had grown up in
care and was totally vulnerable to their brand of
brutality and humiliation. They use it to rule this
place through fear and they are the cause of all
the suicides you have been investigating. I don't
know what you'll do with this information but if
anyone can change things, you can.

I don't think I've truly loved anyone in my life
but what I feel for you is what I always hoped it
would be like. For that reason I so wish I could
change things. But it's too late to stop now.
Be happy – Dom xxx

* * *

It was three months before Megan went back to Balsall
Gate jail. Delva was with her, filming for the documentary
BTV were making about the changes that had occurred
there. Megan was relieved not to be going alone. The loss
of Dom Wilde had turned her world upside down. In the
weeks that followed his death she had seriously considered
resigning from her job at Heartland. She had looked for
posts at American universities; even sent off for details of
a lectureship in Hong Kong. Anything to escape the daily
reminders of what might have been.

She had fulfilled his last request, visiting Elysha while she
was on remand and trying to help her make sense of what her
father had done. And she had included his allegations about

the prison officers in a report she had written for the Ministry of Justice. As a direct result of this, Malcolm Meredith had taken early retirement from his post as governor of Balsall Gate. Al Budgen and Gerry Kirk had been suspended pending a full police inquiry.

But the stress of it all had taken a physical toll on Megan. Her periods had stopped and she had felt so exhausted she had finally gone to see a doctor for a full MOT. The results of the examination had astonished her: she was pregnant. A subsequent scan revealed that she had been so for the past five months. The doctor informed her that although her medical history made conception very unlikely, she had defied the odds.

'How do you feel about it now?' Delva asked, as they walked through the inner courtyard of the prison. 'Has it sunk in yet?'

'Not really, no,' Megan replied. 'When I phoned you yesterday from outside the hospital I think I was in shock. They'd shown me this image on the scanner and I was thinking: this can't be my baby. They must have got it wrong.'

'But you are happy about it?' Delva cast her a worried look.

'Yes. Yes, I am happy.' She said the words slowly, carefully, as if trying them for size. 'It's so hard to describe the way I feel. It's something I never, ever expected but now it's actually happened…' she tailed off, unable to convey the mixture of joy, astonishment and fear that had overtaken her the minute she saw that tiny body on the hospital monitor.

'Have you told Jonathan yet?'

'Not yet, I'm still trying to work out what to say and I'm worried about how he's going to take it.'

'Worried? Why?'

'Well, the relationship ended months ago. It had run out

of steam. A baby can't fix something that's already broken. And to be frank, Del, I don't need a man at this moment in my life.'

'You might change your mind when the baby's born.'

'Possibly. But I don't think so. The main reason it ended was because I hardly ever saw him. I don't want the same for my baby.'

'But what if this changes him? What if he offers to move nearer to you and the baby?'

'Well I suppose he might – it'd be difficult – but I really can't predict how he's going to react. One thing I do know though.' She stopped walking and turned to Delva, her eyes glistening. 'If we have a boy, I'm going to call him Dominic.'

If you enjoyed *The Killer Inside*

you can read more of Megan's investigations in

***Strange Blood*, *Frozen* and *Death Studies*:**

DEATH STUDIES

Chapter 1

It was the girl who found the body.

Llŷr had sent her into the cold, still water while he waited on the muddy bank. As she edged forward the silver stud in his sleek, black eyebrow crept upward. His eyes were fastened on her thighs. Delicate slices of soft white flesh squeezed between dirty green waders and cut-off jeans. The frayed denim trembled as the wind hissed in the reeds. She bent over. Now he could see the top of her knickers. A black thong with a diamanté butterfly. Its wings glinted in the sunlight as she moved her hips. Was this for him?

'Llŷr!' Her child's voice cut through his fogged mind. 'There's something in the water!'

She moved sideways and the sun blinded him. He blinked, shading his eyes with his hand. 'What?' His tone was impatient.

'Something big and heavy.' She half turned, one small breast silhouetted against the sky. 'The line's snagged up in it.'

He sighed and rose lazily from the blanket on the grass. His long black hair fell over his eyes as he spat out the dog-end of a roll-up. He flicked his head back and pulled a band from his wrist, scraping the dark mane into a pony-tail. Then he kicked off his walking boots and wriggled into the waders lying at the edge of the pool.

A skylark fluttered from the reeds as he splashed into the water. In a few strides he was level with her. 'Give me the line,' he said, his hand brushing her thigh as he reached forward. He tugged the fishing twine hard and it snapped.

'Bugger!' He staggered back, almost losing his balance. Then he put his hands beneath the surface, feeling for the thing that had snagged it. There was a loud slosh as he dislodged something flat and hard. As it slid sideways a slick of mud bubbled up from underneath.

The girl let out a shrill cry that sent sheep thundering across the hummocky field beyond the reeds. Llŷr stood transfixed, as a bright, tangled mass broke the surface. 'Jesus Christ,' he whispered. 'Jesus fucking Christ!'

Other titles in the Megan Rhys Crime series by Lindsay Ashford

Death Studies

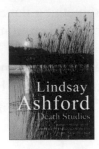

Some secrets haunt the living and the dead…
A windswept seaside strip in West Wales
– sleepy enough, until three bodies turn up
within as many days. A shocking coincidence
or a serial killer?

Forensic psychologist Megan Rhys is
supposed to be on holiday but she can't
ignore the body in her backyard... Her journalist sister Ceri
is being held to ransom by an editor eager to steal a march
on her national red-top rivals, and the closer the sisters get
to the heart of the case the more their careers bring them into
potential conflict...

The third title in the Megan Rhys crime series.

ISBN: 978 1870206 860   £6.99

Strange Blood

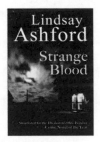

Women are dying with pentagrams carved
on their faces. Satanic ritual or cunning
deception? Forensic psychologist Megan
Rhys is called in to help the police investigate
what they believe is a ritual killing. She feels
that prejudice is taking the enquiry in the
wrong direction and she is suspicious of the
media-obsessed police chief in charge of the case. As more
women die – and as the press, the police, her boss and her
own family turn on her – Megan stakes everything on finding
the killer.

The second title in the Megan Rhys crime series. Shortlisted
for the Theakston's Old Peculier Crime Novel of the Year.

ISBN: 978 1870206 846   £6.99

Frozen

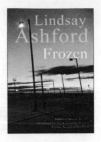

Megan has been asked to advise on two murders: two young prostitutes, dumped like rubbish, seemingly the victims of two men working together. But there is something wrong the the information the police are giving her. Someone is trying to manipulate her. Or are Megan's own prejudices colouring her judgement?

As the killings add up, Megan is being pushed harder and harder towards one solution – and someone is getting into her house. Can she trust her instincts ? Is the killer closer than she realises?

The first title in the Megan Rhys crime series.

"Gritty, streetwise and raw" Denise Hamilton, author of the Eve Diamond crime novels

ISBN: 978 1870206 822   £6.99

Other titles from Honno

Facing into the West Wind
by Lara Clough

A debut novel with an ethereal, deeply felt
focus on characters and relationships. When
Haz meets the rejected and lonely Jason on
the streets of Bristol he decides to take him
home to the family's beach house at Gower.
What follows is a series of confessions and
revelations which will change everything.

"A tender and perceptive tale of secrets" The Guardian.
"A deeply felt and accomplished first novel" Sue Gee

ISBN: 978 1870206 792   £6.99

Girl on the Edge
by Rachel V Knox

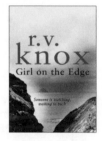

A chilling story of love, betrayal, secrets and
lies…

Just how did her mother die and what did
Leila witness on the cliff top, if anything?
Leila knows that there's something about her
childhood she can't quite remember.. that haunts her dreams
and sometimes her days. This year she's determined to find
out the truth… but someone has tried very hard to keep their
secrets and will go to extremes to make sure it stays that way.

   A compelling psychological thriller set in the moors of
North Wales.

ISBN: 978 1870206 754   £6.99

Hector's Talent for Miracles
by Kitty Harri

A gripping human story set in this century
and the last: heroic, tragic and compelling...
   The small spanish town of Torre de Burros
is known to pilgrims the world over for its
miracles; there Hector Martinez, his mother
and grandmother live in the shadow of
dark secrets. Mair Watkins arrives in a clapped out yellow
Beetle, all the way from Wales, on a mission to find her
lost grandfather. Their meeting is explosive and their lives
revealed as fragile constructions forged in the fire of a vicious
conflict...

  Praise for Kitty Harri (writing as Kitty Sewell) and her
previous novel *Ice Trap*: *"An involving narrative, a sharply
observed cast and an atmospherically evoked and unusual
setting"* The Guardian.

ISBN: 978 1870206 815   £6.99

About Honno

Honno Welsh Women's Press was set up in 1986 by a group of women who felt strongly that women in Wales needed wider opportunities to see their writing in print and to become involved in the publishing process. Our aim is to develop the writing talents of women in Wales, give them new and exciting opportunities to see their work published and often to give them their first 'break' as a writer.

Honno is registered as a community co-operative. Any profit that Honno makes is invested in the publishing programme. Women from Wales and around the world have expressed their support for Honno by buying shares in the co-operative. Shareholders' liability is limited to the amount invested and each shareholder has a vote at the Annual General Meeting.

To buy shares or to receive further information about forthcoming publications, please write to Honno at the address below, or visit our website: **www.honno.co.uk**.

Honno
'Ailsa Craig'
Heol y Cawl
Dinas Powys
Bro Morgannwg
CF64 4AH